SARAH ALDERSON

OUT OF CONTROL

SIMON&SCHUSTER

First published in Great Britain in 2014 by Simon and Schuster UK Ltd
A CBS COMPANY

1 3 5 7 9 10 8 6 4 2

Simon & Schuster UK Ltd
1st Floor, 222 Gray's Inn Road
London
WC1X 8HB

Simon & Schuster Australia, Sydney

Simon & Schuster India, New Delhi

A CIP catalogue record for this book is available from the British Library.

ISBN 978-1-47111-575-2

Printed and bound by CPI Group (UK) Ltd, Croydon, CR0 4YY

www.simonandschuster.co.uk
www.simonandschuster.com.au

For Lauren

1

The policeman is looking at me, his head tilted to one side, a deep line etched between his eyebrows. He taps his pen in a slow staccato rhythm on the edge of the desk. 'What were you doing on the roof?' he asks.

I take a breath and try to unknot my cramping fingers, which are stuffed in the front pocket of the NYPD sweater I'm wearing. 'I was just getting some air,' I say. I sound like an automaton; my voice is toneless, lost. 'I couldn't sleep.'

The policeman's eyebrows rise. He scribbles something on his pad then glances up, catching sight of someone or something behind me. He stands quickly, tossing his pen on to the paper-strewn desk. 'I'm going to get a coffee,' he says, grabbing a mug from among the mess. 'Can I get you anything?'

I shake my head and watch him walk away, scratching the back of his neck. He stops on the other side of the room to talk to another detective, wearing a jacket emblazoned with the word FORENSICS. They glance over at me as they talk. I turn away and stare at the wall. I know what they're saying. They're saying that I'm a lucky girl. That the fact that I'm alive is 'a miracle'.

But if this is a miracle then I don't think I want to know what kind of god these people believe in. A shadow falls over me. I jerk around. The other detective, the one in the forensics jacket, stands in front of me. My eyes fall to the heavy-looking gun in the holster attached to his hip. I recognise it. It's a Glock 19.

'Hi Olivia, I'm Detective Owens. Do you mind?' he asks, indicating the empty chair beside me.

I shake my head and he pulls out the seat and sits down heavily, as though the weight of a thousand dead bodies is piled on his shoulders. His shirt is as heavily creased as his face. He rubs a hand over his eyes. He has saggy grey bags under them but, now he's closer, I can see he's not as old as I first thought; maybe thirty-five, with dark brown hair and a day's worth of stubble.

'So, what I'd like for you to do,' he says in a heavy Brooklyn accent, 'is to walk me through what happened this evening.'

I grit my teeth. I've already done this. I've been through it three times; once with the cop who answered the emergency call, and twice here at the station.

'Just one more time,' Detective Owens says apologetically, trying for a smile. 'I know you're tired, I know you've been through a lot, but we really need your help, Olivia. You're the only witness. If there's anything you remember – even if it seems like something trivial, we need to hear it. It might be the clue that helps us find the people who did this.' He pauses. 'Because, if I can be honest with you, there's not a whole lot to go on right now.'

I nod OK.

'So . . . you get out of bed. What time is it?' he asks.

I frown. 'Around one I think.'

'Can you be any more precise?'

I squeeze my eyes shut, trying to picture the room. There was a clock on the bedside table. I glanced at it when I turned the light out. It was just after midnight. I tossed and turned for at least an

2

hour before I decided to give up on sleep, but I didn't check the exact time.

I shake my head at the detective.

'Why'd you get up? Did you hear something? A noise in the house? Did something spook you?'

'No,' I say, still shaking my head. 'I've not been sleeping very well. I have jet lag.'

'Lucky for you, huh?'

I don't answer. I just fix him with a stare. He holds my gaze for a second and then looks away, down at the notebook cradled in his palm.

'So you get up. Then what?' the detective asks.

I close my eyes and try to remember . . .

I cross to the window. It's sweltering hot, the night air torpid and thick as a quilt, threatening to storm. I'm wearing only a pair of pyjama shorts and a thin camisole top – the same things I'm still wearing now beneath the oversized sweater they gave me at the police station. The house seems to be breathing. There's a clock ticking downstairs by the front door, the hum of an air conditioner, the ticking *tink* of the plumbing and the occasional sound of a car sweeping past on the street in front. Away in the distance a car alarm wails. My third-floor bedroom faces the back garden, a thin band of manicured green, walls stretching high on either side, trees blocking the view of neighbouring brownstones. Beneath my window is a jutting ledge, just wide enough for a foothold.

I don't think twice before I'm crouched in the window frame, my hands gripping the wooden sill, my bare feet slipping through and finding purchase on the crumbling brickwork. I take a deep breath, flattening my palms against the walls, feeling the familiar tightening in my belly, the rush that feels like stars shooting through my veins. I don't look down at the ground four storeys below. I look up, at the moon, a dishwater-dirty half-circle shrouded behind cloud, and feel every cell in my body spark to life.

'Keep going,' Detective Owens says. 'What happens next?' he asks.

I edge slowly along the windowsill, carefully, towards a drain-pipe screwed into the wall. When I reach it I grasp it in both hands and then start shimmying up it, using the brackets as footholds. It's not as high as some I've climbed – maybe ten feet before I reach the roof and scramble on to it, breathless, my legs trembling slightly. I stand, wiping off the dust and dirt from my hands on my shorts and then I balance on the very lip of the roof, my toes disappearing over the edge, feeling the first patter of rain dance on my bare arms. I stare at the tops of trees ink-stamped across the sky, at the water-stained clouds, and the thought whispers through my mind that I'm insane, that if I fell from this height I'd die for sure . . . but then the thought is swept away by a wave of pure adrenaline. I feel light as air, perfectly poised. There's no way I could ever fall.

And then I hear the tinkle of glass breaking somewhere far below.

My arms whirl frantically as I fight to keep my balance. I tumble backwards on to the roof and crouch down low, my hands white-knuckled as they grip the ledge. I squeeze my eyes shut and tell myself angrily that it's just breaking glass, that I'm stupid and just overreacting, and I'm forcing myself to my feet ready to go and investigate when a thud comes from somewhere deep inside the house.

My stomach folds tight, all my instincts, everything I've ever learned from my father and from Felix coming into play: *Steady your breathing, don't succumb to panic, consider your options.*

Maybe, I think to myself, Mrs Goldman woke in the night and spilled a glass of water. Maybe one of them has fallen out of bed. They're old. It's possible. I'm jumping to conclusions that it's something bad. I'm in New York, for God's sake. It's safe here. Saf*er*, at any rate. I throw a leg over the ledge and reach for the drainpipe, readying myself to shimmy down so I can go and investigate, and just then I hear two muffled retorts. I freeze. I know that sound. I hear it in my dreams. I force my leg back over the wall and I cower behind the ledge up on the roof, wrapping my hands around my head, blocking my ears and shutting out the sounds that follow, until, what feels like hours later, a police siren shatters the night air.

2

Detective Owens writes it all down in his little notepad.

'So you didn't see who it was that entered the property?' he asks.

I sigh. Does he not think I would have told them already if I'd seen anything? 'No,' I say through gritted teeth. 'Like I said, I was up on the roof.'

Detective Owens leans back in his chair, chewing on his bottom lip. '

'Why would someone do this?' I finally ask, swallowing the lump in my throat. 'Was it a robbery?'

He glances at me. 'Nothing was taken, far as we can tell. From the looks of it, it was a professional hit job.'

I blink at him in shock, trying to block out the image of the black zippered bags being carried out the house on metal gurneys. 'Why would anyone want to kill them?' I ask.

'That's what I'm trying to find out, Olivia. Mr Goldman was a lawyer, prosecuted a lot of criminals. Maybe someone bore a grudge.'

He hands me a tissue and for a moment I stare at it wondering why he's offering it to me, then I become aware of the tears sliding down my cheeks. I wipe my face. How can they be dead? Just a few hours ago we were all having supper together around their mahogany dining table. Mrs Goldman had made Parmesan chicken. Mr Goldman drank several glasses of wine before heading back to his study to finish some work. They'd been quizzing me about my final year of school and my plans for going on to study dance. And now they were dead. How was that possible?

My mind jumps ahead, another thought surfacing. If I'd been in bed, would the killer have shot me too? If I hadn't been on the roof, if I hadn't had jet lag, if I didn't suffer from insomnia . . . I could be dead right now. That was a lot of *ifs* to bet a life on.

'Why were you staying with Mr and Mrs Goldman?'

I look up at Detective Owens. 'They're friends of my father's. I mean, they *were* friends of my father's.' The lump in my throat expands, threatening to choke me.

'I'm sorry for your loss,' he mumbles.

'I didn't really know them all that well,' I say. 'I was only meant to stay with them a few days, until my dad got back.' I'm rambling, trying to block out the image of the bloodstained headboard and the crimson streaks all over the bed sheets.

'Your father is Daniel Harvey,' Detective Owens asks, 'is that right?'

I nod. He appraises me in what seems like something of a new light.

'And he's currently out the country?'

'He's away on business. I told your colleague. I think they're trying to contact him now.' I glance around. There are several other detectives and police officers in the room, all of them busy. The phones haven't stopped ringing all night. A blackboard on one wall is covered in chalk markings. At the top it reads HOMICIDE in block letters. There are over a dozen cases listed and beside only three are scrawled the words CASE CLOSED. I watch someone write GOLDMAN in small neat letters in the final row.

'Where's your father on business?'

I try to focus on the questions. 'Nigeria. He's working for the government. He's the head of the GRATS task force.'

Detective Owens smiles reassuringly at me, 'What about your mother? Have you tried calling her?'

I shake my head. 'I don't know her number. It's on my cell, which is back at the house.'

'Where does your mom live? We can send a patrol car over so she can come and collect you.'

'I don't think that's going to be possible. She lives in Oman.'

'Oman?' he asks, his eyebrows shooting up to meet his hairline.

'It's in the Middle East.'

'Yeah, yeah. I knew that,' he answers quickly. 'So, both your parents are out of the country and currently incommunicado. Any other next of kin we can contact? You're a minor. If we can't find any next of kin we'll have to contact child services.'

'No,' I say, suddenly alert. *Child services?* 'I'm almost eighteen,' I argue. 'I'll be fine on my own. I can go to my dad's apartment. It's on the Upper East Side. I know the doorman. He'll let me in.'

Detective Owens shakes his head grimly at me. 'Sorry. Rules are rules.' He stands up. 'Have a think if there's anyone you can call to come and get you. I'll go check in with the crime scene folk, see if we can have one of them bring a few of your things over to the precinct.'

'OK,' I nod dumbly. I sink back into my chair as he wanders off and try to think of someone who I can call to come and collect me, but I can't think of a single person. I've only been in New York for a week. The only people I knew were the Goldmans. I suddenly feel like resting my head on the desk and crying. I want my dad. I want this nightmare to be over.

3

'Excuse me.'

A burly policeman with an enormous gut is trying to edge past the desk I'm sitting at. He's got his hand firmly locked around the arm of a boy wearing a dark hooded sweater and jeans, who looks barely older than me. I edge over in my seat to allow them to pass and turn to watch as the cop shoves the boy into a chair just a few feet away from me. The boy's jaw works angrily, his eyes dart once around the room, taking me in with a narrowed look of suspicion before the cop barks something at him that gets his attention. It's only then that I notice the hand-cuffs. He hunches over, almost as if he's trying to hide them from me. I stare at him more closely, wondering what he's been brought in for. Then I remember we're sitting in the homicide department.

'Name,' the cop demands.

'Jaime Moreno,' he answers quietly, spelling it out. He says it with a slight Spanish inflection so it sounds like *Hay-may*. As the policeman writes it down, the boy looks over at me briefly and I see something flash in his eyes – pride or anger, I can't tell which. Maybe it's both.

'You've been read your rights,' the cop says now. 'You got one phone call, Moreno. If I were you I'd use it to call your momma and tell her you ain't gonna be home for a while.' He stretches, reaches for a pencil. 'You know, you could make this go a whole lot easier if you started talking.'

I watch the boy carefully. His face is turned in profile to me. His chin is lowered and he glowers at the cop through the shield of his lashes but doesn't say a word.

The cop leans back in his seat. 'Fine by me, if you don't talk,' he says, undoing the top button of his shirt. 'No sweat off my sack. I'm not the one who's facing twenty-five years in a New York State penitentiary. Maybe I wouldn't be talking either in your shoes. Those some crazy mofos you messing up with. Hell, I'd probably be too busy shitting my pants too if I was the one sitting where you are right now.' He pushes back from the desk, freeing his belly, stands up and stretches. 'I'll just go and see if a cell's opened up.'

Once he's gone, the boy stays sitting there, his shoulders slightly hunched, his jaw working overtime. His lips are pressed together tightly and his hands are clenched in his lap as if he's praying. I almost feel sorry for him. Then I see the board of open murder cases on the wall in front of me and my sympathy magically evaporates. I hope if this boy's guilty they lock him up and throw away the key.

I sit with my back to the boy, my foot tapping, waiting for Detective Owens to return. By the clock on the wall it's nearly five a.m. I've been here three hours, but I'm hoping the detective takes his time as I haven't yet thought of anyone I can call, and I'm still wracking my brains when I hear: 'Pssst.'

I don't turn around.

'Pssst. Hey.'

I do a quick scan but the three cops left in the room are all busy and I can't catch anyone's eye.

11

'Please.'

I turn fractionally towards the boy behind me who's trying to get my attention. 'What?' I ask.

His eyes flit across the room before landing back on me. He keeps his voice low as he bends forwards. 'I need a favour.'

I raise my eyebrows at him in disbelief. What makes him think I'm about to do him a favour? He's a stranger. And he's wearing handcuffs.

As if he knows exactly what I'm thinking – which admittedly, given the look I'm fixing him with, wouldn't be hard to guess – he raises his own eyebrows right back at me. 'What happened to innocent till proven guilty?'

I frown at him. He has me there. But still, there's the fact he's a stranger and I have a feeling that whatever kind of favour he's going to ask me it's not going to be legal.

'You get to walk out of here. I don't. I'm not going to make bail,' he says.

I ponder this for a second. 'How do you know,' I finally say, 'that I've not just been charged with a triple homicide?'

His eyes – a bewildering dark green – light up with amusement. He holds up his bound wrists and then nods at my free hands. 'And besides,' he says, 'you don't really fit the profile. You're wearing a snazzy NYPD sweater. They don't usually hand those out to murder suspects.'

I hold his gaze for a few seconds. His eyes burn into mine – pleading. 'Listen, all I'm asking is that when you walk out of here you call someone for me,' he says.

'Why on earth would I do that?' I ask, incredulous.

He considers me for a beat then sits back in his seat. 'Because you look like you got heart.'

I stare at him blankly. Heart? What's that supposed to mean? 'You get one call, remember?' I say.

'I need that for someone else,' he mumbles.

'Too bad,' I answer with a shrug.

'Please,' he begs, and I catch the waver in his voice and realise this is hard for him to ask. That flare in his eyes – it's pride, not anger. 'I don't want my mom to worry,' he says.

That gets my attention. 'Your mother? You want me to call your mother?' I ask, somewhat sceptically.

He looks at me abashed, colour running into his cheeks. 'I just . . . I want her to know that I'm OK. And that I'm sorry,' he adds.

I flinch back in my seat. *Sorry?* Isn't that as much an admission of guilt as waving a bloodied knife in my face? He scowls at me instantly, seeing my reaction.

'How do I know that you're not just getting me to call one of your friends to pass on some kind of message?' I ask. 'I'm not an idiot.'

The scowl vanishes. His expression turns deadly serious. 'I give you my word. I just want you to call my mom.'

I study him. He looks genuine. I'd go so far as to say desperate in fact. But he's a stranger. And as a rule I don't break rules. If you discount climbing on to roofs. Not even for friends. I learned the hard way. I glance over my shoulder at the far door which Detective Owens disappeared through, hoping he'll reappear and give me a get-out clause.

'If you do this for me,' the boy says, leaning forwards, his hands clasped together, 'I will pay you back.'

'When?' I fire back. 'In twenty-five years?'

He winces and sits up tall in his seat, and I immediately regret my sarcasm. I take a deep breath. Would it really hurt to do this?

But before I can decide, the boy is out of his seat. He throws a quick glance around the room and then he's standing in front of me, pressing something into my hand. 'Please,' he says, staring down at me, his expression begging.

I am too startled to do anything but stare up at him.

'OK,' I say quietly, kicking myself mentally as soon as the word is past my lips.

He drops my hand and gives me a grateful nod, the relief rolling off him in a wave that makes his whole body sag.

'Moreno!'

The boy is back in his seat, wearing a smoothly innocent expression, by the time the cop lumbers over to us. 'He bothering you?' he asks me.

I shake my head, my fingers closing around the small scrap of paper in my palm.

'Leave the pretty lady alone,' the cop says with a growl. He unsnaps one of the boy's cuffs and locks it instead around the leg of the desk, which is bolted to the floor. 'And stay put,' he tells him gruffly.

4

The cop walks past me and the piece of paper scalds my palm. There's a waste paper basket right by my foot. I could easily toss it in and turn my back on the boy. I know I should do this. But for some reason, possibly to do with the fact he looked so relieved when I said I'd do it, I don't. Instead, I slip the scrap of paper into the front pocket of the sweater I'm wearing and then I stand up. I tell myself I am going to find Detective Owens before this boy tries to get me to do anything else for him. But really, it's because I can feel his gaze burning the back of my neck and it's making me feel tense, like I'm sitting on an anthill.

I manage two steps before a gunshot from somewhere in the building jolts me straight back into my seat. For a split second everyone in the room freezes, all heads turned towards the door. And then three, four, five more shots ring out in succession and the sound of screaming bursts through the walls; bloodcurdling screams, screams that are cut terrifyingly short by another round of gunfire, this time closer.

The three cops in the room go running past me in a blur, all heading for the door. The first two pile out into the corridor, guns already in their hands, shouting commands to each other. The third – the one who just cuffed the boy to the desk – hovers in the doorway. He looks over his shoulder. 'Stay here. Don't move,' he shouts at us, clearly forgetting that he just cuffed one of us to a desk, and then he takes an uncertain step out into the corridor, following his colleagues.

He is blown instantly backwards, the force of the bullet throwing him several feet across the room. Gunfire detonates all around. But I don't notice. I'm just staring at the body of the cop, lying on the floor not fifteen feet from me, his face no longer recognisable as a face, just a crater foaming with red, with shards of white poking out of it.

Everything funnels in that moment; the world reducing to a shattering hum and the completely unreal image of this cop dead at my feet. And then, as if I'm the epicentre of a bomb, reality explodes around me, everything sharpening, noise and heat rushing back in as though filling a vacuum. I become aware of someone yelling at me.

'Get these off!'

I turn slowly. The air feels suddenly dense as tar, as though I'm wading through it. The boy is shouting at me. He's standing up, straining against the cuff that holds him to the desk, the muscles in his neck are so taut they look like they're about to burst through his skin, and for a moment that's all I can focus on.

'Keys! Grab the keys!' he yells. He's pointing with his free hand in the direction of the dead cop.

For a few seconds I sit there unmoving. I *cannot* move. Then his shouts manage to break through my daze.

'They're in his pocket!'

I tumble out of my chair to my knees and start crawling towards the body, ducking automatically as bullets roar over my head. The glass above the door explodes, shards flying like daggers.

16

On the far side of the room a police radio crackles to life. A disembodied voice on the other end cries for help before a storm of static drowns it out.

I reach the cop and my hand hovers in mid-air as I stare down at the mass of red and grey pulp where a head should be. Oh God, my body starts to shake, nausea rising in a solid block up my throat, hysteria gaining a foothold in my brain. I breathe through my mouth and force myself to focus. Which pocket?

'Hurry!'

The boy's voice punches through the panic and my brain suddenly throws a switch. It stops computing. Somehow I stop seeing the blood and the gore. I no longer feel the sticky wet warmth beneath my bare knees. I stop noticing the bullets. All I can hear is the gallop of my pulse thundering in my ears and Felix in my head ordering me to stay calm.

Without thinking, I shove my hand deep into the front pocket of the cop's trousers and find the key. I tug it out and crawl as fast as I can back to the boy through the carpet of broken glass which now litters the ground between desks. The boy snatches the key from my outstretched hand and jams it into the tiny hole. The cuff springs apart, freeing him.

Instantly, he throws himself on top of me. 'Get down!'

A bullet smacks itself into a filing cabinet just behind us as we tumble to the ground. His chest presses down on mine, my face is buried in his shoulder. Quickly he rolls off me and pushes me towards a desk. I scoot underneath it, banging the side of my head on the sharp metal corner of a drawer unit. I let out a cry.

'Shhh.' His hand clamps over my mouth.

I tug his arm away. 'What's going on? What's happening?' I whisper.

Before he can answer me, the shooting stops and a silence falls that is even more terrifying than the gunfire. The boy and I both freeze, staring at each other unblinking, just a few millimetres between us. Together, enclosed in the tight space beneath the desk, we strain to listen, and over the radio static and the whir of the air conditioner overhead, I pick out faint cries coming from somewhere in the distance; the unnatural keening howl of a wounded animal.

The boy shifts his weight. His back is pressed to one cabinet, his feet to the drawer unit. Carefully, he peers around the edge of the desk then ducks quickly back, breathing fast. A bead of sweat trickles down the side of his face.

'Shit,' he murmurs, resting his head back against the cabinet and closing his eyes.

'Wh—' I begin, but stop when I hear the sly creak of the door being pushed open. A boot crunches on glass. The boy's eyes flash open and lock on mine, holding me in place, silencing the scream that has risen up my throat and is threatening to tear free. My legs begin to shake from holding still in a crouching position. The boy's right hand squeezes my knee hard – another warning, his eyes wide and burning fiercely into mine, telling me: *Do not move.*

Something topples off a desk on the far side of the room and, over the boy's shoulder, through a gap between two filing cabinets, I glimpse the back of a man's leg. Whose? Is it a cop? Where is everyone else? What happened to the cops who ran out into the corridor?

No. I shut off the thought, not wanting to go there.

The man in the room is standing stock-still with his back to us. What is he doing? I can't see. He's facing the wall – the chalkboard with all the homicide cases listed on it. The seconds seem to extend into whole hours, days, centuries, and I'm holding my breath and the boy's hand is still squeezing my knee and my heart is bursting, literally bursting, as though too much blood is pumping through it. My leg muscles are on fire and, without warning, my foot slips. Not far. But it bumps the edge of the desk. The man spins instantly in our direction. The air rushes from my lungs and the boy shifts beside me, a single word that I don't catch, falling from his lips like a dying man's prayer.

The man starts to head in our direction, is almost on us, when someone somewhere else in the building shouts something that's instantly swallowed in a storm of gunfire and the man rushes out into the corridor.

The boy darts his head out and then he's out from under the desk and reaching for me.

'Move!' he says, pulling me to my feet.

I glance around, holding on to the desk for balance. The room seems to spin and dip as though it's a fairground ride.

'We gotta go now!' the boy says, dragging me towards the door.

I dig my heels in, my grip tightening on the corner of the desk. The boy yanks on my arm, 'Come on!'

I shake my head at him. 'This way,' I say, pulling my hand free from his and heading for a glazed door at the other end of the room; the way Detective Owens went. The boy glances once over his shoulder towards the corridor and then hurries after me. I weave between the desks, feeling adrenaline finally cranking through my system, erasing all other thoughts from my mind except for one: RUN!

5

The door opens into another room similar to the homicide department; there are rows of empty desks and chairs, blinking computers, even a ringing phone. But there's no one in sight.

A door into another corridor hangs ominously ajar. The building seems to echo with silence. I glance around. What do we do? Hide? Find a way out? But this is a police station. It's designed to keep people in. There are no windows. I try an unmarked door. It's locked. I hear movement on the other side. People hiding? Shit.

The boy is already at the doorway to the corridor, peering out.

'It's clear,' he whispers over his shoulder.

I run to his side. The corridor is deserted. He's right. It is empty. Except for the bodies. I count them. One. Two. Three. All cops in uniform. All of them dead. The nearest is barely two steps away from where we stand, lying face down in a pool of blood. I stare at the spreading slick of it. And then suddenly, I'm moving. I'm not sure how. Until I realise the boy is pushing me ahead of him, towards a fire door at the end of the corridor.

'Hold up.'

I turn. He's crouching down beside one of the bodies. I hesitate, glancing over my shoulder at the fire door and then back down the corridor. There's no time for this. I run back to him.

'What?' I hiss. 'Come on, let's go.' My feet dance on the sticky linoleum.

His hands are working fast, fumbling at the cop's waist. I bend down, grab hold of the boy by his hood and try to haul him to his feet, but then I see what he's doing. He's trying to work the cop's gun free from his hand.

'Help me,' he says through gritted teeth.

I stare at the dead man's knuckles, drenched in his own blood, and take a faltering step backwards. The boy manages without my help, unclasping the gun from the cop's cold-fingered grip. He gets to his feet, breathing heavily, his face set, and together we turn and slam through the fire escape. The boy spins and catches the door with his hand before it can slam, and eases it shut. We're in a stairwell. Up or down? I look at the boy and without a word we both dart to the right, heading down. We're on the ground floor, but it seems like the basement will offer more exits than the second floor will. We take the steps three at a time, crashing into the walls. The boy is right behind me, urging me forward, his hands against my shoulder blades.

When we hit the bottom, he pushes me aside, reaching for the door handle first.

'Get behind me,' he says, holding the gun to his chest.

I glance at the gun in his hand and am about to argue with him but he's already throwing open the door so I duck behind him, my hands balling his sweatshirt, my face pressed to his shoulder blade.

The door smashes against the concrete wall on the other side. It's an underground car park, filled with police cars and unmarked vehicles. The boy steps through, with me tripping on his heels. We scan the space simultaneously. To the right of the door is a small booth. I hear the boy's intake of air, a sudden sharp gasp, before I register the body on the floor – another cop, this one sitting propped up against the wall with his legs splayed and a ragged black red hole where his left eye used to be – but I don't even have time to process it before we hear footsteps thundering down the stairs behind us.

The boy leaps over the dead cop's legs towards the booth, but I just stay standing there, staring at the body, as the footsteps ring out closer and closer.

My mind is yelling at me to move, to keep running, but the sound of those footsteps, the sight of all that blood, gloss black against the concrete, holds me in place like a hypnotist's trick.

And then the boy is suddenly standing in front of me, waving a set of keys in my face. He takes my arm and starts dragging me across the parking lot, and my legs feel heavy and too slow but it doesn't matter because he's running hard enough for both of us, propelling me forward. I hear a beep and a car's lights flash on the other side of the lot. The boy changes course, veering wildly around a pillar, heading towards it.

We're three cars away when we hear someone burst through the doorway. We both duck, scurrying between a pillar and a car. We edge silently around it until we're hidden behind the back of a van. Have we been seen? No one is shooting at us.

For a second I think that maybe it's a policeman chasing us, that it's someone coming to tell us everything's safe now, that we don't need to run, but my instinct says otherwise. My instinct says that unless we get out of this underground car park in the next thirty seconds, we're dead.

The boy scoots along until he's at the edge of the van and then darts a look down the row. *Let's go*, he mouths to me, and I follow him, keeping low, my heart crowding my chest. We make it to the car. The boy nods to the passenger side and I nod back at him in understanding, then start inching along towards the door as he slips silently around to the other side.

My hand slides under the door handle and I try to ease it up silently, but there's a muffled click and a second later a bullet whizzes right past my face and smashes into the pillar beside me. Through the high-pitched whine that fills my ears I hear the boy yelling at me. I throw open the door as another bullet smacks into the front fender of the car.

The wheels are already spinning as I dive inside, and the boy straightaway tears out of the parking space without even waiting for me to shut the door. It swings open and I try to grab for it even as he throws us around another corner, and I see the man then, see the gun raised and pointing straight at me, see the black hole that the bullet comes spinning out of, and I hear the smack as it hits the wing mirror. The car door slams shut as we tear around another corner.

'Get down, stay down!' the boy shouts and I do. I cradle my head in my arms and duck low.

The engine screams as we fly up a ramp. I'm aware of the boy's hand, gripping the gearstick, close to my face, moving it fluidly, punching it up and down the gears. He lets go at one point and grabs the handbrake, jerking it up violently and we spin two-seventy degrees, the wheels screeching, before he hits the gas and I fly backwards against the seat and then forward, smashing into the dash. A second later we bump over something and go careering around a corner before slowing abruptly to a normal speed.

'Buckle up,' the boy says, looking over at me.

6

I straighten up, glancing at the street as I reach with shaking hands for my seatbelt. The boy cruises for several blocks, making a few sharp turns. His eyes stay glued to the rear-view mirror the whole time. I twist around to see if we're being followed but the streets are eerily deserted. There are a few garbage trucks and some early-morning commuters, but that's all. The sky is saturated purple and grey. The lights of the stores we pass are bright and glittering. I realise it's been raining heavily, though now the storm has passed. The sidewalks shine like new.

The boy takes a left at the next block and pulls over into a loading bay outside a shuttered restaurant. He keeps the engine running and for a few seconds we just sit there, both of us in silence. My heart is still pounding. My head whirring as it tries to process what I just witnessed.

'What the hell just happened?' the boy asks finally. His voice is a hoarse whisper. His hands grip the wheel tightly, as though he's still driving.

I shake my head, unable to formulate coherent thoughts, much less words. My head feels as though it's wrapped in clouds – all my thoughts are foggy and half formed, images of that dead cop's face overlaying them like a scratched red filter.

'Did you see?' he asks, turning towards me. 'Did you see him?'

24

I nod and we stare at each other in the gloom of the car. He looks just as horrified as I do.

'What do we do?' I finally ask.

'I'm getting outta here,' the boy says, snapping suddenly into action. He starts rooting in the pocket of his jeans for something and then he pulls out the key he put there. I watch as he unlocks the handcuffs that are still dangling from his left wrist. He tosses them into the back of the car and I contemplate for the first time the fact that I'm sitting in a stolen unmarked police car with a murderer who I just helped escape from custody. I guess that makes him a fugitive. But then, what does it make *me*? Oh God. I can't even think it through. Does it even matter, I wonder, after what's just happened? Does *anything* matter? My gut writhes as I remember the three dead cops in the corridor and the detective who was shot and killed right in front of me. Will anything ever matter again after seeing that?

The tang of blood and smoke still fills my nostrils, the memories of all those bodies making me want to retch. The boy is still staring at me, wide-eyed, though his hand is already on the door. My eyes track at the same time as his to the gun he took from the cop, which sits in the seat well between us.

I swallow, keeping my gaze on the gun. 'We should call nine-one-one,' I say evenly. 'We were witnesses. They're probably looking for us.'

'I think they're probably too busy counting dead bodies to be out there looking for us,' he says, with an edge to his voice. 'Besides they're not going to be looking for you anyway.'

My head jerks up at that.

'Listen,' he says, more softly now. 'If you want my advice, stay away from the police.'

25

I take a deep breath in, though it's like I'm breathing in water and not air. Every time I blink, the shooter appears on the back of my eyelids; the image of him scored there indelibly – his gun pointed at us, his face blank as a corpse, all except for his eyes, which were glittering and hard as ice. It wasn't his eyes though that sent a chill through me. It was the uniform he was wearing; dark blue trousers, a lighter blue shirt, polished shoes, and the metal glint on the lapel which revealed who he was. A cop.

'Are you OK?'

My eyes fly open. I realise that I'm shuddering violently, my shoulders heaving up and down as I try to suck air into my shrunken lungs. I'm vaguely aware of the boy's hand resting on my shoulder, his voice sounding like he's talking to me from the top of a mountain while I'm sitting on the bottom of the ocean.

'Just try to breathe,' he says. 'It's OK. It's over.'

His hand draws tentative circles on my back as I try to do as he says and just breathe, in and out, before the darkness that is threatening to close in on me does. I focus on his voice, just his voice, soothing and low until I feel the darkness easing.

'Hey, look at me,' the boy says. 'Look at me.'

I raise my eyes slowly, pushing back my hair, which has come loose from its hastily tied ponytail.

'Do you have somewhere you can go? Someone you can call?'

I blink at him. 'My dad,' I say, trying to pull myself together.

'You have a phone on you?' he asks.

I shake my head. All I have on me is what I'm wearing. I don't even have change for a payphone.

The boy reaches across the handbrake and opens the compartment beneath the dash. There's a stick of gum in there, some paperwork, a torch. He shuts it again and flicks open the ashtray, which is full of loose change. He scoops up a handful and pours it into my palm. 'There's a phone over there,' he says, pointing to a payphone on the opposite side of the street. 'Why don't you go call your dad?'

I hesitate. I don't want to leave the safety of the car. Stepping foot on the sidewalk seems too risky, too exposed. Frankly, crossing the street seems like insanity.

'I'll wait for you if you like,' the boy says, as if he senses my nervousness. I glance at him out the corner of my eye. He's tense, his jaw is pulsing like it did back in the police station when the cop was taking his details, he keeps looking in the side mirror, checking the street. Before I can tell him not to worry, that I'll be fine, he gets out the car and I'm forced to follow. He's eyeing the street in both directions, running an anxious hand over his closely shorn hair before tugging up his hood.

Despite the early hour it's humid, the air muggy, and I pull my NYPD sweater away from my body. I feel almost feverish; shivering and sweating simultaneously. My legs are bare, my pyjama shorts are so short that they just skim the top of my thighs, but I have goosebumps prickling my legs. I jog across the road and stand in front of the phone for several seconds before I pick up the cracked receiver. It takes me another thirty seconds before I can remember the number to my dad's cell phone and then my finger shakes so much as I try to dial that it takes me three attempts to place the call.

As it starts ringing in my ear, I turn around and check the street. It's deserted. The boy has vanished. My stomach tumbles away as though I've been pushed off a ledge. The sense of panic that was sitting inside me, crouched down like a frightened animal, rears up once again, scratching at my throat. I whip around, a gurgled cry rising up my throat. The street is empty. He's gone. He lied. He said he would wait. The car is still there but there's no sign of him. I take a step, the phone falling slack in my hand, but then there's a click on the line and a *'Hello?'* and I press it quickly back to my ear.

'Dad . . .' I sob, feeling such a blast of relief at hearing his voice that I have to lean against the phone box to stay upright.

'Liva?' my dad says, his voice filled with desperation. He must know. He must have heard. 'Where are you? What's going on?' he demands. 'The police rang me. Someone said you were at a police station, that something had happened to the Goldmans. What's going on?'

'The police station – it . . .' I break off, unable to describe the massacre I just witnessed, and press my forehead against the grimy metal of the phone box. 'Everybody's dead,' is all I can manage.

'What? What are you talking about?' my dad asks. I can picture him on the other end of the line, in some hotel in Nigeria, his hands gripping the phone tighter to his ear as he sinks down into a seat. His tone has changed, become more businesslike. It's the voice he uses for work calls. 'Tell me where you are.'

'I don't know,' I say, glancing in a daze at the nondescript street. 'We were in the police station and then there was all this gunfire and . . .' I shake my head, trying to dislodge the images stuck there.

'What do you mean, *gunfire?*' my father demands. 'Where are you now?'

'We got away,' I whisper into the receiver.

'Who got away? Olivia, you're not making any sense.'

'Me and . . . this boy,' I say, scanning the deserted street.

28

'OK,' my dad says, the authority in his voice making my attention snap back to him. 'Listen—'

'And the Goldmans, they're dead,' I interrupt, suddenly remembering the reason I was at the police station in the first place.

'I know. Liva, I know,' my dad says softly. 'The police called to tell me and I got cut off halfway through the conversation. Liva, I'm trying to get back. I'm going to be on the next flight out of Lagos, but I need you to hold it together. Are you listening?'

'Mmm,' I mumble, staring at the phone cord biting across my palm. My vision keeps swimming.

'Liva.' My dad's voice cuts through my trance. 'Can you tell me what happened? Did you see the shooter? Did you see what he looked like?'

I take a deep breath. 'It was a policeman,' I say.

My dad doesn't speak for a few seconds and I wonder if he's heard me, but then he says, 'I'm sending someone to pick you up right now. Give me your address.'

'Um . . .' I lean backwards, stretching the phone cord to its limit. There's a street sign at the end of the road and I squint through the strengthening morning glare to read it and then give him the address.

'OK. Listen to me,' he says. 'Don't move. Just hang tight. I'm going to call someone from my team to come and get you.' He pauses. 'It's going to be OK, sweetheart,' he says more gently, but I hear the anxiety running like a fault line through his words, and the voice in my head asks whom exactly he's trying to convince. My blood starts to run a little cold and I shiver some more.

'Liva,' my dad says, with slightly more conviction, 'I promise. It's going to be OK. I'm about to leave for the airport but there's

29

not a flight for a few hours, it's going to take me a while to get back. I'll be with you by the morning.'

I suck in a breath. The morning? As in another twenty-four hours?

'I'm going to hang up now and make a call,' my dad continues. 'Someone from my team will be with you in ten minutes. This will all be over soon, I promise.'

And then he rings off and the coins drop with a cascade of clinks into the box and I rest my head on my forearm and feel myself sway. What was he talking about? I think to myself. It's over already, isn't it?

7

Someone taps me on the shoulder and I jump, slamming my fore-head into the side of the phone box. Scalding liquid splatters my bare legs.

'Ow,' I yell.

The boy dances a few steps backwards, the two cups of coffee he's holding spilling over his hands and splashing the sidewalk.

'Here, I got you a coffee,' he grimaces, shaking off the burning drips and offering me one.

I take it, blinking at him in shock. He's still here. He didn't leave. He just went to get coffee. Relief swamps me as I reach for the cup. I stare at him as though he's a mirage.

'Drink up,' he says, nodding his head at the coffee in my hand.

'I don't drink coffee,' I say.

'You need some sugar.'

I frown at him, not sure whether to tell him that I don't eat sugar either.

'You're in shock,' he says as though I'm being stubborn. 'You look like you're about to faint. You should drink it.'

Grudgingly, I admit he's right. I feel like I'm surfing the world's largest break of adrenaline and my legs are about to give out from under me. I take a sip. It's so sweet I almost gag. He must have poured seven or eight packs of sugar into it then topped it with some Sweet'N Low.

'Thanks,' I say, instantly feeling the hit as the sugar floods my bloodstream. My fuzzy head clears and for the first time I take a good look at him. I notice he's taken off his hooded sweater and slung it over his shoulder. Automatically my eyes scan the length of him, checking him out, as though I'm in a ballet studio and he's my partner. He's about five eleven, muscled but lean, with good shoulders and narrow hips. He's got the body of an athlete or a gymnast for sure, though I can't see him in a leotard somehow. If I had to guess I'd say he works out, plays something involving his arms, maybe basketball . . . My gaze lifts to his face. He's drinking his coffee as he scans the street. Stubble is darkening his jaw and I realise with something of a jolt that the word *boy* is an understatement.

I study the rest of him surreptitiously as I take another few sips of the oversweet coffee. His jeans are loose fitting and his sneakers are scuffed, the laces fraying. He has smooth coffee-coloured skin, which contrasts against the brilliant white of his T-shirt. I'm guessing he's part Mexican or Costa Rican perhaps, definitely something Latin American. His eyes are the most stand-out thing about him. They're an unusual greeny-grey colour, tinged with brown and framed by long dark lashes. A scar runs through his right eyebrow dividing it almost in two, if anything accentuating his eyes even more. If it wasn't for the close-cropped hair and the permanently wary, slightly hardened look in his eye, I could easily imagine him gracing a billboard advertising some hipster fashion brand. Instead, I think to myself, he's posing for mug shots. It's then that I notice the bandana hanging out the back pocket of his jeans. I quickly look away and start studying the cracks in the sidewalk. I know what that little scrap of material signifies. He's a gang member.

I shake my head to myself. Why am I even surprised, given where I met him?

'What did he say?' the boy asks. I glance up, feeling like I should avoid looking at him directly, but it's kind of impossible to because he's staring right at me. He's cradling his coffee in both hands, balancing on the balls of his feet. He doesn't look like he needs any caffeine, he looks like he's still flying on the adrenaline from earlier. His foot hasn't stopped tapping the entire time we've been standing here.

'He's sending someone to pick me up,' I tell him.

The boy nods, seemingly relieved. 'Who?'

'Someone from his team.'

His head shoots up at that one. 'His team?'

'Yeah,' I say, suddenly putting something together. 'You might want to leave before they get here.'

'Why?' he asks, his foot falling still.

'My dad's the head of the GRATS task force. That's who he's sending to get me.'

'GRATS?' the boy asks, frowning at me in confusion.

'Gang-related active trafficker suppression.'

He frowns some more as he puzzles out the acronym and then I watch his eyes go wide as he figures out the meaning. 'Police?' he asks.

I nod, offering him a half-apologetic shrug, but he doesn't notice. He's thrown his still half-full coffee cup into the trash can by the phone and is already jogging towards the car. He doesn't look back or say goodbye, he's in too much of a hurry. I watch him jump behind the wheel, my arms slumping to my sides. He guns the engine and screeches out of the parking spot, this time not bothering to check his mirrors.

I don't know why but it's like I've been punched in the stomach. I made it out of that police station because of him, and I'm not ready for him to leave just yet. I feel like I need to talk it all through, figure out what just happened and why. I need to understand it – and he's the only one who might be able to help me do that because he was right there with me. But then I hear police sirens, coming closer, and realise that I'm too tired to run any more. Whereas this boy clearly has to. Well, he doesn't *have* to, but it's obvious he's not planning on turning himself in.

I spin on my heel, ditching my coffee cup in the same bin, and then start heading towards the corner of the street where I told my father I'd be waiting. The sugar hit is wearing off and my body feels sluggish, my muscles all aching and bruised, like I've just finished an all-day dance rehearsal and haven't warmed down.

The noise of a car engine makes me jerk suddenly around. It's the boy. He's crawling the kerb beside me.

'You never told me your name,' he says through the open window.

I study him for a few seconds – this stranger whose life I saved and who saved mine in return – and decide that it can't hurt to tell him.

'Olivia,' I say.

His serious expression doesn't alter. He just nods as though satisfied and, holding my gaze, says, 'Thanks, Olivia. For back there. I owe you.'

I nod in return, without smiling. There's nothing to smile about after all. And he drives away.

8

I stand on the corner, trying to shrink into the shadows cast by the building opposite. I wrap my arms around my chest to cover the NYPD logo stamped there like a giant bullseye. This does not look like the kind of area where advertising an affiliation to the cops would go down very well.

How long has it been since I hung up the phone? How much longer before they get here? My dad said ten minutes. Surely it's been ten minutes already. It feels like ten hours. The police sirens I heard faded away. My muscles are so tensed I can't ever imagine them relaxing again and my breathing is coming in short fat bursts that sound more like the gasps of someone whose respirator just got switched off.

My head flies back and forth, searching in every direction, my eyes peeled for anyone in a cop's uniform. I think I spy a familiar blue jacket in the distance and my heart leaps into my throat, pulsing violently. But then the person comes nearer and I see it's a woman wearing a pale blue shirt, and my heart plummets back into my chest as I tell myself to relax. It's fine. I'm safe now.

I glance around at the graffiti painting the walls and metal shutters of the stores behind me. Torn posters advertising gigs and yard sales are glued to every available patch of wall. This part of Brooklyn (if we're even still in Brooklyn) is a lot more run-down than where the Goldmans live – *lived* I remind myself, squeezing my elbows hard and welcoming the shard of pain that shoots up my arms. The Goldmans' house was a large brownstone on a leafy avenue in Brooklyn Heights. Another world away. Another lifetime away. All of a sudden the knowledge of how alone I am strikes me anew and panic fills my body, leaking into every cell and cavity like noxious gas.

I barely know New York, have only ever been here once before, five years ago. My father brought me with him on a business trip. He took me to the ballet and we talked over dinner about which dance schools I might try out for when I was older. The ballet was *Swan Lake*. It was Christmas. Snow dusted the ground like icing sugar. The hotel room had thick velvet drapes that I wrapped myself in, pretending that I was the black swan unfurling her wings. I try to focus on those memories, I even force myself to run through the steps for the *danse des petits cygnes* in my head, counting off the sixteen *pas de chat*, all to avoid thinking about what just happened.

But it's useless. My mind won't stay focussed and all I can hear is a voice asking *Why? Why did all those people have to die?*

I look around automatically for the boy, as though he might be able to explain it to me. Then I remember he's gone. He left without telling me his name, but I remember it. I heard him spelling it out for the cop that booked him – *Jaime. Jamie Moreno*. I jig up and down on the balls of my feet. It's OK, I tell myself over and over, until I'm almost humming it. It's going to be OK. My dad is on his way back. And they've probably caught the guy by now. Or maybe he's shot himself. Isn't that what they always do? Turn the gun on themselves once the killing rampage is over?

Just then a car speeds towards me and pulls up to the kerb. The windows are wound down and a woman leans her head out. She's about thirty-five, pretty, with dark brown hair pulled back in a ponytail.

'Olivia?' she asks.

A headrush of relief. I nod.

She smiles at me and jumps out of the car. She's wearing a dark grey suit, a starched white shirt beneath. She flashes a badge at me but flips it shut before I can get a really good look at it. I do notice the worn leather gun holster under her arm though as she shoves the badge back into her pocket. Through the open door I glimpse the driver – a black guy in his late thirties who stares straight ahead at the street, his face half hidden behind mirrored sunglasses.

'I'm Agent Kassel,' the woman says. 'This is Agent Parker.' She indicates the driver, who still doesn't look my way. 'Your father called us and asked us to come get you. We heard what happened at the police station. Come on, get in the car, let's get you somewhere safe.'

The urgency in her voice doesn't pass me by. Her hand is already gripping my elbow and she's steering me towards the car. The driver leans over his seat and throws open the back door and now the woman's hand is on the small of my back. I glance into the car, noticing the lack of door handles, and a warning signal flares in my body that I instinctively try to quell. She's a woman, I tell myself. My father sent them. I'm safe now, just like she said. But if that's the case then why are the hairs on the back of my neck standing on end? Why is every nerve ending in my body currently feeling electrified?

I hesitate. I hear Felix in my head, telling me always to listen to my instincts, always to trust them because, unlike people, instincts never lie.

The woman senses my indecision and her hand presses more firmly on my back. She's trying to force me into the car.

'Olivia,' she says, her tone more strained now, 'please, get in the car.'

I twist so I'm facing her and, as I do, I realise what it is that's bothering me. She called herself an agent. Yet my father runs a task force made up of police, with a few civilian experts. There's no FBI or other government agency involved in it. 'Where are you taking me?' I ask her.

She pauses and her eyes flick over my shoulder. Something doesn't feel right, is not adding up. After everything that's happened today trusting anyone, let alone someone who claims to work in law enforcement, feels like madness. I take a small step backwards and Agent Kassel's hand moves instantly for her gun. Before I can make a move, the barrel is pressed to my stomach. Through my sweater I feel the blunt roundness of the muzzle like the snout of an animal trying to bore its way under my skin.

'Just get in,' Kassel hisses, jerking her head at the open door.

I stare down at the gun. My pulse skips erratically and then starts to race. I don't have any option but to get in the car. But just then the sound of tyres tearing up asphalt makes us both whip around.

A car is speeding towards us down the narrow street, its engine whining. I catch sight of a flash of blue behind the wheel and my gut lurches. Agent Kassel yells something and out the corner of my eye I see Agent Parker throwing open his door and drawing his weapon.

He and Agent Kassel both start firing at the car heading towards us. Bullets bounce off metal, thud into concrete, spit off the sidewalk. The car coming towards us swerves and there's a lethal squeal of brakes . . . and that's when I take off. I push past Agent Kassel, ignoring her yells and I just run.

I reach the end of the street and dive sideways straight into traffic, narrowly avoiding a yellow taxi that has to slam on its brakes to avoid me. A torrent of abuse is hurled through the open window and I hold up my hands in apology and then turn and keep sprinting, the sound of bullets flying and cars honking pushing me forwards.

I make it a block, then turn down a side street that's barely more than an alleyway, my pace never slowing, my arms piston pumping . . . And I'm ten feet from the end when a car slides right in front of me, blocking my path, its wheels spinning. I thrust out my hands to break my speed and they slam down on to the hood, my knees banging against the fender. My head jerks up and I stare at the driver, breathing hard. It's him. I blink. It's the guy in the cop uniform.

Time seems to slow as though it's slipped into freeze-frame mode. Half the windshield is a blizzard of broken glass but through the spiderweb cracks I watch as his hand moves to the door handle, and I'm dimly aware that there's someone beside him in the car, in the passenger seat, and that they're reaching for their door handle too, and the voice in my head is screaming at me to run but my legs are paralysed – they may as well be encased in concrete. All I can do is stare at the man, at the semi-automatic in his hand – a Colt with a varnished wooden handle – and it's amazing that I can notice the detail of the gun and the bloodstains on his shirt front but that I can't make my legs move.

The doors fly open and a tightness grips my chest. Somewhere off to the side someone screams. And next thing I know I'm in the air. The car is buckling and crumpling beneath my hand, lifting off the ground, taking me with it. The shriek of metal grinding metal rips the air around me and I'm suddenly on the ground, splinters of glass showering down over me, and I watch in dumb shock as the car slams headlong into a lamppost, bending it like it's chicken wire.

Another car has rammed into the cop's car from behind and, as I scramble to my feet, I realise that it's the car Agent Kassel was in, the same black saloon, but I don't stand around to find out what the hell is going on. My body has caught up with my brain finally and the adrenaline is shooting through my veins like wildfire. I elbow my way through the handful of people who've gathered on the sidewalk to stare at the carnage and start sprinting, my legs at first wobbly and unsure but then certain and strong as I get into my stride.

Up ahead I see a subway entrance and my heart leaps. If I can make it to the subway, I can disappear. I can jump the turnstile. I can find a tunnel. I can – I don't know what. But right now the subway feels like my only shot at salvation. I skid to a slower pace to try to blend in with the sparse crowd, just in case they're following. Sweat trickles down my back, I'm panting, sucking in air as though I'm drowning. People veer out of my way, shooting me strange looks.

The subway sign is getting closer. I increase my pace, weaving around a woman pushing a pram, then hopping out of the way of a man who is jogging along bare-chested, pulling two giant poodles behind him on a leash. I register the fact he's coated in sweat and that he's singing along to his iPod without a care in the world.

But then, from behind me comes shouting and another gunshot that seems to fracture the air like it's made of glass. I glance over my shoulder and see him – the cop in the blue shirt. He's striding down the centre of the sidewalk and people are diving out of his way. His gun is in his hand and as he strides he brings it up to shoulder level and points it straight at me. My feet trip over a loose paving slab and I let out a cry and stumble but manage to keep my balance. The subway seems to be getting further away, not nearer.

Someone starts screaming hysterically behind me, and I start running again, dodging around a woman who's standing frozen to the sidewalk, eyes wrenched wide in terror as she stares at the cop stalking towards her, as if he's coming for her. But I know something she doesn't. He's not coming for her. That's what I know with a certainty that makes my blood turn to ice in my veins.

He's coming for me.

And then suddenly my legs go out from under me. The woman with the pram has rammed me from behind in her panic and my knees smack the sidewalk and I roll, landing heavily on my shoulder as she goes screaming past.

When I blink away the tears stinging my eyes, I see the shooter striding even more purposefully towards me. His eyes are locked on mine, cold and unreadable. But his lips are turned upwards in a smile.

I scrabble backwards on my hands, my feet kicking out in front of me, pathetic and useless. And now he's so close I can see the embossed letters on the silver shield pinned to his shirt, the empty glacier-blue of his eyes. I open my mouth but nothing comes out. This can't be happening, I think in stunned amazement. And then—

'Olivia!'

I look over my shoulder.

41

A car has pulled up on to the sidewalk right behind me, the engine roaring. 'Get in!' Jaime yells, throwing open the door.

I grab the door handle and haul myself to my knees, diving into the passenger seat and slamming the door just as the shooter reaches me. His hand snatches for the handle. His fist pounds the window, threatening to punch right through it, but Jaime puts his foot to the floor and swerves us out into oncoming traffic. He roars through a red stoplight, spinning one-eighty in front of a school bus that has to stamp on its brakes, and then he cuts down a side street, almost mowing down the jogger with the two poodles who is still singing along to his iPod oblivious to the chaos around him.

Jaime keeps driving with his foot to the floor, while I cower in my seat, cradling my shoulder, words playing on a loop in my head, pounding with unceasing rhythm against my skull.

He's coming for me.

9

Gradually I become aware of other things besides my hammering heart and the fact that I'm still alive. My cheek is stinging and I raise a hand to my face and wince as a needle of pain inserts itself behind my eye. My shoulder throbs like a bass drum. Then I notice my legs are scratched and bleeding – the blood jumps out bright as day against my skin, as though I'm wearing 3D glasses. My vision blurs and I force myself to look away. I focus on Jaime instead, on his hands gripping the wheel, manoeuvring the car fluid and fast through traffic as though he's playing a video game. I wish it *was* a video game, I think to myself. Or a nightmare. Something that I could unplug myself from, or wake up from.

Jaime looks over at me quickly. He's pale beneath the tan of his skin and I can see his pulse firing rapidly in his neck.

'Why were you there?' I ask him.

'I just had a feeling,' he says, his eyes back on the road. 'I doubled back and parked up. Wanted to make sure you were OK.' This last bit he mumbles.

I take that in slowly and with an element of wonder – the knowledge that right now I could be dead – *would* in fact be dead for certain, if not for him.

'Thank you,' I say, though two words never felt so insubstantial. I want to say his name but it stalls on my lips.

He looks my way briefly before slipping across traffic and taking the exit just before the bridge. I wonder where he is going, but don't ask. I don't care, so long as we keep moving . . . It feels like we're trying to outrun an avalanche. I keep checking back over my shoulder to see if we're being followed.

'I owed you,' he says under his breath.

I sink back into my seat and study him out the corner of my eye, feeling a rush of gratitude spill through me. How did we get mixed up in this together? I wonder.

He is quiet, studying the cross streets. I catch glimpses of brown – the sludgy East River – and snatches of towering, glittering skyline rising up between clumps of greying buildings and concrete expressway. Without warning we make a sudden right turn, Jaime spinning the wheel hard and fast. We jolt over uneven ground into some kind of abandoned lot beneath the expressway. There are no other cars in sight. No people. Though the cardboard boxes and tarpaulin stretched between concrete pillars suggest that the place isn't completely abandoned. The roar of traffic from the expressway overhead can be heard even through the closed windows. Jaime pulls the car into the shadows of a pillar and yanks on the handbrake. He places his hands on the wheel and takes a deep breath. I note the strips of muscle running the length of his arms and the fact that they are trembling ever so slightly. But then again, I'm shaking too. I'm having to stop my teeth from chattering.

'Where did you learn to drive like that?' I ask. It's a stupid question and I'm not really asking because I want to know the answer. I'm asking because I don't want to talk about what just happened. I'm trying to convince myself that if don't say out loud what the voice in my head is trying to force me to acknowledge, then maybe it won't be real.

The faint trace of a smile ghosts across Jaime's lips before fading completely. 'That's what I was being booked for back at the police station,' he says, glancing sideways at me. 'Grand Theft Auto.'

'Oh,' I say, staring at him in shock. He's a car thief? Well, that figures. I stare at him slightly dumbfounded though. I mean, what are the chances that the guy I escape from a police station with happens to be a car thief who also happens to know how to drive like one of the guys from *The Fast and the Furious*? I reassess him in the light of this information. Grand Theft Auto. So, not a murderer then. I guess that's a positive.

A flare of defiance lights Jaime's eyes as he watches my reaction. They burn green, challenging me. He raises his eyebrow in a gesture I'm coming to recognise as defiance. 'What? You thought I had killed someone?' he asks with a smirk that pulls up the corner of his mouth.

I shrug. 'You were in the homicide department. What else was I supposed to think?'

'I was in the Major Crime Unit. It works out of the same room as Homicide.'

'Oh, Major Crimes, well that's *so* much better,' I throw back, rolling my eyes.

He looks like he's about to say something else, but then he's distracted by the blood on my legs. His eyes widen as he stares at my thighs. Now my body is winding down, everything has started to sting or burn. In fact, it feels like I've been lashed with nettles and fallen down several flights of uncarpeted stairs. Jaime unbuckles his seatbelt and leans across me, and for a second I wonder what the hell he's doing and am about to shove him backwards into his seat, but he's only going for a box of tissues in the side of the door. He dabs at my leg ineffectually with one a few times

45

before looking up at me. His cheeks flare briefly and he hands me the tissue. 'You better do it,' he mumbles.

I take the tissues and try wiping up the blood. The tops of my thighs are strafed with tiny cuts from the broken windshield and my knees are still scratched up from when I crawled through the glass back at the police station – I hadn't even noticed until now . . . I frown at the dark stains blotting my knees. So much blood. Where did it all come from? And then, with a sickening feeling, I remember.

I spit on the tissue and start rubbing frantically at my knees, ignoring the sharp wincing pain as slivers of glass which must have buried themselves beneath the skin are driven deeper.

'What are you doing?' Jaime says, grabbing for my wrist and pulling my hand away from my knees.

'It's not mine,' I say, trying to wrench my arm free. 'The blood. It's not mine. I want to get it off.'

Jaime opens his mouth then shuts it. He lets go of my arm and just stares as I keep scrubbing, handing me tissue after tissue in silence. It's not my blood. It's the cop's. Images sear themselves on to the back of my eyelids like the lightning bursts of a camera flash. I thought my brain had switched off, had stopped computing back at the police station when I slid the handcuff key from that dead cop's pocket, but it obviously did no such thing. It was merely storing the images, archiving them, and now it's decided to play them back to me.

I grind my teeth together and rub harder, sucking in a breath as an invisible fragment of glass buries itself deeper, so deep it scrapes the bone.

I bite my lip to stop from crying out and he takes my hand then, wrestles the tissue free from my clenched fingers and forces me to look up at him. 'Stop,' he says. Then again in a firmer, yet quieter voice, 'Stop.'

I let my hand drop and very slowly, his eyes not leaving my face, he starts dabbing a clean tissue just by my eye. His other hand is still gripping mine. Or is it me? Am I gripping him? I can't work it out. I stare at him, aware of the silence building in the car like flood water behind a dam. His lips are half parted as he wipes up whatever's on my cheek and there's a faint frown line between his eyes.

Someone just tried to kill me. More than once. And we're studiously avoiding talking about it, though the elephant in the car is stomping its feet demanding to be acknowledged. I snatch the tissue suddenly from Jaime's hand and fall back into my seat, staring at the bright droplets of blood staining it, like something out of a fairy tale. A wave of exhaustion so thick hits me that I think about sliding down into the seat well and falling to sleep for a hundred years.

'What just happened?' Jaime asks me.

I close my eyes and take a deep breath. When I open them I find him staring at me. 'I thought someone from your dad's team was coming to get you?'

'Yeah, that's what I thought too.'

'Was that the woman I saw get out the car?'

I frown at him before remembering he was watching me from down the block. 'Yeah,' I say, picturing Agent Kassel with her swept-back hair, crisp white shirt and shiny badge.

'Why didn't you get into the car with her?' Jaime asks. 'Why'd you hesitate?'

'She pulled a gun on me.'

Jaime's eyes go wide. '*She what?*'

I shrug at him. 'It didn't feel right. She said she was an agent, but there are no federal agents on my dad's team. I didn't want to get in the car.'

'So she pulled a gun on you?'

'Yeah,' I nod.

'OK,' he says slowly. He seems calm but I note his fingers are back to gripping the wheel as though he's considering tearing it from the steering block. 'So, this woman shows up claiming to work for your father, but she pulls a gun on you and tries to force you into a car, and then the next thing you know the cop with the gun and the trigger-happy hard-on turns up. Outta the blue. Just like that. What's the connection?' He stares at me, checking that I'm following his thought process. But I'm not just following him. I'm way ahead. He's only just joining the dots but I joined them even as the guy was striding towards me on the sidewalk, even as I was contemplating the psycho smile on his face my synapses were firing, making the connection.

I'm the connection.

We stare at each other as the traffic rumbles on and on over our heads. I'm grateful for the noise as it fills up the car, interrupting the graveyard silence.

'Why were you at the police station earlier tonight?' Jaime suddenly demands.

'What?'

'You were a witness right? To something?'

'Yes,' I say. 'No. I mean – I didn't see anything. The people I was staying with. They were . . .' I can't finish the sentence because I just joined another dot. A light bulb pings in my head. Maybe in fact Jaime is ahead of me after all.

'Killed?' Jaime asks.

I nod.

'Were they shot?' he asks.

I nod again.

'And then the police station gets hit.' He raises his eyebrows at me to emphasise the point he's trying to make. 'Then the same gunman comes after you on a crowded street.'

I just keep staring at him.

'Don't tell me that's a coincidence.'

'I wasn't going to,' I say. Coldness saturates me, has soaked through my muscles, through my bones, like alcohol has been rubbed on my skin.

'The odds of a single person mistakenly being caught up in a gunfight three times in one night are pretty—'

'Slim,' I finish for him. 'I know.'

He waits a beat. 'I was going to say non-existent. This side of Basra at least.'

There is nothing but screams filling my head. It is me. It is *me*. It is *my* fault all those people are dead. I'm the cause, the reason. It's bigger than me – the knowledge is a pressure so huge, squeezing me from all sides, that all of a sudden I feel like if I don't escape it, if I don't get out of the car, I'm going to die. Simple as that. My lungs are going to be crushed, my skull is going to implode. I scratch for the door handle and then I'm tumbling out on to the ground, my bloody knees scraping concrete, my forehead pressed to the dirt.

I try to suck air into my lungs, to draw it down, but the world is closing in, the sky darkening, the roar of traffic vibrating in my bones. Arms come around me, lift me to my feet, hold me upright.

'Olivia.'

I open my eyes. Jaime has me by the tops of my arms. My head is lolling backwards and he's staring down at me.

'Why?' Jaime asks. 'Why is someone trying to kill you?'

I laugh then. A horrific sound but I can't stop it. I feel as though I'm cracking open.

His hands tighten and he shakes me. 'Olivia!'

I can't answer that. I might have joined the dots but I don't know what the hell the picture is of.

'I don't know,' I say, almost spit.

We stare at each other, both of us breathing hard, both of us angry and scared too. He glances over his shoulder, at the road, as though looking for an escape, and tears start slipping silently down my cheeks. He looks back at me, then, sighing, he pulls me against his chest.

10

It should feel weird being held like this, by a near stranger. It should feel wrong to have my lips pressed against his neck, to feel his arms wrapped around me and his chin resting on top of my head. But it doesn't. It feels like there's no other place for me to be while these waves of panic and terror wash over me. So I just hold on tight, feeling as though if I let go I'm going to be swept away.

After a few seconds I press my face against his shoulder and take several deep breaths, forcing myself to stop crying. Tears aren't going to get me anywhere. They're a pointless waste of energy. I need to lock everything down, reel every stray emotion back in, and keep a clear head.

I hardly ever cry. The last time was when Felix died. My dad has no time for tears or tantrums and I learned as a kid that if I wanted to get something, or was angry about something, crying wasn't going to help my case. Crying didn't bring back Felix either.

I pull out of Jaime's arms and walk a few steps away from him. Straightaway my body tries to turn towards him, as though acting on a reflex. I want to be back in his arms. There's no thought to it. It's just an urge. I shake off the feeling, the sharp stab that goes with it, and wrap my own arms around my body, but it's much smaller comfort. I stub my toe into the ground. These people are chasing after me, someone wants to kill me, someone else who may or may not be a government agent is also trying to kidnap me. I need to stay focussed if I'm going to get out of this alive and in one piece. And another truth is becoming apparent. I can't drag another innocent person into this.

After I think I have pulled myself together I turn to face Jaime. He has walked off a few paces in the other direction and has stuffed his hands deep into his pockets. He's watching me with a mixture of wariness and worry, as though I'm an unexploded landmine.

'You shouldn't stay with me,' I say. 'If I'm the one they're after then you're not safe.' I tail off, staring at the ground, angry that my voice cracked.

Jaime doesn't say anything so I glance up. He's staring at me fiercely, his jaw clenching and unclenching as though he's trying to dislodge a tooth. 'I'm not about to leave you here on the street,' he says, gesturing at the empty lot.

'Someone's trying to kill me,' I point out. 'And someone who may or may not work for my father is also trying to kidnap me.'

His head is bowed and he looks up at me through his lashes. 'Looks that way,' he says.

'And you want to hang around and wait to get shot at again?'

That ghost of a half-smile again. 'Call me old-fashioned.'

He doesn't want to take the out that I'm offering. Relief makes my pulse leap through the stratosphere and I struggle to contain it.

Suddenly Jaime stalks towards me.

'You said you didn't see anything. Last night. You said you didn't witness the murder, but what if he doesn't know that? What if the killer thinks you did?'

I blink at him. I'd dismissed that thought because I didn't witness anything. But could he be right? I think it through some more, then shake my head. 'So, what? To cover your tracks you kill a dozen more people, in a police station of all places, and then walk down a crowded street firing a gun?'

Jaime chews on that one, his eyebrows drawing together in a scowl. 'And if he's a cop, he would know from your statement you didn't witness anything,' he adds.

'You think he even is a cop?' I ask.

Jaime shrugs. 'Who knows? Maybe he just borrowed a uniform.'

Both of us pause as a truck thunders overhead. The ground rumbles beneath the soles of my feet and for a moment it feels as though the earth is about to crack open and swallow me whole. And for a moment I wish it would.

'If he wanted you dead, why'd he not take the shot?' Jaime shouts over the noise. 'He had a clear shot at you. I saw him. He didn't shoot you, not in the basement. He shot at the car. At me. And he didn't shoot you on the street either. He shoots everybody else, no questions. Explain that.'

He's stopped a foot in front of me, squaring up to me, the energy bursting off him like infrared rays.

'I don't know what they want,' I say, but lights are flashing in my head, images dancing just out of reach.

His head snaps up immediately, his eyes widening. '*They?*'

I lose the thought I was trying to snatch at. 'There was someone else in the car. I saw him.'

Jaime takes that bit of knowledge and absorbs it silently. He rubs a hand over his shorn hair, then he places both hands on the roof of the car and rests there with his head bowed.

'Jaime,' I say quietly after a minute has passed and he still hasn't moved or said anything. I shift from foot to foot, glancing over my shoulder. We need to be moving again. We can't stay here. But where are we going to go? And should I really let him come with me? Is that even fair? He could go home, hide, pretend this never happened. I could . . . I falter. I could what? If he takes the car, where exactly am I going to go? And how am I going to get there? I have no money, I'm wearing an NYPD sweater and a tiny pair of shorts. And I look like I've just been mugged. Out the corner of my eye I spy the pile of cardboard boxes and the thought actually crosses my mind that I could just crawl beneath them and attempt to hide out right here. But then I imagine what the homeless person who lives there would say when he or she came back to find me cowering in their spot.

'Jaime,' I say again, taking a crunching step towards him.

He looks at me over his shoulder, a crease running between his eyes but his lips pulling upward into that curious smile he uses a lot. 'How'd you know my name?' he asks.

'I heard you telling the cop,' I shrug.

The smile widens, showing a brief flash of dimple. 'It's Jay,' he says finally, taking a step towards me and holding out his hand. 'Jay to my friends. Jaime to the cops and my mother.'

It's my turn to shoot him the quizzical look. Is he classifying us as friends? Or is it simply that I don't qualify in the cop/mother bracket? I stare at his hand for a while before I take it. His wrist has a raised, bloodied band all the way around it from where the handcuff bit into his skin, but he seems oblivious. His fingers grip mine, firm and sure. *Same way he drives*, I think before I can stop myself.

'Liva,' I say, shaking his hand. 'It's Olivia to the cops and my mother.'

'Nice to meet you, Liva,' he says, the smile now reaching his eyes.

54

11

'Come on,' Jay says. He starts striding across the abandoned lot.

I jog after him. 'Hold up. Where are we going?' I ask. Out of the shade it's hot, at least ninety degrees already. I'm sweating in my NYPD sweater but I'm not wearing a bra under my camisole top so I keep the sweater on. 'Why aren't we taking the car?' I ask.

'We have to ditch it. The cops will put an APB out soon, once they figure out it's missing. It might even be tagged. We gotta move.' He ups his pace, checking to make sure I'm keeping up. I match his stride. He's heading away from the expressway.

'Do you still have the gun?' I ask quietly.

Jay pats the small of his back. I see a bulge under his T-shirt and frown. I hope for his sake he knows how to check the safety is on, otherwise he's going to blow a hole in not just the seat of his pants.

'Where are we going?' I ask. I think it would be a good idea to figure out a destination before we start walking, otherwise we're wasting energy.

'Away from here,' Jay says though, 'then we'll figure it out.' He marches off again.

Reluctantly I follow him. It's not like I have any suggestions either. We walk in silence for a few minutes until the thunder from the traffic fades and the street starts to become less war zone

55

and more green zone. Clapboard houses are coming into view. We hurry past a woman pushing her toddler on a scooter. She double-takes when Jay walks by, her eyelashes fluttering, but my bloodied cheek, pyjama shorts and cut-up legs don't register on her radar at all. Maybe I don't need to worry about calling attention to myself after all.

'Why didn't your dad come and get you?' Jay asks as we walk. 'Why'd he say he was going to send someone instead?'

'He's in Nigeria.'

'Nigeria?' He shakes his head as though this piece of news just added immeasurably to the bad day he is having. Hell, it's not making my day much better either, I feel like telling him.

'He's not going to be back until tomorrow morning at the earliest.'

His eyes roll slightly, his jaw tensing in that giveaway tell. He'd be hopeless at poker. 'So we have twenty-four hours to keep out of trouble,' he says to me.

I slide a glance in his direction. Judging from the way he's now grimacing at the sidewalk and the fact that I met him in a police station where he was being booked for stealing a car, I'm guessing that staying out of trouble is not his forte.

We walk a few more paces, both of us deep in thought. I'm the opposite of Jay. I've been in trouble twice in my life. The first time was when Felix was killed five years ago, and the second time was when I was expelled from school, which was just over a month ago. Both were a direct result of disobeying rules. After Felix's death I thought I had learned. I became obsessed with never stepping a toe out of line, of always obey-ing authority, even if I silently questioned it. The expulsion was an aberration, a mistake. Up until then I had been trouble free for five years. Not a blemish, not a mark, not a grade less than an A. I slow my pace trying to piece it all together. Is this all happening to me because I broke some kind of rule or because I did something wrong? It can't be. But then again, if they're coming after me, I must have done *something*. Or maybe they think I'm somebody else? Maybe that's it. Maybe they have the wrong person.

I come to a stop in the middle of the sidewalk. 'How did they find me?'

Jay turns back. 'What?'

'How did they know I was going to be there? At the pick-up point?'

He thinks about that for just a instant, which makes me wonder if he'd already been considering the same question himself. 'They must be tracing calls to your dad's phone,' he says. 'Or maybe they have access to his team's phones. Who knows?'

I bite the inside of my cheek until I taste the tang of blood on my tongue. He's right. It's not a case of mistaken identity. Not if they are tracing calls. They want me. And if I can work out why, if I can work out the connection – the final dot – I might be able to figure out why.

'But no more phones,' Jay says. 'No more communication with your dad. No more communication with *anyone*. Deal?'

'Deal,' I say and we both start walking again. I don't add that there's no one else I could call anyway. There's my mum, but what use would calling her be? What could she do from the other side of the world? She must be worried, but then again, she might not even know what's happening. In a way, I hope she doesn't. She'd only start raving hysterically and then find a way to blame it all on my dad.

The only person I wish I could call is Felix, but that would require a line to the beyond. His voice still rings clear in my head though. I thought I'd lost it – that it had faded, just like the memory of his face has – but when I needed him back in the police station when I let panic overcome me, he was there, strong and loud in my mind, barking instructions at me. I miss him. My stomach clenches even as I walk. If he was here, what would he tell me to do? I try to listen, to see if he's still there. I even offer a silent, tentative *Hello?* And then I shake off the idea that I've got my very own Obi-Wan giving me advice from beyond the grave. Even Felix would laugh at that one.

We're heading towards an intersection; it's busy with traffic and people. I slow my pace. The thought of going anywhere near people puts me on edge.

'Here are the options,' Jay says, noticing I'm slowing and coming to a stop himself. 'We could go to a motel. But we don't have any money.'

'How is that an option then?' I ask.

He glowers at me. 'I'm not done. We could go to Queens.'

I glower back at him. 'Queens?'

'To my place. But getting there is going to involve walking through the part of town we just came from.' He jerks his head at the street up ahead of us.

I shake my head and cross my arms over my chest. 'No way.'

He gives a one-shouldered shrug. 'We don't have to walk.'

I narrow my eyes at him. What's he suggesting? And then I get it. 'NO! No way!' I yell. 'I thought you didn't want to do anything that might get us noticed. Stealing a car is going to get us noticed.'

He holds up both his hands. 'Woah, chill. I wasn't talking about stealing a car.'

'Then what were you talking about?' I ask.

His lips purse and his annoyance is barely contained when he speaks. 'Calling a friend. I don't make a habit of stealing cars. Just so you know. It was a one-time thing.'

'Sure,' I say, toeing the cracks in the sidewalk with my shoe.

'Whatever,' he says, shaking his head as he walks away.

Panic, which I thought I'd managed to put down, rears up again, gripping hold of my insides with talon-claws. 'I don't think calling a friend is a good idea,' I stutter. 'No communication. You said it yourself. Let's not bring anyone else into this.'

Jay turns back to me, his eyes tentatively meeting mine. My muscles relax a fraction.

'We could walk over the bridge and lose ourselves in the city,' he says but then tails off, wincing at my legs. 'But in those clothes you're going to get noticed. And in this city, that's saying something.'

I feel indignant, even thought he's right. 'It was the middle of the night. I was dragged out the house by an army of police. If I'd have known what today was going to bring I would have dressed for the occasion.' *I'd have worn a bulletproof vest.*

He struggles to swallow his smile. 'We need to be inside somewhere,' he says. 'We need to sleep. And eat. And you need a change of clothes.' He rubs a hand across his eyes.

'You don't need to do this,' I say. It's clear he's having second thoughts about agreeing to stick with me.

His eyes flash to me. 'I know,' he almost growls. 'You don't need to keep reminding me. Let's just say I'm repaying a debt. Not just to you. A karmic one.'

He believes in karma? It's my turn to raise an eyebrow. After what I saw today I don't believe in God or karma. Not that I did before. After what happened to Felix when I was twelve years old, I stopped believing in God or justice and started believing only in man's capacity for evil and in the intrinsic unfairness of life. What good did karma do the Goodmans or the cops that died in that police station?

'I'll stay with you until you can get to your dad. Until I know you're OK. Then I'm gone.'

I nod at the ground. I want to say thank you, but I'm not sure how he'd take it.

'We just need to find somewhere to hole up.'

'There's always my dad's apartment,' I blurt. 'We could grab some clothes, some money. I could leave him a note.' I'm aware that I'm talking fast, rattling on, trying to make a case. 'There's cash in the safe. For emergencies . . .'

'Your dad's apartment?' Jay interrupts. He's biting the bottom corner of his lip and his left eyebrow – the one with the scar dissecting it – is raised.

'Yeah,' I say, excited now. Why didn't I think of this before? It was staring me in the face. 'It's in Manhattan,' I say. 'We're near the bridge. We can walk. It's only a couple of miles.' I glance around me. Actually I have no idea how many miles it is because I don't even know where we are, but I suddenly feel energised enough by having a plan that I don't care if it's ten miles, or even twenty. 'Come on, let's go,' I say, starting to march faster back towards the river. We need to find a bridge.

'Liva.'

I look over my shoulder. Jay hasn't moved from his spot standing in the shade of a tree. It's casting shadows over his face, hollowing out his already tired eyes.

'Yeah?' I say. Why isn't he moving? We have to get off the streets.

'They found you in the house tonight. They found you at the police station. They even found you at the pick-up point. You don't think they'll have thought to find you there? At your dad's place?'

The air hisses out of me like I've been punctured. Goddamn it. I sink to the kerb. He's right. Why does he have to be right? I rest my head on my arms. It feels suddenly as heavy as a bag of bricks. I am so tired. I need some water. I need a shower. I need for everything to stop and to go back to the way it was. Why is this happening? It's Monday morning. I should be making my way to dance class, taking the subway for the first time on my own. I should not be sitting on the street with some gang member who steals cars, trying to figure out how to stay alive for the next twenty-four hours.

'Maybe I should just go to the police,' I mumble to my feet.

'Because it's been proved that police stations are really safe and that the police do not have it in for you. At all.'

'Well, where then?' I yell, surprising both of us. 'Where do I go? Who can I trust?'

Jay doesn't answer me. And after glaring at him for as long as I can, I rest my head back on my knees and shut my eyes.

'OK,' Jay says finally. 'We go to your dad's apartment. We got no other choice.'

My head flies up.

'We case it first though,' he says, eyeing me warily. 'We don't just walk straight in. We sneak in. We do as you say, grab a change of clothes, some money, leave your dad a note and then we're gone.'

I ignore the fact he used the word *case* as casually as I use the word *OK* – as though casing joints is something he does regularly. 'It's an Upper East Side apartment. You can't just sneak in,' I point out, already starting to walk towards the river.

'We'll see about that,' Jay says, running to catch me up.

12

It's not about me being a witness. The final dot materialised a while ago in my mind but I kept ignoring it, shoving it aside, not wanting to face up to the picture that was slowly taking shape. When Jay asked me why they hadn't shot at me I told him I didn't know. But I did. Or I had an idea at least. I just didn't want to admit it to myself, let alone to him. But as we climb the steps on to the bridge the picture is revealed as surely as the skyline of New York right ahead of us.

I was twelve. We were living in Nigeria. My dad's company was doing business with a lot of the oil companies in the region. We lived in a compound like every other ex-pat who didn't have a death or kidnapping wish, and I went to an international school that had more security around it than the Pentagon. We had maids and a driver and I had my very own bodyguard – Felix. Sound over the top? Not to my father – his company is a private security firm. Felix was one of his men. And at twelve years old I didn't know any different anyway. Before Nigeria we lived in Pakistan – not exactly Disneyland. My whole childhood was spent behind electronic gates, around adults who packed firearms and spoke in military-sounding acronyms about things like collateral, targets and marks.

My father is paranoid – he says he has to be. Paranoia keeps his clients – and he has many of the wealthiest people in the world on his client roster – alive and in good health. His company provides surveillance and close protection to oil barons, royal families, government officials and bank personnel in developing countries – the kind of people who are often targeted by criminal gangs. He also supplies private contractors in places like Iraq and Afghanistan – that's another more polite term for mercenaries – people who basically get paid to play *Call of Duty* for real and who work for the highest bidder rather than for king, country, or because they're inspired by that little thing called patriotic duty.

The specialist work, which my dad mainly handles himself, involves dealing with hostage-taking and kidnapping cases, especially in countries where corruption is so endemic the police can't be trusted. A lot of the time the police are the ones behind the crime in the first place. Maybe that's why I'm so sceptical about trusting them now.

Felix was with me from the age of seven. A constant at my side, with a Glock 19 in a holster under his jacket and my schoolbag over his arm. He came with me to school and he picked me up at the end of the day. He took me to ballet class and sat and watched me plié and curtsey and try to pirouette. He even used to pin my hair in a bun when it came loose; his scarred, rough hands more used to stripping gun parts, gentle as could be as he tried to figure out how bobby pins worked. He came with me on play-dates and more often than not he *was* my play-date. He taught me to swim. He taught me darts. He taught me to play poker (when my dad wasn't around). He taught me bad jokes, and basic self-defence moves like sticking thumbs in eyeballs and aiming for the balls. He taught me how to read body language and to recognise the little tells when someone is lying – the heightened pitch of a voice, a lack of hesitation when answering questions – things like that. He taught me how to make bacon caramel popcorn and he taught me not to be afraid of the dark.

He died on a street in broad daylight, his blood draining out his body before my eyes.

He died because of me.

They weren't trying to shoot me then either, the three men who cut us up in a rusting van on the way back from school and jumped out waving shotguns and yelling – they were trying to kidnap me. That's what my father told me later, weeks after Felix's funeral, when I was just coming out of my catatonic state of shock but still refusing to speak.

They had thought I was some diplomat's kid. At any rate a kid with parents who were rich enough to send her to the international school in the centre of Lagos in a blacked-out Mercedes car. The kidnappers couldn't actually tell us what they were thinking or why they chose me, because they were all too dead to talk. Felix shot and killed two of them during the gun battle that ensued and the third – well, he died too, shortly afterwards. My dad claimed the police had caught him and he'd been shot attempting to escape custody, but I have a theory that it wasn't the police that caught up with him at all. It wasn't like my father to rely on the police for anything. He would have had someone from his team straight on it. He never leaves stray threads hanging.

I guess the kidnappers should have done their research better when they picked me as a target.

*   *   *

As I walk along beside Jay that's what I'm thinking of. I'm thinking of Felix and about the similarities between that day and this.
They didn't shoot me then, they shot Felix and they shot my
driver. They needed me alive to get the ransom. But if they are
trying to kidnap me, who is Agent Kassel and what does she have
to do with anything?

Jay glances over at me. 'What's up?' he asks. 'You look like you
just saw a ghost.'

'Nothing,' I mumble. 'Just tired.'

He mutters something under his breath.

'What is that?' I ask. 'Spanish?'

'Yeah,' he says.

We're halfway across the bridge. The view from here is incredible. The whole of Manhattan lies gleaming and proud. If any city
can be said to thrust, then it's Manhattan. The spit of land it sits
on thrusts out into the water and the buildings thrust up into the
sky. Even the Freedom Tower, which stands close to where the
Twin Towers once stood, is tall and proud and defiant. The iconic
Brooklyn Bridge straddles the river just down from us, a moving
cloud of people swarming over it like locusts about to descend on
the city and strip it bare. I'm glad we chose the Manhattan Bridge
route. It's almost devoid of pedestrian traffic, though trains rumble
across regularly above us, and from the Lycra on display it seems
to be popular with joggers.

We've been walking for an hour and I've given up on trying to
wipe away the sweat. My hair is plastered to my neck and my lips
are dried and cracking. My knees sting and smart with every step
I take and my shoulder is so tender that it jars with every stride.

'Where are you from?' I ask, squinting at Jay.

'New York,' Jay replies, offering me a sardonic look in return.

'No. I mean, your heritage,' I say, pressing on. 'Where are your family from, originally?'

'I'm half Cuban. The better-looking half at least.'

'And the modest half?' I ask.

He laughs under his breath. 'My father was Irish-American. He ran out on us though when I was three. So I hope I didn't inherit shit from him.'

Fair enough, I think to myself, studying him anew. Half Cuban, yeah that makes sense. The eyes, the tan skin, the way he moves, cruising a very fine line between sexy and *don't mess with me*. Hell – did I really just think the word *sexy*? Clearly I'm delirious with dehydration, shock and endorphin overload. He's a car thief. And he's a gang member. *Really* not sexy. I need to get a grip.

'You not hot?'

'Excuse me?' I ask, wondering if my heat-addled brain misheard.

'You look hot.' He rolls his eyes in the face of my dislocating jaw. 'I meant you're sweating. Why don't you take off the sweater? It's kind of attracting attention, little Miss NYPD.'

What's beneath will probably attract more, I think to myself. I shake my head at him and increase the length of my strides, even though it makes me sweat even more.

'Suit yourself,' I hear Jay say, then after a few seconds he catches me up. 'Wait, are you naked underneath that?'

'No!' I yell, staring at him. God, what is with the interrogation? 'What's it to you anyway?'

'Nothing. I was just going to offer you my T-shirt to wear if you needed it, you know, to protect your modesty.'

'Really?' I ask, not sure if he's joking.

'No. Not really,' he answers, grinning at me. He glances down at his T-shirt. 'It's kind of filthy.'

I shake my head at him, then exhale loudly, blowing my hair out of my sweaty face. I'm so hot. If I have to keep wearing the damn sweater I'm probably going to collapse from heat stroke and dehydration. 'Don't stare,' I warn him. 'If you stare I'm putting it back on.'

'Hey,' he says, doing that *I surrender* gesture with his hands again, 'It's your call. I'm just saying. You look hot . . .' He presses his lips together to rein in the laugh. 'Sweaty, I mean.'

I walk ahead of him a few steps and tear off the sweater, instantly relishing the prickle of air against my sweat-coated skin. I glance down. At least it's not a white camisole top. It's pink. I pull it away from where it's stuck to my skin and hear Jay make a whistling sound through his teeth behind me.

I whip my head around. He is of course looking in the opposite direction. But I can tell he's grinning. I ball up the sweater and hold it against my chest, my cheeks on fire. If I didn't need it to cover myself with it I'd throw it at his head.

'You're making a lot of joggers very, very happy,' Jay says. He's snuck up behind me, walking in my shadow, and his breath hits the back of my neck making me shiver. Or maybe it's just the wind off the East River. Or shock working its way out of my system. I grit my teeth and say nothing, marching on ahead of him, refusing to let on he's riled me. He catches me up.

'So how far is it from here?' he asks, his attention on the city-scape stretching out ahead of us like it's a stage set cut out of card.

'I don't know,' I admit, eyeing the never-ending spread of skyscrapers against the achingly-blue, painted sky.

'How can you not know? It's your apartment, right?'

'No. It's my dad's apartment. I only just moved here to live with him.'

Jay sidesteps out of the way of a jogger. 'Where were you living before?' he asks.

'Oman.'

His eyebrows shoot up. 'In the Middle East?'

I glance at him, trying not to look surprised that he knows where Oman is. Normally when I tell people I get asked things like: *Is that a state in the Mid-West?* Or, *Is that where they found Osama Bin Laden hiding out?* 'Yeah,' I say.

'Bet you wish you'd stayed put.'

I press my lips together, remembering my last few days there. They weren't much fun either. My mum yelling at me for getting expelled, my father trying to convince her to let me come to the States with him, friends treating me as if I was contagious or just plain mental.

'You're American though, right?' Jay asks.

'Half,' I tell him, 'like you.'

'The hot half or the modest half?' He's nudging me with his eyes, trying to get a reaction or a smile out of me, but I feel like I'm running on empty. I have no smile to give.

'My dad's American,' I say tiredly. 'My mum's half English, half Russian.'

I can feel his eyes skimming me, checking me out in the light of this new information, and I stare straight ahead, focussing on the rooftops getting closer, wishing I could take a flying leap from the bridge like Spider-Man and find myself clinging to the top of the Empire State Building.

Jay's gaze burns. I have my mother's pale English skin and Slavic features – overly-full lips, blue-grey eyes that slant a little, and my father's poker-straight brown hair. It's a weird combination. It took me a very long time to grow into my features and some days I'm not sure I have or that I ever will. I hate people scrutinising me. My shoulders pull back and my chin lifts as though I'm standing in a ballet studio in front of an examiner. I will myself to shrink a few inches and for my hips to get smaller, even as I squeeze the sweater tighter against my chest. My skin prickles with heat.

Jay doesn't make that sucking noise through his teeth. He doesn't make another comment in fact about my looks or my family or where I'm from. All he says is, 'This crime that you witnessed, it wasn't at the apartment, right? We're not about to walk into a place that's criss-crossed with yellow tape and overrun with police?'

'No,' I say. 'I was staying with friends of my father's in Brooklyn for a few days while he was out the country.'

'The old man doesn't trust you not to party while he's away?'

'No. He just likes to know where I am.' *Kind of goes with the territory*, I add silently.

After the attempted kidnapping in Nigeria we moved to Oman, where it was safer, but my dad never eased up on the whole personal security. In fact, he doubled it. I was the only kid in my new school with not one, but two personal security guards to accompany me on the school run. It was one of the reasons my mother left him and hooked up with Sven, the doctor with as much personality as a jar of pickled herring. My father was obsessed with tracking our every move, and it got too much for her.

My dad only eased up on the close protection in the last year or so, realising finally I think, that his paranoia had cost him his wife and was about to cost him his only daughter. I mean, try going out for dinner accompanied by a six foot two Israeli bodyguard who likes to flash his gun every time your date leans in too close.

Yeah, having a bodyguard did wonders for my social life, but as Jay and I head down off the bridge and enter the grid of streets that make up Manhattan, I muse on the realisation that maybe my dad had a point with the close protection after all.

13

I tell Jay the address and he heads us in the right direction. At least I think he's heading us in the right direction until he crosses the road and I see he's making for a subway entrance.

'Woah,' I say, grabbing his arm. 'I thought you said we didn't have enough money for the subway.'

'We don't. But I'm not walking five hundred blocks.'

'It's not that far.'

'It's not that near either. If I'd have known your dad lived in Trump Tower I would never have agreed to walk. I thought you knew where we were going and that it was within walking distance. In case it's escaped your attention Manhattan is BIG.'

'He doesn't live in Trump Tower.'

'Close enough.'

'How are we going to get on the subway? We don't have any money.'

'Trust me,' he says with a touch of impatience.

'Stop asking me to do that,' I say, equally as impatiently.

We glare at each other for a second before a smile starts to curve his bottom lip, though it doesn't quite reach his eyes. 'Then at least stop doubting me,' he says.

I don't even know you, I want to yell. Instead I let him walk ahead of me down the stairs and I follow, albeit dragging my heels.

It's hot as a sauna in hell down in the subway. Jay has stopped at the bottom to tie his shoelace. Except he's not really tying his shoelace, he's *casing* the ticket hall for uniforms. I slump beside him, leaning against a wall as tides of people push past me. My body decides to speak up and declare mutiny. It's had enough of walking and being dragged through one-hundred-degree heat. It's had enough of running and adrenaline cranks and being tossed around like a garbage bag. It wants a bath and a rub down with Deep Heat and my shoulder is begging for some liberally applied ice.

Jay glances up at me, shaking out the change from his pocket and counting it up. 'OK, we got enough for one ticket,' he says.

He strides to the machine and inserts our change. I force myself to ignore the aches and pains and tiredness which want to drag me to my knees, digging deep to find whatever energy remains. I push away from the wall and head over to join Jay by the machine. He hands me the ticket that it spits out. 'After you,' he says motioning to the turnstile.

I slit my eyes at him. If this is going to end in us having to run anywhere while people chase us, I'm not sure I can take part.

'Just walk through. I'll be right behind you,' he urges, his hands on my shoulders. I shudder. Last time he had his hands on my shoulders like that, a man was after us with a gun and he was trying to get me to run faster.

I slide through the turnstile gate and, once through on to the platform side, I look back. Jay is over by the exit turnstiles. He glances once over his shoulder, then places a hand on the turnstile and hops it, graceful as a panther. He takes my hand as he strolls past me, whistling, and pulls me after him down the stairs two flights to our platform. No one yells. No whistles or alarms ring.

I yank my hand free so I can keep my arms crossed over my chest and I let out a deep breath.

We wait at the far end of the platform beside a group of four-teen-year-old Russian girls wearing what can only be described as clothes inspired by a Victoria's Secret runway show, a fact that Jay seems oblivious to. He's too preoccupied with scanning the plat-form, eyes darting in every direction, his body angled closely into mine, as though he's trying to shield me from view, and I find myself leaning ever so slightly in towards him too, until I realise what I'm doing and shift away, edging more towards the girls.

I can pick up a few words here and there, though I'm far from fluent in Russian. My mother only spoke it on the phone with my granddad and quit trying to teach me when I was about nine and he died.

Jay might not have noticed the girls, but they have noticed him and are talking about him in a way which I'm sure would shoot his ego into the stratosphere if he understood what they were saying – something about wanting to know what's under his shirt and inside his . . . I frown then wrinkle my nose. Oh God. Since when did fourteen-year-old girls get so precocious?

'Come here,' Jay suddenly says, jerking his head at me.

I stare at him.

'Come here,' he says again, reaching for me and pulling me towards him.

I resist but he's stronger than me. He has one arm locked around my waist and the other reaches behind my head and for one totally crazy, surreal moment I think he's going to kiss me and my heart starts to beat like it's trying to drill a hole through my ribs, but all he does is yank my hair-elastic free so my hair falls down around my shoulders.

'What did you do that for?' I ask, annoyed. He's still holding me around the waist and I can feel my face flushing.

He lets go of me, but his other hand strokes my hair gently, positioning it over my cheek. 'There,' he says, 'covers the scratch. Makes you less noticeable.' His gaze falls to my legs, which no amount of spit-scrubbing could get clean, and he pulls a face. 'Kind of.'

The train tears into the station and we push on board. It's busy – rush-hour commuters filling up every inch of available space. The Russian girls squeeze on behind us. Jay reaches up for a handrail and I stretch almost so I'm *en pointe* and take hold too. At least the air conditioning is ratcheted up to a degree just south of a cryogenic lab so I can luxuriate in the feeling of sweat evaporating off my skin finally, goosebumps rippling in its wake. With so many people pressing in on us I actually feel safe, shielded, hidden. I glance up at Jay, who's swaying in rhythm with the train, the shadows under his eyes looking like bruises in the halogen strip lighting, and for the first time I start to believe that maybe we can make it through twenty-four hours. Could I say the same if I was alone?

'If I'd have known that it was Lingerie on the Subway Day today I'd have worn my best Calvins,' Jay murmurs suddenly in my ear. 'Between you and them,' he says, indicating the Russian posse giggling and swaying purposely into his back, 'I feel kind of overdressed.' I feel his eyes skimming the top of my breasts.

'Yeah, you're hating every second of it. I can tell. Eyes up, Moreno.'

He grins over the top of my head. 'Oh, it's Moreno now, is it?'
I shake my head. 'How can you smile?' I whisper as the train

grinds to a halt in a tunnel and I'm thrown irritatingly against him. 'With everything that's going on?'

He shrugs as I find my balance again, but his smile fades as though I've taken an eraser and wiped it clean off his face and I feel my own body react as though someone's pulled the plug out of the power supply to my muscles, and my mood dips instantly. I didn't realise how Jay's upbeat humour was actually getting me through this, was carrying me along like a tidal force.

When we reach Lexington, I let Jay push a way past the giggling, hair-flicking Russian girls wearing only their underwear and follow him off the train with a tightening sensation in my gut. We switch to the 6, heading uptown to 77th Street. Emerging back into the light I'm tentative, like a prairie dog peeking out a hole. It's like we've entered a whole new city, one that's buffed and polished to a high sheen – a *Gossip Girl* set poised and waiting for someone to yell *Action!*

The sidewalks are wider and cleaner, the traffic moves more fluidly. It even smells better. You can take a breath without being hit by a waft of burning pretzel, diesel fumes and hot dog grease. Jay makes that whistling sound through his teeth as he checks out the smart awnings bridging the sidewalks, each one manned by a doorman in a uniform. A lady in quick-clicking heels wearing mutantly-oversized sunglasses and walking her mutantly-under-sized dachshund, gives him a very wide berth, clutching her designer handbag tighter against her body. Jay gives her a smile that reveals a deep dimple in his right cheek, though a flash of anger lights his eyes like a stone striking flint. I'm surprised the woman doesn't set her dachshund on him.

From the tiny pull of muscle at the edge of Jay's eye and the tension in his shoulders I can tell that he's as on edge as I am though – and not because of the looks he's getting. What if he's right and they're here waiting for us?

'OK, this is it,' I say as we approach the corner of 80th and hover outside a gourmet deli admiring the watermelon selection.

'Is there anyone else in the apartment?' Jay asks.

'Like who?'

'I don't know. Your mum? A housekeeper? A butler?'

'My mum and dad are divorced. She's still in Oman.' *With Sven the pickled herring gynaecologist.* 'And no. There are no staff. The cleaner comes Mondays and Thursdays.'

Jay mutters under his breath, shaking his head in what I guess is disgust. I wonder what he'd say if he knew how many staff we had in Oman. My mum has two nannies just to look after my half-brother Oscar and then there's the cook, driver, housekeeper and gardener as well.

'So how exactly do we case the place?' I ask quickly.

'Well, you're going to stay out the way and I'm going to check it out, see if there's anyone sketch hanging around outside.'

'Sounds foolproof,' I say drily.

'Would you just trust me?' he snaps, glaring at me.

I narrow my eyes. Trust is a commodity as rare as unicorn horns, Felix used to say. If someone has to ask you to trust them, generally speaking it's best not to. Like all Felix's advice, I've tattooed it on my brain. There was one time I ignored it, with my ex-boyfriend Sebastian. He told me to trust him – that he knew exactly what he was doing. After it became clear that he really did not have a clue what he was doing, I decided to never make the same mistake again. But as I study Jay, who's still busy glaring at me, his nostrils flaring like a horse, I remember the fact that he's a car thief. And a gang member. Checking things out, *casing things,* is probably his day job.

'Give me that,' Jay suddenly says, pointing at my chest.

'What?'

He grabs the sweater from my hands before I can argue and shakes it out. I stare at him indignant, crossing my hands over my chest.

'What are you . . . ?' I stop when I see he's pulling it on over his T-shirt.

He rolls down the sleeves that I'd rolled up and then offers me that trademark grin of his. 'How'd I look?'

'Like someone in a really lame cop disguise.'

He grins some more and, with a flourish, pulls something out the back pocket of his jeans. I think he's going for the gun and throw myself forwards, grabbing his wrists and pushing my body against his, trying to hide it from view. We're on a street. Is he a complete asshat? He cocks his head at me in amusement, glancing down at my chest pressed against his and smiling. Then he nods to his hands, which are crushed against my stomach, and shows me not the gun but a police department badge and ID.

'Where did you . . . ?' I break off once again and draw in a guttering breath. He took it from the same cop he stole the gun from. The dead cop, that is. I stare at it like it might be contaminated. The boy has balls. And he knows it. Right now he looks as pleased as if he's just won a grand slam. He probably wears the same expression when he manages to put his underpants on the right way round.

Seeing the ID in his hand spins me right back to the cop station. For the last hour I'd managed to stuff the memories into the far recess of my brain but now the stream of images from last night blasts me again in a full-on military-style assault – dead bodies, streams of blood, the *rat-tat-tat* of heavy weapons fire. I swallow rapidly, trying to force the grotesquely frozen stills of bullet-ridden bodies and a pair of ice-blue eyes out of my head.

After the attempted kidnapping in Nigeria, I stopped talking, I was trucked off to a therapist who gave me some techniques for managing the panic attacks and flashbacks that I was having. I learned to concentrate on my breathing, to focus on a totally innocuous object and start describing it in my head until I stopped freaking out. Often I run through ballet steps. This time I choose the spire at the top of the Empire State Building, which is just visible if I crane my neck backwards. I picture myself climbing it. I try to imagine what it would feel like up there with the wind sawing at me, the spiralling view down to the sidewalk below – people as ants, noise just a memory. My pulse starts to race. But in a good way. In a way that's not connected to fear.

When the playback of the night before fades I turn back to Jay. 'What are you planning on doing with your fake cop costume?' I ask.

'Hey, these are bona fide cop props,' he answers, plucking at the NYPD sweatshirt and shooting me a hurt face. 'And to answer your question I'm going to walk into your fine apartment building and tell the doorman I'm an off-duty cop.'

My eyebrows raise another half inch. 'Because off-duty cops walk around the city wearing sweatshirts advertising they're cops all the time, never mind it's a hundred degrees outside. And never mind you look like the youngest cop ever recruited in the history of policing.'

He *tsks* at me. 'Have you never seen *21 Jump Street*?'

I close my eyes and take a deep breath.

He carries on, shoving the ID back into his pocket. 'I'll tell them I'm investigating some suspicious activity a member of the public alerted me to.'

'Suspicious activity?'

'Yeah, maybe an attempted burglary. There a back entrance?'

'Excuse me?'

'To the building?'

'Yes,' I say. 'There's a fire escape that leads into a little square at the back. But it's locked.' I feel the need to gain control of this situation. And fast.

'I'm going to open it,' he tells me. 'You're going to be waiting out there. And you're going to sneak in when I distract him. Got it?'

Actually, it's not a bad plan. Considering it's the only one we have. 'OK,' I say, grudgingly.

'What apartment number?' he asks, brusque now, down to business.

'Twenty-five. Twentieth floor.'

'I'll see you up there. Wait for me in the fire escape.'

'How are you going to get up there?' I ask.

'I'll figure that out. Don't worry.'

Don't worry. Up there with *trust me.*

'No,' I say, not willing to leave this all in his hands, '*I'll* figure it out.'

14

Five minutes. Ten minutes. My foot taps and a teardrop of sweat trickles its way down my spine, soaking into the waistband of my shorts. Where is Jay? Why hasn't he let me in yet? I'm crouching down behind the garbage and recycling bins in the yard area. The stench of rotting food fills my nostrils, and my stomach, which had been growling with hunger fifteen minutes ago, roils now with nausea.

Jay circled the block before on his own, eyes open for anyone suspicious – or anyone in a cop's uniform. We figured that whoever is after me may have caught a glance at Jay when he pulled up alongside me and threw open the car door, but not for long enough that they'd recall him.

After he had cased the block for anything sketch and was satisfied it was all clear, we walked down the side alley and Jay gave me a boost over the gate that leads into the yard before he headed on around to the front modelling the NYPD sweater and a swagger straight out of *Miami Vice*.

This was a bad idea. I stare at the back door willing it to open.

As I squat amid the recycling, waiting, I try to wrap my head once more around what's going on. Is this another attempted kidnapping? I press the heels of my hands into my eyes, trying to force some clarity of thought through the spongy mess that is my brain.

It doesn't feel right. Most kidnappers wouldn't keep coming after the first attempt failed. That's not just relentless. That's *Terminator* determined. Shit. *Think. Think it through.* Why would someone be trying to kidnap me? My father's wealthy, but he's no Bill Gates, so money doesn't seem like much of a motive. Which leaves love, lust or loathing – they're the only motives behind any crime, according to my dad, though I think he stole that particular saying from Hercule Poirot. I think it's safe to discard love and lust as motives, which leaves only loathing.

So, either someone hates me or . . . the wheels spin . . . they hate my father. There are a couple of people who probably would put their hands up and admit to hating me – but Oscar is only three and hates everyone who dares tell him 'no', and my ex-boyfriend Sebastian may post vicious slander on Facebook but I highly doubt he'd go this far.

A lot of people, however, do hate my father, including but not limited to my mother, though I discount her automatically. Could it be something to do with my father's new job? With this gang task force he's heading up? That doesn't make sense either though. If there was any risk whatsoever to my safety my father would have assessed it and would never have left me alone, not even to go to the bathroom, never mind out of his sight for a week in New York.

For a split second I hear Felix, his voice a whisper behind me. I spin around, half expecting to see him there, crouching down behind the garbage bins alongside me. There's nothing of course, except some trash bags spilling their guts. I try to imagine what Felix would do in this situation, but the fact remains that I'm not an ex-SAS soldier, trained in military tactics and survival.

Work with what you got, Felix used to say. I glance down at my polka-dot pyjama shorts and scratched-up hands and legs. That's not that helpful, as advice goes. But then I realise that I do have something. I've got my brain. And everything I've ever learned from my father and Felix, which might not make me Nikita, but it's not like I'm totally helpless either. And I'm not alone – I've got Jay, that has to count for something.

For the first time since all this began I realise that I've been letting everyone else call the shots and I've just been reacting – letting shock and panic rule me. I need to lock those down, push back the fear. I need to be smart. I've been worried about playing by the rules, but there are no rules any more. For an instant I get a hit, similar to the one I get when I stand on the edge of a building and feel the wind pummelling me. The sense of empty air, dead space all around, stars flying through my bloodstream.

My head tips backwards then, taking in the bulk of the building. There's more I can work with up there in my dad's apartment. I just need to get in.

So where is Jay? What is he doing in there? Asking the doorman on a date?

I get up, intending to scoot closer and see if I can peer through the small pane of glass set high in the door, when all of a sudden it flies open and Jay appears. My heart rockets into my mouth and I fall back on to my haunches, ducking down behind the bins once more.

'Yes, sir, you're right,' Jay says over his shoulder to someone. 'There's no one out here. Good to be sure though.'

He turns away but his heel catches the door, stopping it from slamming. By the time I make it across the yard he's gone, but the door is wedged open with a piece of folded paper that Jay has stuffed against the doorjamb. I prise it open as carefully and quietly as I can. I can hear voices heading away back towards the lobby – Jay and the doormen talking animatedly about a game, something about the Yankees being on a winning streak – and I take the opportunity to slip inside and make for the stairs.

I run up the first flight and when I hit the second floor I fly through the exit on to the landing and head straight for the elevator. It feels like an hour I stand there waiting for the doors to ping open, and once they do I dart inside, relieved that it's empty. I shove an empty Coke can, taken from the recycling bin outside, and wedge it into the groove so that the doors won't shut, and then I hit the emergency button.

The elevator lets out a wail and the doors start dementedly bashing the Coke can as they try to close. I head straight for the stairwell and am on the fourth floor already before I hear the doorman heading upwards, his breathing laboured, cursing the damn elevator alarm under his breath.

I'm glad I called the elevator on the second floor and not the fifteenth, or he'd be dead from a heart attack before he even made it, and then we'd have that on our hands too. The doorman eventually huffs his way out on to the landing and a split second later I hear quicker, lighter footsteps running up behind me. I lean over the banister and see Jay taking the steps three at a time. He's on me in no time and then whipping straight past.

'I thought you were going to wait for me on the twentieth,' he says as he runs.

I grit my teeth and follow behind him, having to use the banister to haul my way up, pushing past the burn in my thighs and my muscles, which are ready to go on strike. I overtake him on the twelfth floor and have put a flight between us by the time we make the twentieth. I wait for Jay, sucking in large gulps of air and unsticking my top from my sweat-coated skin. Jay reaches the landing and stands there panting for a few seconds, before he pulls the gun out from his waistband and hovers behind the door. I place my hand on his shoulder and my other hand on top of the gun and prise it carefully out of his hands.

'What?' Jay asks.

'You've left the safety on,' I say, showing him how to release the catch. I check the chamber and then release the clip to check how many bullets we have. Then I look up. Jay is staring at me with his mouth hanging open.

I ram the clip back into place. 'My dad owns a security company. I grew up around guns.'

He frowns at me. 'Hell, if I had known I was on the run with Rambo I would have let you lead the way from the start.'

I push past him. 'Get behind me.'

'With pleasure,' he says, stepping aside.

I reach for the door handle.

'Hang on!' He catches my arm. 'The doorman reported no unexpected visitors, but that's not to say they couldn't have snuck past. I mean, that guy's hardly Mr Aware. I could have flashed him a toy truncheon and a pair of fluffy handcuffs and he'd have spread his legs. What if we burst through here and they're on the other side of the door or they're waiting in your apartment?'

I take a deep breath and settle my shoulders, staring at the door trying to visualise the cop-killer on the other side. 'I'm a good shot,' I say, but my voice shakes as I say it. *What if there are two of them?* the voice in my head points out. I ignore it. There's no room for second-guessing.

Jay blinks at me. 'Right,' he says and his hand falls away from my wrist, leaving a burning patch of skin.

I *am* a good shot – my dad made sure of that. I've been taking lessons every week since I was thirteen. But like anyone who works in close protection or in the military will tell you, firing at a paper cut-out of a person and firing at an actual person are two very different things. It's not uncommon, I've heard, for people to freeze when faced with a flesh-and-blood target. My hand shakes and I cup the elbow on my firing arm to steady it.

Jay waits for me to nod and then opens the door for me, just a crack. I nudge it with the barrel of the gun. It eases open and we both let out a breath. The hallway is empty. We step out of the stairwell, our footsteps cushioned by the deep tread of the carpet. It's like walking through a snowdrift, but I'm not complaining. Silence is an asset. We move slowly down the corridor, our ears straining for any sounds, until we're standing in front of my dad's door. It's closed and the keypad beside it is blinking red. No one's tried to tamper with the lock. I let the gun fall to my side.

'Woah,' Jay whispers close to my ear. 'What's with the high-tech entry pad? What's wrong with a good old-fashioned key?'

I don't answer because I'm concentrating on tapping in the eight-digit code. The pad beeps and invites me to press my thumb against it.

'Holy shit,' Jay murmurs as the light flips to green and the door clicks. 'Is this when you tell me your dad is actually Jason Bourne?'

We step into the apartment, which is ghostly quiet and still, as though it's holding its breath, waiting to ambush us. I wait for the air to settle, holding up my hand for Jay to be quiet. Finally, when I'm sure I can't sense anyone, I turn around and ram the three bolts across the door.

When I turn back Jay is already making himself at home, throwing open doors and making an appreciative noise when he finds the kitchen. He heads straight for the tap and sticks his head under it, gulping down water and soaking his entire face and half the kitchen floor in the process. When he comes up he shakes himself like a wet dog and I dance out of his way as water sprays me. I reach past him and grab two glasses from the cabinet above and hand him one. We both drink until we're gasping, holding on to swollen stomachs.

'You know, I think this might be the safest place to hang out after all,' Jay says, opening up cupboards. 'It's not like they're getting through that door. And we have food. It's like a five-star panic room.'

I place my glass on the side and stagger towards the hallway. Jay is wrong. We need to be quick. I need to get my stuff together, leave my dad a note, and then we need to get out. They've tried three times and failed. They're not about to stop now.

'We're not staying,' I tell him as I walk out the room.

15

We have to get out of here but, first things first, I need a shower. Half my brain argues with me about the stupidity of taking a shower at this particular moment in time, but the other half of my brain doesn't give a damn. I'm rank and disgusting, and if I don't get under a scalding jet of water in the next sixty seconds then I'm going to melt down. I want to scrub the blood from my legs, along with the memories of this morning. I want a shower even more than I want to eat. Even more than I want to sleep.

Even more than you want to live? I hear Felix yell at me.

I stop stock-still in the middle of the hallway as though his ghost is standing right in front of me. The words ring in my ears. The reason Felix died was because I didn't listen to him.

Ever since then I've done my best to follow orders, to do what I'm told. To the point of accepting the Israeli bodyguard accompanying me on dates. But now there's no one to tell me what to do – I have to rely on myself. And right now I am making the call that it's safe to take ten minutes to regroup and grab supplies. I'll live with the consequences. But I take the gun into the bathroom with me and set it down on the side of the bath.

I lock the bathroom door and step towards the mirror, flinching at the horror film extra staring back at me. Jesus. That's not pretty.

I turn around quickly and tear off my clothes, then step under the shower, letting out a groan that quickly becomes a hiss when the water hits my thighs. Ignoring the sting of flayed flesh, I soap myself and my hair, before quickly rinsing and jumping out. I grab a towel and wipe the steam from the mirror. My face stares back, clouded and distorted, pale and wide-eyed, with dark shadows beneath my eyes and hollows below my cheekbones. Still not that pretty. But better. The cut close to my eye is just a scratch, a fading red line beneath my eye.

When I step out in the corridor I hear Jay banging around in the kitchen, but I head straight to my bedroom and stand in the doorway taking stock. Nothing appears any different to how I left it. Not that I was expecting it to. The bed is made. My books are lined up tidily on the shelf. The photograph of me and Maddie – my best friend back in Oman, who I'm not sure is still my best friend, given the fact she's not talking to me – still sits at the same angle on the corner of my desk beside the stack of information about the two-week dance intensive I was meant to start today. My alarm clock blinks the time: 10.07 a.m.

I take a step into the room. My ballet certificates and awards are framed and hung on the wall – one of my father's efforts to make me feel at home. He was so happy I was moving to New York to live with him that he ran straight out and bought new covers for the bed and tried to fix up my new bedroom to make it as welcoming as possible. Though his idea of what a seventeen-year-old girl might be into was slightly off, I was so relieved he wasn't angry with me about the expulsion that I just smiled politely at the sight of the pink comforter on the bed and the teddy bear wearing ballet shoes he'd propped on the pillow.

He even took me shopping for new clothes, handing me his credit card and encouraging me to spend whatever I wanted.

I slide open the wardrobe doors and stare at the few things I did actually buy, most of them still wearing their price tags. For a moment I stand there like a bunny in the headlights. Then, with an elastic snap, my brain kicks into gear again; I need something that blends in, something with pockets, something with a waistband. I snatch a pair of shorts, a tank top, clean underwear and a bra. I need to be quick. We need to move.

But first I need to treat my legs. They feel like jelly, as though I've climbed Everest and slalom skied down it. And there are still those slivers of glass that I need to get out. Beside me on the bed are tweezers and disinfectant I brought from the bathroom. I wrap the towel tighter around me and bend over my thigh with the tweezers in my hand. The first couple of splinters come easily enough but the third one has me sucking in air through my teeth and cursing like an Israeli soldier.

'Do you need a hand?'

My head jerks up. Jay's standing in the doorway. My first instinct – to tell him tersely that I'm fine – is overridden by the look on his face. Gone is the smirk and that almost permanent flicker of mocking amusement which lights his eyes; instead he looks as wasted and shell-shocked as someone who's just walked unharmed out of a high-speed car crash that killed everyone else. I guess the adrenaline supply has finally cut out and he's crashing as hard as I am.

I nod and he walks towards me, feet scuffing the floor. I notice the beads of water still clinging to his hair and the fact that his T-shirt is sticking to him like a second layer of skin, revealing every line of muscle. He glances around the room and a smile tweaks at his lips when he sees the pink comforter and the teddy bear sitting atop it. I glare at him, daring him to say a word. Perhaps it's the look I give him or maybe it's the sight of the gun on the nightstand, but either way he thinks twice and the smile fades.

'Here,' he says, shoving something at me. It's a bag of frozen soybeans wrapped in a tea towel. 'For your shoulder,' he says, nodding towards it.

I take the frozen bundle, murmuring thanks while wondering when he even noticed my shoulder was hurting. He drops to his knees in front of me, taking the tweezers from my hand without a word.

I squeeze my knees together and pull the towel closer, but he doesn't seem to notice that I'm to all intents and purposes naked but for a small rectangle of Egyptian cotton. He puts his hand under my knee and pulls my leg gently closer. I inhale sharply, though not because it hurts.

'I haven't even touched you yet,' Jay says under his breath.

I watch his dark head, bent over my thigh, and my heart rate accelerates as fast as I've seen Jay drive. Angrily, I try to rein it in, trying to dismiss it as the toxic effects of the adrenaline and shock leaching through my body. I press the ice packet to my shoulder, hoping that the cold will somehow counter the effect of his fingers, but no joy. His thumb gently grazes the top of my leg, looking for the splinter, and I almost leap a foot off the bed.

'So, your dad – this GRATS thing – what is it exactly? You said it was something to do with the police,' Jay asks, seemingly unaware that my leg is jerking like it's in spasm with every pass his thumb makes across my skin. I wince as the tweezers suddenly dig in.

'Kind of,' I say through gritted teeth as he pulls the splinter free. 'It's a task force and it works with the police. But it's government-led. They're looking at ways to stop gangs trafficking.'

Jay grabs the bottle of disinfectant and pours some on a cotton pad. He starts wiping it over my knees and thigh and I hiss loudly and grip the edges of the bed. 'Trafficking what? Guns? Drugs?' he asks.

I hesitate for a second before speaking. 'People,' I finally say.

He blinks at me, confused. 'What?'

'People,' I say again, watching him carefully. 'Girls, mainly.'

I wait for him to figure it out and watch his face closely as he does. He pulls back away from me, grimacing.

'Shit,' he says.

'Yeah,' I say. 'It's the fastest growing criminal activity in the world. Over two and a half million people each year, mainly women and girls.'

I sound like a walking, talking UN report. But that's because I'm quoting directly from one I found on my dad's desk a week ago and skim-read.

'The task force is trying to find a way to stop the gangs from trafficking. They asked my dad to lead it because of his background. We used to live in Nigeria and there's a big trade from there into the US. And, like I told you, he has a private security company. He's led hostage rescue and special ops missions in countries where the UN and Western forces won't step foot.'

I know I sound like a woman on a PR mission and it makes me cringe. The need to paint a glossy picture of my dad's line of work is deeply ingrained, and has been since I was about thirteen and figured out that he makes his money from some of the dirtiest people on the planet – banks, oil companies, obscenely wealthy people protecting their obscenely vast amounts of wealth. Even warlords who need hired guns. It doesn't sit comfortably. It doesn't sit at all, actually. And I question it daily, believe me. It's why I don't like taking money from him. I spent the last two years teaching dance to little kids, saving every penny for the day I turned eighteen and left for college. I only moved to New York to live with him because I had to. No school in Oman wanted to take me. And then my dad took this job consulting for the government and I felt like it redeemed him slightly. It made moving here easier anyway.

Jay's resting back on his haunches. He's breathing shallow and fast but his gaze stays level and unfaltering as it meets mine. And that's when the final dot shimmers into view dizzyingly fast and the picture waves in front of me like a Bridget Riley painting, making me lurch backwards, nausea bubbling in the pit of my stomach.

'And you didn't think to mention this sooner?' Jay says, his voice laced with disbelief. He stands up and I have to tilt my head back to see him. 'It didn't cross your mind that maybe, just maybe, there might be a link between the fact your father is running a police task force cracking down on gangs that traffic people and the fact someone is out to get you like you are the goddamn *prize*.'

I can feel my breathing scattering all over the place. My internal organs feel like they're being speared on the ends of my ribs. 'Yes,' I whisper.

Jay stares down at me, his lips half parted and his eyes hooded.

'When you questioned why that cop didn't take the shot when he could have, yes,' I say quickly, too scared to look him in the face. 'Then I started to think maybe it *was* a kidnapping attempt. But . . .' I shake my head more violently, trying to find some kind of grip. It's like my thoughts are sliding around on ice in there. 'It just didn't add up. It still doesn't. I mean, my dad's insanely obsessive about security. You saw the door! My whole life I've been followed around by a big man with a big gun. Growing up I had more security than the freaking president. I don't just know how to fire a Glock 19,' I say, pointing at the gun I've left on the corner of my desk. 'I can strip, load and fire an M4 machine gun too. You know of any other seventeen-year-old girls who can do that?' Jay stares at me as though I've just walked straight out of the pages of *One Flew Over the Cuckoo's Nest*. 'If I was at any kind of risk from the people he was working against,' I say, my wet hair going flying, 'if there was even the smallest *whiff* of danger, my dad would never ever have just left me in New York unprotected. No way.'

Jay studies me warily, backing off. Maybe it was the comment about the M4.

'Look,' I say, my voice dropping, 'does it matter why they're coming after me?' I say. 'Really? What does it change?' I stand up and push past him. 'Nothing,' I spit angrily. 'It changes nothing.'

Jay doesn't say a word.

I turn to face him. He's staring at me with an expression I can't decipher – half glaring, half pained. 'You don't have to stick around. I can look after myself,' I tell him.

A shadow passes across his face but vanishes almost instantly. What was it? Hurt? Annoyance?

'I'm in this just as much as you now,' he says quietly. 'You think I can just walk out that door,' he gestures wildly towards it, 'and forget everything that's just happened? Go home and act like none of it occurred? Is *still* occurring?'

There's a pause that seems weighted on a gossamer strand and I'm aware of how important the next words out of my mouth are if I don't want to snap it . . . If I want him to stay.

'I need to get dressed,' I say, speaking the words softly and holding his gaze. 'Then we should go.'

He takes a second to process then he just nods once and leaves the room without another word and I let out a long breath. I'm not sure what scares me more right now, them coming through the door, or Jay walking out of it.

16

Thirty seconds later I am standing in the kitchen, which looks like a homemade bomb exploded in the middle of it. Jay is standing with his back to me, orchestrating some kind of clean-up, or possibly he's just rummaging through the debris seeing what further damage he can do.

'Wow,' I say, staring at the ripped-open packets and gaping cupboard doors spilling their contents happily to the floor. 'Make yourself at home.'

'Here,' he says, turning around and handing me a bowl piled high with pasta. 'I made you this.'

'You just made this?' I say, staring at the mountain of spaghetti.

'Yeah,' he says gruffly, grabbing his own plate off the side.

I open my mouth to tell him that we don't have time to stop for a sit-down meal and that we should just pack whatever we can stuff in a backpack and get the hell out of this place, but then my stomach overrides my brain cells. The smell of carbonara sauce hits my nostrils and I almost suffocate by sticking my face straight into the bowl and inhaling the contents.

Jay heads past me to the living room at the end of the hallway. We drop on to the leather sofa opposite the floor-length windows offering a view all the way to Central Park.

'Who needs a flat screen when you have a view like this?' Jay asks, gesturing with his fork.

I can't answer because I'm too busy forking spaghetti into my mouth.

'Is this the penthouse floor?' he asks.

I nod, swallow, and then glance down suspiciously at the contents of the bowl. 'Is there cream in this?'

Jay pauses with his fork halfway to his mouth. 'Are you serious?' he asks. 'You're worried about cholesterol? Never mind the fact you have a psycho killer chasing after you, you're worried about having a heart attack?' He shakes his head at me in disappointment. 'Priorities, man.'

I feel my cheeks burning.

He stuffs his mouth full of spaghetti. 'You don't drink coffee, don't take sugar, don't eat cream. What are you,' he asks through his mouthful, 'anorexic?'

My back teeth gnash together. 'No. I just . . . I have to watch what I eat,' I say to the spaghetti strangling my fork.

'Why?' he asks. 'You got a—' he breaks off, clears his throat, 'you got no worries there. You should see my cousin Maria. She's one Krispy Kreme away from having her own zip code.'

I fork another mouthful of the pasta into my mouth. I'm not sure if it's because I'm starving and my body is literally screaming at me like a drill sergeant to fill it with calories, but this pasta is very possibly the best thing I've ever tasted in my life. 'Look, it doesn't matter,' I say, forking up another mouthful. 'See, I'm eating it. It's good.'

'Yeah,' he says, eyeing me suspiciously until I swallow. 'My mom taught me to cook.'

His mum. My hand flies to my mouth as I remember the piece of paper Jay passed to me in the police station with her number on it. 'You never called her!' I say. In the next instant I'm remembering his fingers pressing against mine – that instant surge, like a connection being made, that made all my thoughts scramble, overrode my judgement and made me agree to help him.

'No,' he mumbles. 'Not yet.'

'Maybe you should.'

'Yeah,' he answers, stabbing at his food. 'Let's get out of here first.'

We eat like it's our last meal, not stopping to savour but only to refuel. Then we're both on our feet. My head and limbs feel unnaturally heavy, as though my blood has been replaced with liquid lead, and I remember that's why I normally avoid eating carbs and cream. It makes me feel sluggish. As well as the fact that when you're standing in front of a mirror in a leotard every day you become hyperaware of the smallest ounce of fat going somewhere it shouldn't. I freaking hate the body Nazism that goes hand in hand with a career as a dancer.

'I'll get some stuff together while you shower,' I say, trying to shake off the fog of tiredness that's descending.

'We got time?' Jay asks, though his face has brightened immeasurably at the thought.

It only seems fair, seeing how I had a shower, so I just shrug. 'I can get you a T-shirt to wear if you want to get rid of that one.'

'OK,' Jay says, following after me. 'Though I don't think we're the same size.'

Even though he's behind me I can feel his eyes scrolling down my body checking me out. I walk into my dad's bedroom.

'You can borrow something from my dad,' I say. I throw open the door to my dad's en-suite bathroom and Jay makes a beeline straight for it, while I head over to my dad's closet.

My dad only wears discreet designer clothes, all serving to make him blend in and project the image of him as professional and serious; exactly the kind of guy you'd want co-ordinating your rescue if Somalian pirates happened to kidnap you in the Gulf of Aden. His T-shirts are stacked in a neat pile in a drawer. I shake one out. My dad's a big guy. He's ex-military and still stays in shape, but it'll have to do. Jay's not exactly small either. With the T-shirt in hand I scan the closet. There are two dozen suits hanging on a rail, shoes polished to a high sheen lined up beneath them, and there on the shelf above the suits is the thing I am looking for. It's just a small black backpack, but when I grab hold of it, and feel the weight of it on my shoulder, I feel instantly better.

I head to the bathroom to give Jay the T-shirt. It's not until I'm standing in the doorway that I realise the shower is running and it's too late to turn away before I catch a glimpse of Jay stepping naked into the shower stall. He turns around and I have to fight to keep my eyes from flying to his chest and, well . . . lower. *Really* fight. I shut my eyes, toss the T-shirt in his direction and blindly stumble out of the room making some kind of mumbling apology as I go. The image of his ass is now scored on to my retina with a laser gun.

I smile to myself for the first time since all this started.

The keypad on the safe stares blandly back at me as though it's telling me not to waste my time. I stare it out. I'm on my knees next to my dad's desk, where the safe is hidden behind a panel in the wall.

My dad's codes might be uncrackable to strangers, but I know him. He doesn't go for the obvious – birthdays, telephone numbers, anniversary dates – he uses seemingly random sequences.

Except, they're not random. One time he was opening his safe and he quoted, out of the blue, a line from *Henry VI, Part 2* – *The first thing we do, let's kill the lawyers.* (This was just after my parents divorced.)

It took me ages to figure it out – that he was using the scene, act and line number as the combination. But once I had a theory I tested it at the first opportunity and, hey presto, it worked.

The Complete Works of Shakespeare sits open in front of me now, lifted from the shelf in the living room. But Shakespeare wrote a lot of words. A ridiculous amount of words. How could one person write so many words? I ponder as I flick quickly through it, my hands clumsy with urgency. The thin paper rips. On the fourth flick through, I'm starting to panic. If I can't get into the safe we're in trouble. We need what's in there.

Just as I'm about to toss the book and start raiding through all my dad's suit pockets for small change or anything that might be pawnable, something catches my eye. I flatten the page and see a small biro mark in the inner margin beside a quote from *King John*.

How oft the sight of means to do ill deeds makes deeds ill done!

Scene 2, Act 4, line 114.

I spin the dial. 2 – 4 –11 – 4.

The click is a beautiful sound. Almost as beautiful as the sight of what's inside. A stack of cash – probably enough to get Jay and me to the furthest corner of the South Pacific if we only had fake passports – a platinum credit card in my father's name, and one of his guns – a Smith & Wesson with two extra magazines lying beside it. I scoop it all out and shove the cash into the backpack I took from my dad's closet – his *go-bag*. The credit card I slip into the back pocket of my shorts. I check the gun and then push that into the bag too, along with the extra magazines and the Glock 19 we took from the policeman. For a brief moment I see myself – a girl on her knees pushing a wad of cash and a gun into a bag – and want to laugh at the absurdity of it all. Who have I become? But then I hear the shower cut out and jump instantly to my feet.

I reach across my dad's desk and scrawl a note on a Post-it.

Dad, I'm OK. Meet Tues 9 a.m., same place we bought the Statue of Liberty. Be careful. I love you, Liva

I shove the piece of paper into the safe, spinning the dial to lock it. I can only hope that my dad finds it, and that he knows where I'm talking about. It was the only place I could think of in a hurry, but it's a good meeting place – lots of open space, lots of people, lots of escape routes if necessary.

I run back into the hallway, opening my mouth to yell for Jay to hurry, and then I freeze. My stomach drops a thousand feet and slowly, very slowly, I cock my head towards the door. There it is again, a gentle *scrape scrape* sound – someone tampering with the keypad. With my heart audibly smashing into my ribcage I tiptoe backwards as quietly as I can, my eyes fixed on the front door the entire time.

I fumble without looking for the door handle to my dad's room and slip inside, closing the door gently behind me and twisting the lock. Then I run to the bathroom. Jay has a towel wrapped around his waist and is just bending to pick up his jeans from the sopping wet floor. He looks up in surprise when I burst in and straightens up slowly, giving me a slyly amused smile, as though he thinks I've burst in here specifically to catch another look at him naked, but then his expression switches to alertness when he sees the pure panic on my face and the go-bag in my hand.

'Someone's trying the door,' I whisper.

Jay tosses the towel instantly aside and starts pulling on his jeans. I twist my head automatically away but turn towards the mirror and manage to catch a second glimpse of him naked. He sits on the edge of the bath to pull on his socks and shoes as I crane to listen. The touchpad makes it harder to get through the door – no lock to pick. And the bolts will delay things, but at the end of a day it's just a door. And nothing has stopped them so far.

'Is there another way out of here?' Jay asks as he ties his shoes.

Our eyes meet in the mirror. Water is dripping from his hair and running in rivulets down his chest. I nod. 'Yes.' *But you're not going to like it,* I think silently to myself.

17

Jay jumps to his feet, snatching for his T-shirt, and I notice the NYPD sweatshirt lying by the laundry bin and grab for it, shoving it in the backpack. It's proved its worth already.

'Let's go,' I say, motioning for Jay to be quiet as he follows me out into my dad's bedroom.

There's a crash that makes us both freeze – the sound of someone slamming their whole body with force against the door. Once they make it through we'll have about ten seconds before they find us. I sling the bag on to my front, spin on my heel and grab hold of the window, sliding it open.

We're twenty floors up. The wind barrels into the room with hurricane force.

'What the—' Jay starts but his words are whipped away by the snap of the curtain and the noise from outside that's rushing in to fill the vacuum.

'It's the only other way out,' I tell him, shouting over the wind.

He gives me the look again, the one that tells me he thinks I'm certifiably insane. 'Two choices,' I tell him, jerking my head in the direction of the apartment door, where the crashing is only intensifying. It's not going to hold much longer.

A gunshot, followed instantly by the smack of a bullet ricocheting off metal, makes Jay jump. He inches to the window, arms spread wide. 'You have a parachute or something?' he asks.

'We're not going down,' I tell him, nudging him aside. 'We're going up.'

He leans through gingerly beside me, holding on to the wall for anchorage, and I point to the roof just a foot above us. There are more advantages to living in the penthouse than the view – something I discovered the first time my dad left me home alone.

Jay pulls back inside, fear turning his features waxen. He shakes his head violently and mutters a string of words in Spanish. He glances one more time at the door as though actually weighing a confrontation with a bullet as a more appealing option.

I ignore him and fit myself into the window frame, my hands finding the corners.

'Jesus Christ. You're not seriously going out there?' Jay asks, his fingers gripping my wrist.

I look at him and nod, and his hand falls away as he realises I'm deadly serious.

I take several deep breaths, trying to quiet my body. The stillness falls. It's the same feeling I get the split second before I step on stage, when the world falls away and it's just me and my breath and every cell in my body coming alive, attuned to every vibration, running totally in synch. On the out-breath I move, bracing for the impact of the wind. It tunnels into me, whipping my hair in front of my face and flattening my clothes against my body, but I'm in the zone and it's barely a hindrance. I slide my hand along the face of the building until I find the thin groove that marks the start of the guttering and then I take a step.

Jay swears under his breath, but I keep going, inching along the ledge. I don't look down, I just concentrate on keeping my balance, which is slightly off centre thanks to the weight of the bag. Once at the guttering, I ease my hand slowly under the metal bracket and grip tight before I step one foot off the ledge and swing my body around so I'm now face to face with the length of plastic tubing that runs down the side of the building. I hook my other hand around another metal bracket and my feet, stepped wide in a ballet stance, hold fast.

I turn my head. 'Come on,' I say to Jay, who is leaning out the window staring at me with eyes so wide they almost eclipse his face.

For a second I actually think he's going to say no and disappear back into the room but then there's an almighty sound of plaster and wood splintering and in the next second he's balanced in the window frame.

'Don't look down. Go slow,' I urge him.

His eyes lock on mine and I have to fight the urge to reach a hand out to him. My heart jerks to a halt in my chest as I watch him take a deep breath and step out on to the ledge. I breathe for him, willing his body to relax. He doesn't look down, he looks right at me the whole time, and I hold his gaze tight, as though it's a rope connecting him to me. He edges bit by bit towards me, until we're close enough for our fingers to touch.

'OK,' I say to Jay over the roar of the wind. 'See where my hand is? You're going to copy what I do. Exactly. OK?'

I can see he wants to argue with me, but then he changes his mind and he just nods, swallowing away his fear as best he can. He closes his eyes and presses his head back against the brickwork and I see him mumble something that sounds a bit like a prayer.

I twist around, aware that my hands are starting to sweat – that my grip is slipping. I don't have long. I grit my teeth and then I climb. It's not hard. The guttering is well bolted and my feet are nimble. I've got enough upper body strength to pull myself up without too much difficulty. It's all about forgetting what's beneath. If you lose concentration for one second and start thinking about the drop to the sidewalk below, then you're done for.

The last part of the climb is the hardest. I need to let go of the guttering with one hand, pull myself up with my arms and haul my leg over the ledge. I manage it and roll straight on to my front to look down. I expect to see Jay frozen to the guttering beneath me but he's already climbing, following in my footsteps, sure now and confident in his movements.

His hand appears on the ledge and I grab it and start pulling him, hauling him over the ledge. He collapses, panting, on to his back, clutching his side and breathing hard.

I lean over him, throwing the bag on to my back and tugging on his arm. 'Come on, get up.'

His eyes flash open. He stares at me as though he's seeing a stranger and it jolts me – but then he's on his feet again, lurching slightly.

I take his hand and pull him towards the fire escape that clings to the side of the building. I'm doubting anyone will follow us up on to the roof, which means their only option will be to retrace their steps and try to meet us at the bottom. They even have a head start. I do the calculation halfway across the rooftop and come skidding to a stop, almost tearing Jay's arm out of its socket.

'What?' he asks.

'They'll be waiting.' I say and start pulling him in the other direction, away from the fire escape. He doesn't pause even for a second, he turns with me, understanding. The other side of the building runs flush with the neighbouring apartment block. There's a drop though. Fifteen feet or so. Jay goes first, hanging over the side and landing in a crouch. He stands and catches me around the waist when I drop. He seems to have shaken off the side effects of the climb and is now sprinting way faster than me. I have to push to keep up with him and, as if he senses the gap widening, he slows and holds out his hand to me. I take it while still running and together we leap on to the fire escape that clings to the side of this building, sending shock waves reverberating hard through my bones with the impact.

The whole thing shakes as we slam down it, grabbing the railings and launching ourselves down whole flights in one leap. We're both high on adrenaline by the time we make it to the bottom and have to jump another twelve feet to make it to the sidewalk below. A few people have stopped to stare. Jay ignores them, swinging nimbly to the ground and then holding his arms out to catch me again. It's practised this time, almost choreographed. He places me down lightly and we sprint around the corner. Jay dashes straight into the road, ignoring the traffic, and the cars that swerve around him, honking. He flags down a yellow taxi by standing right in front of it so it has to emergency brake, then he throws open the door and we dive inside, panting, both of us yelling at the driver to *go*. The driver shakes his head at us but he puts his foot to the floor and obliges.

Sliding down low into the seats Jay and I peer nervously out the windows. Apart from a few people standing open-mouthed staring at us, and a few pausing to glance up at the fire escape as though wondering where the fire is, it doesn't look like anyone is following. There's no sign of the guy in the cop uniform.

We beat them.

We fall back against the seats, both of us breathing hard, and it's only then I realise we're still holding hands, our fingers linked tight. Jay seems to realise at the same time. His eyes meet mine and after a beat I feel him squeeze my hand and, without even thinking, I squeeze back. Then Jay rolls his head against the seat and starts laughing, gasping for breath, his free hand clutching his stomach. I stare at him wondering if he's lost it, but then a laugh bubbles up inside me too and bursts free, and in the next instant we're both laughing so hard that tears are falling down our cheeks. Just as suddenly though the laughter cuts out and we fall silent as if on cue. We sit, staring out our respective windows, our hands still linked across the back seat.

The driver, finding his moment, finally gets a word in. 'Where to?' he asks.

18

Jay looks at me. 'Did you get money?'

I nod, patting the bag.

'So, where do we go? A hotel?'

I shake my head. It's too obvious. And whoever it is that's after us, they're organised, meticulous and have access to online data and communications systems – how else did they tap my dad's phone to find me at the pick-up point? Hotels have to check ID. Hotels keep records. And if two people our age turn up without bags or ID we'd raise more than a few eyebrows.

'Too dangerous,' I say, glancing out the window and trying to think. An idea starts to take shape, thin and nebulous at the corner of my mind, then jumping fully formed into view in the next second. I turn back to Jay. 'We need to do the opposite of what they'll expect us to do. We need to confuse them.'

Jay's staring at me with this odd look on his face, as though he's trying to fathom me.

'Can you take us to an electronics store?' I ask the driver, who grunts in response.

'Electronics?' Jay asks, looking worried.

'We need a phone.'

He visibly relaxes and I wonder what he thought I wanted to buy – ingredients for a cluster bomb?

'What else is in the bag?' Jay asks.

I slip my hand from Jay's and unzip it, noticing that my fingers are trembling slightly. To be honest, other than the things I tossed in there from the safe, I'm not entirely sure myself what's in it. It's my dad's go-bag. Anyone in his line of work always keeps a bag like this at the ready in case of emergencies. I'm glad I thought to look for it in his wardrobe.

Keeping my eyes on the driver, who's separated from us by a scarred Plexiglas window, I pull out the NYPD sweater and quickly push the pile of cash and the guns to one side of the bag. Then I start rooting through the remaining contents, pulling them out and laying them on the tacky vinyl seat between us. There's a small wind-up torch that I test. It works. Of course it works. My dad probably checks this bag every month or so to make sure everything in it is fit for purpose. I toss two trauma bandages and a tourniquet on to the seat and Jay stops playing with the torch to watch. Next is a full water bottle, some dummy cords – small lengths of stretchy rope – a notebook, a permanent marker, a small pair of binoculars, and a switch-blade with a laser-sharp edge that makes Jay inch back in his seat when I flick it open. I open the front pocket and pull out some plastic flex cuffs.

'Kinky,' Jay says, admiringly.

I toss some small packets of honey on to the seat beside them.

'Even kinkier,' he says, his eyes dancing to me. 'If you were to combine the two.'

'It's for sugar hits. Instantaneous energy,' I say, ducking my head so he can't see the blood that's rushed to my cheeks. I want to ask him how handcuffs and honey equals kinky, but my mind has already wandered there, combining the two with the image seared on to my retina of him pulling on his jeans and coming up with a very graphic answer. One that makes the blood pump even faster around my body and takes my head places it shouldn't. I don't even know how it's managing to do that. I don't need distractions right now and the way that Jay is making me feel, that tightening in my stomach whenever I sense his eyes on me, is distracting, among other things.

I don't want to name the other things.

I focus on the remaining contents of the bag – digging up some energy bars and a rubber doorstop and tossing them on to the growing pile.

'What the hell? Did you pack the kitchen sink as well?' Jay asks.

'I didn't pack it. It's my dad's go-bag.'

'Go-bag?'

'Yeah, the bag you keep packed and ready if you ever have thirty seconds' warning to run for your life.' I risk a glance at him. He's playing with the handcuffs still and my skin scorches as I suddenly remember the way his hands felt around my waist when he caught me, how much trust he put in me to follow me out that window and up on to the roof.

'What's the doorstopper for?' Jay asks, picking it up and examining it as though it might have a secret compartment or a hidden lever that when depressed transforms it into a blow dart or a block of plastic explosive.

It is just a doorstopper though, unfortunately.

'It slows down someone trying to sneak into a room or force entry. It can buy a few seconds,' I tell him, remembering the time my dad explained the contents of his go-bag to me. He was getting ready for a trip to Afghanistan and I was watching him pack while my mum huffed downstairs, pouring herself one extra-large gin-and-tonic after another. My dad didn't know it but I had nightmares for months after he showed me the contents of his go-bag, worrying about him being in a situation where he might need it, my imagination taking me to some very dark places, fuelled partly by having watched *Star Wars* the week before, followed by several CNN reports on Al Qaeda. It was only when Felix reassured me that Sand People weren't real, and neither was Darth Vadar, that I began to relax. He also told me that my dad was the best soldier he'd ever known – an ex-recon marine no less – and that if I was going to worry, it should be about the people who were stupid enough to choose him as a target. Thinking about that now makes me feel slightly better. My dad will be back soon. And then whoever is chasing me is going to regret every single bullet they've fired.

I do a final check of the bag and my fingers close around something small and soft. I pull it out, my heart already skimming close to my ribs. I stare in amazement at the tiny worry doll, made from wool and beads, slightly battered and faded, that sits on my palm.

'What's that?' Jay asks. 'A cunningly disguised grenade?'

'No. It's . . .' I pause, staring at the doll. I haven't seen it in almost ten years, not since the day I slipped it into my father's bag. The same day he showed me the contents and explained their uses. I wanted him to have something to remind him of me – of home – if he ever found himself on the run from baddies. That he's kept it all these years makes tears sting furiously behind my eyes and my throat constrict as if the tourniquet is wrapped tight around it. 'It's just a good luck charm,' I manage to say, dropping the doll back into the bag.

As I start to pack the other things away, my hand brushes a tag attached to the bottom of the bag. With a tug, I tear it free, hearing the tear of Velcro. Beneath the false bottom of the bag, is an envelope. I wrestle it free and pull it out the bag.

Jay watches as I turn it over, catching my eye briefly, nervously, as I slide my finger inside the flap and rip it open. Inside is a photocopy of my father's passport, his birth certificate, and then another scrap of paper with a series of numbers on it. A phone number perhaps? Jay's head is pressed against mine as we study it.

'What do you think it is?' he asks.

I'm about to shrug when the taxi driver interrupts. 'OK. Electronics store. That'll be ten dollars fifty.'

My head jerks up. We're outside a Best Buy. I shove the rest of the things into the bag and peel off a twenty-dollar bill from the stack in the bag, pushing it to the driver and telling him not to bother with change.

19

We walk out of Best Buy fifteen minutes later with two no-contract smartphones and six extra SIM cards.

'Where now?' Jay asks, carrying our booty.

'Payphone,' I say, already scanning the street for one.

'We just bought two phones,' Jay says, holding up the bag and waving it in my face.

'Yeah, I know.'

Jay, to give him credit, doesn't ask any more questions, but as we walk I shoot him several sideways glances and note that the muscle in his jaw is working overtime, and although he's tired – the shadows under his eyes have shadows – he's still on high-alert, his head twisting left to right, eyes quick, ready to register any movement or person that's out of place. I wonder whether I should have kept one of the guns on me, stuck it down my waistband, but that's a stupid place to stick a gun. And besides, the last thing we need is to get arrested and find ourselves in another police station. That thought is quickly followed by a sobering reminder that Jay is technically a fugitive.

When this is over, how much trouble is he going to be in? My fingers itch to reach out and take his hand again. I'm not exactly sure why. Maybe to let him know that I'm grateful he's stuck around? That I'm sorry for dragging him into this? Or maybe because I want to make sure he's not going anywhere?

But I stick my palms to my sides. Back in the cab it felt like the most natural thing in the world, holding hands, feeling his pulse feeding my bloodstream. It felt like we were somehow invincible so long as we stayed inseparable. But now, out on the street, it would be just weird. Out of place. I mean, we're still strangers, more or less.

I try to shut down all my thoughts about it – about him. In less than a day he'll be gone – either he'll have to hand himself in to the police or he'll be a fugitive for the rest of his life. Either way, it's not like I'm ever going to see him again.

We walk in silence for two blocks before we find a payphone that works. The downside to the world going digital and to everyone owning a cell phone is the gradual disappearance of payphones from the world. Like horse-drawn carts they're a quaint icon from another time. At least we've found one that actually works, even if it *is* coated in something that appears to have been secreted by some kind of prehistoric sea creature.

I ask Jay to hail a taxi and have it sit with the meter running at the kerb and then I start making phone calls. It takes Jay all of about ten seconds to hail one and then he sits inside it with the door hanging open, watching me, his foot tapping on the sidewalk. I have to turn my back, but that doesn't help much as the feeling of sitting on an anthill returns.

When I'm done with my calls, I pick up the bag and walk over to the cab. Jay scoots along the bench seat and I slide in beside him.

'The High Line please,' I tell the driver, pressing my temples in a futile attempt to head off the headache that's starting to thump behind my eyes.

'What was that about?' Jay asks. 'Who were you calling?'

I hold up my dad's credit card. 'I just booked a flight leaving from La Guardia to San Francisco.'

Jay's eyes flash dark. He rocks backwards and away from me.

'And a ticket from Grand Central to Philadelphia.'

Now his frown becomes a scowl.

'And a double room at The Greenwich. All on my dad's credit card.'

The scowl fades and a grin slowly eases across his face. 'You think they're monitoring his card?'

I shrug. 'Maybe. Probably. And if they are, then that should keep them busy for a while. Even if they don't fall for it, they'll still need to check, just in case.'

'Why didn't you use one of the cell phones we just bought?'

'Because if the number turns up on any of the switchboards I just called they'll be able to trace the SIM card to the Best Buy and then they'd know what we bought and the other SIM numbers. And a payphone's a payphone. We'll be long gone before they figure out that we used this one.'

Jay shakes his head at me, still smiling. 'You're cunning. Man, you're nothing like I thought you were when I saw you in the police station.'

I bite my lip and let my hair fall in front of my face. *What* did he think I was? I want to know. But sure as hell, I'm not going to ask.

He fills me in anyway. 'You got balls,' he says.

I slice my eyes in his direction.

'OK,' he flounders, 'not actual, *literal* balls but, you know, balls of steel.'

I finish packing up the bag, zippering it shut a little too forcefully. I'm not sure I want him thinking I have balls – literal or actual *or* made of steel.

*   *   *

116

'You don't want to risk the room at The Greenwich?' Jay asks as he sinks back into the ripped vinyl seat of the cab. 'Jesus, that sounds good right about now.'

I risk another glance sideways at him. He's grinning at me but there's that flicker of something behind his eyes, like shadows flitting across a storm-drenched sky. 'We could test out some of the contents of that go-bag,' he adds, a touch of mischief sneaking into his voice.

I arch my eyebrows at him, even though my insides have just looped around my stomach and pulled it into a stranglehold.

'The doorstopper. I was talking about the doorstopper,' he says plastering an innocent expression on his face. 'What did you think I was talking about?'

It's on the tip of my tongue to tell him that the only thing we'd be testing out would be the sharpness of the switchblade, but all of a sudden his expression changes. His attention has switched to the TV screen in front of me. Another downside to the march of progress – non-stop media wherever you go. In New York the taxis all seem to have TV screens broadcasting at you; a mixture of lurid, totally biased news read by supermodels and uber-tanned, strangely wrinkle-free older men, interspersed with advertisements. Jay is leaning across me, hitting the volume button.

It's the news channel – same set-up as always – the woman newscaster looks like she just stepped off a runway show at NY Fashion Week. She's the eye candy while the male newscaster beside her lends the grey-haired gravitas. This is one of the many reasons I don't watch the news in the US.

I'm about to ask Jay to turn it off when the male newscaster puts on his grave face and starts talking in a sombre baritone about the shocking events of this morning. My blood starts to thicken and turn cold, and suddenly images appear on the screen of the police station that Jay and I escaped from just a few hours ago. The camera's pointed at the front of the building, which is swarming with police in blue NYPD jackets. Crime scene tape barricades a battalion of press, and several vans are parked in the way, partially obscuring the view of the front steps. As the newsreader talks about an unknown assailant attacking the 84th Precinct Police Headquarters in Brooklyn, in the background we watch trolley after trolley of black-bagged bodies being wheeled out into the waiting vans.

The ticker tape across the bottom of the screen announces that thirteen policemen and civilians have been killed and a further six wounded.

Without realising it, I'm gripping Jay's hand, crushing it, and his other hand is on my right knee, doing the same.

An image of the shooter then flashes on to the screen. It's a grainy image, taken from CCTV somewhere in the police station. A shudder races up my spine just as a cold sweat breaks out all over my body.

'Turn it off,' I whisper hoarsely.

Jay shakes his head slightly. 'No,' he says, 'we might find out something useful.'

The camera returns to the brightly-lit studio where the super-model and the granddad are posing with their shocked faces on for the camera.

'The Police Commissioner has refused to comment on the likely identity of the killer or the motive behind this terrible atrocity,' the man says, 'though they are claiming that the killer is not, I repeat, *not* a police officer. Members of the public should not approach him under any circumstances, as he is armed and considered extremely dangerous.'

After that I catch a few words about panic, public disorder, demand for answers and the Mayor of New York sending condolences, before Jay frees my knee from his grip and punches the off button.

We both fall back against the seats, barely breathing. Neither of us says anything for a long time and I shift my gaze from the blank screen to the streets outside the window; to the Chelsea townhouses and tourists in sneakers holding guidebooks, to the achingly hip couples strolling hand in hand, to the storefronts and billboards screaming at me to buy overpriced jeans and perfume and to call 1-800 GET THIN, and for a moment it's hard to tell what's real and what's not. It's like watching a television show. But I can't tell which side of the screen I'm on any more.

20

The High Line is an old freight railway that runs for almost two miles from the meatpacking district up Manhattan's West Side. Some nice folks, my dad included, sponsored its transformation a few years ago from derelict rail line into a park that's now frequented by supernannies who dress in designer clothes and push thousand-dollar prams, awed tourists with their frayed Lonely Planets, picnicking school-kids, and New Yorkers looking for some sunshine and peace amid the chaos. It's an oasis. And the reason I like it so much is because it's elevated. It sits above the streets, offering a panoramic view in all directions.

Up here the world looks different. The blazing heat still scorches down but, thanks to the breeze off the nearby Hudson, it's bearable. The ever-present honking, screeching and sirens that make up the background chatter of New York is distant and almost comforting at this volume. The city looks beautiful from up here. I watch Jay eyeing it all suspiciously.

'I didn't even know this was here,' he says, looking with confusion at a Lilliputian-sized statue of a giraffe planted in the grass before dancing out of the way of a parade of children wearing fluorescent bibs who are following their teachers towards a patch of shaded grass.

'My dad brought me the last time I came to New York,' I say.

Without a word we both head towards a row of wooden sun loungers, arranged beneath the shade of some trees, and drop down heavily on to them.

'So you like heights then,' Jay says lying back and putting his hands behind his head. He seems more relaxed now, less on high-alert, though I can tell by the pitch of his voice and the way he keeps rubbing between his eyes that the tension hasn't gone anywhere.

I shrug and drag myself into a position where I can start to stretch out my hamstrings and glutes before they seize up. All the running and climbing and the adrenaline spikes and crashes is going to create pain later unless we rub down. I know this from a decade of ballet classes and am already dreading how I'm going to feel when I stand up after resting.

'You'd done that climb before, hadn't you?' Jay asks.

I nod, bending forwards to increase the stretch. 'Yeah.'

'Holy shit.' He shakes his head at me baffled. 'Why would you do that?'

I shrug again.

'No. Come on. You just pulled some crazy Spider-Man moves back there.'

'So did you,' I say, switching legs, feeling my whole body – bones, tissues and cells – screaming as though they're being fed through a shredder. 'And anyway, it's not like it was that difficult. It wasn't the Brooklyn Bridge or anything.' I grin, despite the pain. 'Now that would be a climb.'

Jay just stares at me uncertainly, as if he can't tell whether or not I'm joking. I'm not. 'You would climb the Brooklyn Bridge,' he asks, 'just for kicks?'

I shrug at him. The Brooklyn Bridge has been in my sights since the day I first saw it. That swirling mass of water below, the immense power and beauty of the structure. I can only imagine the exhilaration and freedom that would come from climbing something like that.

I nod at his legs. He's lazing back so languidly you'd think he was hanging out at a day spa. 'You should stretch,' I tell him.

'Why?' he asks.

'Because otherwise you're going to get stiff.'

Straightaway I regret my choice of words but before I can revise them he sits up and says, 'No. Why'd you decide one day to climb out the window of a twenty-storey apartment building and climb on to the roof? Why would you want to climb the Brooklyn Bridge? I need to understand, because that to me is insane or suicidal or possibly both, and you don't seem like you're either.'

I release the stretch and sit up to face him, aware of the way his eyes are searching my face and feeling heat rising up my neck like mercury in a thermometer. 'Why'd you like to drive so fast?' I ask him.

His face splits straightaway into a grin. 'It feels good. It's a rush.' The grin grows even wider, revealing his dimple. 'There's only one other thing that feels better.'

'Exactly,' I say, breathlessly. He gets it! And then I realise what he's just said and my cheeks catch fire because it's clear that the one other thing he's talking about is sex, and so I add quickly, in something of a mumble, 'I mean, yeah, maybe.'

Jay's eyes narrow like a wolf's scenting blood, his smile becoming curious, and I feel that if it was possible to die of embarrassment I would already be on the floor turning blue.

I've had sex only once and let's just say I would have traded the whole experience for a bowl of Ben & Jerry's, or even a night in reading a book (a boring book too, like one of my dad's tomes on Byzantine military campaigns). It came nowhere near close to the feeling I get from scaling a tall building.

I can feel Jay's eyes tracing laser pathways over my skin, and I stare down at my lap and keep on talking, hoping that the sheer volume of my words will distract him, as well as help erase the image that has just sprung into my mind of Jay naked, having sex. With me. Thank you, brain.

'The first time I climbed out on to the roof it was because I was trying to get away from someone,' I blurt.

'Who?' Jay immediately asks.

'My bodyguard.'

'You have a bodyguard?' he asks.

'I did. This was back in Oman,' I explain. 'Anyway, this guy was ex-Israeli Special Forces. His name was Liron.'

'Lion?'

'No, Liron. It's Hebrew for *I have joy*, which was completely ironic because this guy never smiled. Not once. I used to tell him jokes to see if I could get him to laugh – but nothing. He could have been a cyborg. One with a faulty personality chip.'

'So what'd he do to make you want to run away?'

'Nothing, really. I was just sick to death of being followed everywhere. I'd go on a date and he'd be sitting at the next table drinking coffee and freaking out the other diners with his killer robot stare.'

'Wow.'

'I know. I couldn't even go to the bathroom without him waiting outside the door.'

'I mean *wow*, boys actually had the balls to ask you out?'

123

'Not many. Well, just one.' Not that I was complaining about that. In fact it was about the only benefit to having a bodyguard who carried more firepower than a character from Halo. Boys tended to give me a wide berth.

'Is that what you were doing? Giving him the slip so you could meet up with your boyfriend?'

It doesn't pass me by that he is asking a lot of questions about boyfriends.

'No,' I say slowly. 'I just wanted to escape. It was like living under house arrest all the time.' I pause. 'And the only escape was through the window. So I climbed up on to the roof and I spent the night up there. I didn't sleep. I was so high.' I smile at the memory, at what it felt like to heave myself over the ledge and then stand on shaking legs looking out over the compound below, the realisation that for the first time in my life I was completely alone, that no one knew where I was. It was like being reborn. For so long after Felix's death I'd locked away my feelings, walked around wrapped in a blanket of numbness. But up there on that roof, I felt like I'd shaken off the blanket and was standing there naked. *Alive.* That's how I felt. Like anything was possible. Like I could pluck the stars right out of the sky.

I glance at Jay who's still sitting up, his arms resting on top of his knees, watching me closely, and I take a breath. I want to explain it to him. I want to have him understand. There's something in his expression, the light in his eyes, that makes me think he'll get it. 'When I'm climbing, when I'm balanced on the edge of a roof,' I say, 'I get this feeling,' I press a hand to my navel, ' in my stomach. It's incredible, like my blood's made of light particles. Like I weigh less than nothing.' I let out the breath I'm holding. 'That night was the first time in my entire life that I felt . . . completely free.'

Jay starts nodding. 'It's the same reason I got into racing,' he says.

'You race?' I ask, surprised.

'Yeah. I started when I was fourteen. Moment I got behind the wheel and put my foot to the floor I felt like I could take off, go anywhere, *be* anything. There was nothing could stop me. Like you, I guess, it felt like an escape.'

I want to ask him what he wanted to escape from, but before I can he shakes his head and says, 'It's funny, back at the cop shop I thought you were this uptight rich chick . . .' He breaks off, seeing the look on my face, then shrugs his shoulders apologetically at me. 'You wouldn't even turn around when I was trying to get your attention.'

'What do you expect?' I say. 'We were in the homicide department. And you were wearing handcuffs. And anyway, what do you mean, *uptight?*'

He grins at me, holding up his hands. 'Hey, you thought I was a murderer, so cut me some slack. All I'm saying is that you were sitting there, all straight-backed, sounding like someone from a Bond movie.'

'Excuse me?'

'It's the British thing. You sound like that woman, you know, the secretary in the Bond movies.'

'Moneypenny?' I ask, my voice so shrill it scares a bird out of the branch overhead.

'Yeah, or the Queen,' Jay continues, oblivious to the depth of this insult. He's just compared me to a frumpy secretary *and* to an octogenarian, both in the same breath. 'And you wouldn't even give me the time of day.'

My mouth is opening and shutting like I'm a demented goldfish. 'You were trying to get me to break the law. And I didn't know you from Adam.'

'I was just asking you for a little favour. It wasn't breaking the law. It was just maybe bending it a little.' He holds his fingers up to demonstrate how little. 'For a moment I even thought you were going to leave me there, chained to the desk.'

He looks at me as if to say, *I know, crazy, right? My bad,* and I shake my head at him, trying to look appalled that he could ever have thought such a thing, yet at the same time my gut squirms like live bait, because he's right. I did contemplate for a moment whether I should let him go.

'Goes to show you can't judge a book by its cover or by the NYPD sweater it's wearing,' he says, winking at me.

'Or the boy by the cuffs he's wearing.'

'Hey, that was the only time I've ever been arrested,' he says, his smile fading, replaced instantly with a scowl.

I look away and don't say anything. The sudden reminder of who he is – a gang member and a felon – is a slap, bringing me sharply back to the present. I stare at the mud-brown water straight ahead of us.

'What?' I hear him say. 'You never once broke the law before today? Never did anything stupid? At all? Other than climb on to a roof?'

'Nope,' I say, turning back to face him.

He looks at me sceptically. 'You never once had a beer? Or smoked weed?'

I shake my head at him. I've had a few glasses of wine at birthday celebrations with my parents but I've never drunk beer. Even if beer contained zero calories, drinking just doesn't appeal, nor

126

does getting high, not when I have to be in a ballet studio by seven most mornings. And even if I had ever felt like getting drunk, just try sneaking alcohol past an Israeli Defence Force soldier. That ain't happening.

Jay shakes his head in wonder. 'Yeah, well, different worlds I guess,' he says and turns to look in New Jersey's direction.

'What's that supposed to mean?' I ask him.

A light shrug. 'Just that we grew up different. You grew up in Nigeria. I grew up in Queens. You've lived all over the world. I've never even seen the West Coast of America. Hell, I've never even seen this part of Manhattan before. I had to learn how to throw a punch in kindergarten and you've grown up surrounded by body-guards.' He laughs under his breath and shakes his head. 'Though where's a killer robot Israeli bodyguard when you need one, huh?' He turns again to stare out across the water. 'We're just different, you and I, is all.'

Anger bubbles up but I keep the lid on it.

'And anyway,' Jay says, glancing over at me and smiling ruefully, 'I guess it would be kind of hard to do anything with Lion – or Liron or whatever his name was – shadowing your every move. That's gotta make stealing a car difficult.'

I laugh under my breath, though inside I'm mulling on what he's just said and starting to seethe. 'We're not so different,' I say finally, thinking of how we both craved escape from our lives. He's making all these judgements based on the little he knows of my life and I guess I'm doing the same of him too. It's not surprising. That's what people do. We judge people, calibrating and recali-brating our feelings and thoughts about them by what they say and do. But it frustrates me. I know after today I'm never going to see Jay again, but for some reason, maybe even because of the fact

I'm never going to see him again, I want him to see more than that. I want him to see the real me. Though is that even possible? Can you ask another person to see you when you're not even sure you can see yourself?

I pause and take a deep breath. 'It's not because of the bodyguard.'

Jay looks puzzled. 'Huh?'

'I don't break rules because the last time I did someone died.'

Jay's head whips around. 'Who?' he asks.

'His name was Felix. He was my bodyguard. Before Liron. We were living in Nigeria.'

Why am I telling him this? I don't know. I haven't told anyone this before. Not even my therapists ever got all the details out of me. But for some reason I have a sudden urge to tell Jay about Felix and about what happened. Maybe it's because I think Felix would have liked Jay, would have liked his sense of humour, as well as his sense of loyalty. He always did rate humour and loyalty above all else.

'Is he the one who taught you everything you know?' Jay asks, his expression softening.

'Like what?' I say, tying my hair up and out of the way. 'Like what a doorstopper is for?'

He smirks at me. 'No. Like how to shoot bad guys.'

'I've never shot anyone before,' I say, then add quickly before we can get to thinking too much on that, 'My dad gave me shooting lessons. But Felix taught me other things.'

'Such as?' Jay asks.

I relax back into my sun lounger. 'He taught me to play poker,' I say, grinning suddenly at the memory. 'And how to tie really complicated knots.'

'All essential skills,' Jay says smiling. Then the smile fades. 'My dad didn't teach me shit.'

The loophold around my stomach tightens. I start to speak, to tell him that Felix wasn't my dad, but then I realise that he knows that and it strikes me all of a sudden, like a knife blade slashing through nerves, that that's exactly why it hurts so much still. Felix *was* like a father to me. That's why I miss him so much. Why have I never realised that?

I go quiet, remembering him pottering around the little kitchen of his apartment over the garage, trying to teach me sailing knots while simultaneously trying to cook his dinner over the tiny gas stove. He'd stop occasionally to lean over and check what I was doing. He had this habit of rubbing the top of my head with his knuckles when I got it right.

'He was a really bad cook,' I tell Jay as the memories start to flood in. 'But he could make the best and weirdest popcorn on the planet. Flavours that should never ever, according to all scientific reason, actually work.'

Jay grins, 'Like what?'

'Like bacon caramel. And pumpkin blue cheese jalapeno.'

Jay muses on it. 'That could work,' he says. Then after a beat, 'He sounds cool.'

I stare out at the strip of Hudson glinting blue in the distance. 'Yeah,' I say, 'he was.'

'How'd he die?'

The pain rushes in like it always does, like a gust of wind threatening to knock me over the edge. I take a deep breath, focussing on Jay to keep me steady.

'Some people tried to kidnap me.'

Several expressions pass over Jay's face at once; anguish,

consternation, weariness, pain. I can almost guarantee he's regretting his last question. Yet he pushes on. 'What happened?'

'You really want to know?' I ask.

Jay nods. 'Yes.'

I pull the water bottle out of the bag and take a sip. 'I was in a car with him and our driver and they attacked us. These three guys – they pulled out across the road, blocking our way. I don't really remember exactly what happened. It was all so fast. They shot the driver and shot out the tyres and then Felix was suddenly hauling me out of the car. He tried holding them off.'

Jay is staring at me wide-eyed. I can see that he's right there, with me, back on that street in Lagos, hearing the bullets ricocheting off the car – spitting up dirt from the road. That he can hear my heart hammering in my chest, that he can taste the fear rising like bile in my mouth. He can see Felix, his face pressed to mine, his hand gripping my arm tight enough to leave a circle of bruises around it that would last a month.

'He told me on the count of three I was to run. Run as fast as I could back towards the school. It was just a block. I could see the gates. He said he'd be right behind me.'

'And?' Jay asks quietly.

I swallow. 'And I didn't run. I stayed. I didn't want to leave him.' I can picture Felix's face. He was always so calm. Always. But in that moment I saw the absolute terror in his eyes. That's what froze me to the spot. I couldn't leave him because I was so scared for him. What I didn't realise at the time was that he was scared for me.

'He died,' I say, the disbelief still evident in my voice. 'He got shot in the chest right in front of me. Trying to shield me.'

After a minute I raise my eyes, expecting to see what I saw on the faces of therapists even though they tried to hide it, that flash

130

behind their eyes that signified blame. But there's nothing like that on Jay's face. Rather, his expression is a mixture of fury and sympathy. He reaches across and takes my hand, keeping his gaze locked on mine. 'It wasn't your fault,' he says, as though he can force it to be true just by saying it. His fingers squeeze mine.

This time I don't squeeze back. 'You weren't there,' I say weakly.

His jaw tenses. 'You were a kid,' he says. 'You weren't the one firing a gun at a child. Felix died protecting you. That was his job.' He squeezes my hand for a few more seconds but when I don't respond he takes it away.

'If I had listened to him he'd still be alive,' I say quietly.

Jay shakes his head once, firmly. 'You don't know that.'

The silence settles between us, soft as a quilt. On one level I know Jay's right. I just can't bring myself to accept it. It's been so long I doubt I ever will.

'It's the same with what's happened today,' I say. 'They're all dead because of me. All those people.' My voice peters out. My throat burns but the tears don't come. It's wrong that there aren't any. I want to cry. But I'm all carved out, dried up.

Suddenly Jay's hand is beneath my chin, tilting my face up to meet his.

His eyes are alight, the green blazing. 'You're not responsible for all the shit in the world, Liva.'

I look away, at the little children all seated on a row of steps, eating their sandwiches, laughing and chatting.

'You saved my life,' Jay tells me still holding on to me, forcing me to turn back.

I blink at him. We both breathe in, tight, as though our ribs are bound. And then suddenly he pulls me against his shoulder and his arms are around me. My face is buried in the warmth of his neck and I breathe in the clean soap smell of him, the musky undertone scent of his skin beneath, and for a moment I feel myself letting go, falling off the edge of that building, dropping into oblivion.

'You saved both our lives,' he whispers into my ear.

21

I move away first, my heart beating uncertainly, and start busying myself rummaging through the bag, pulling out our new phones and the NYPD sweater. Jay kicks his legs up on to the sun lounger that's flush to mine and leans back with his arms behind his head again. A small part of me wants to curl up against him and bury my head in his shoulder once more. It felt safe when his arms were around me. For a moment I was able to forget about everything else going on and let my guard down. I was able to believe that maybe he was right – that maybe what happened to Felix wasn't my fault after all. But now I'm jittery again, my pulse skidding then slowing, skidding then slowing, as though it can't figure out what speed to run at.

I can feel Jay watching me as I open the phones and insert the SIM cards, and my skin feels like a feather is being trailed slowly and deliberately over every bare inch of it – an electrified feather. My hands shake. God. What is with me? I'm not even sure if I'm imagining the intensity of his stare. Maybe he's not actually staring at me at all. Maybe he's just admiring the view. Or checking we've not been followed. I rub my eyes. I'm so tired. I can't ever remember being this tired before. I glance around at the happy chattering tourists and picnicking school children and feel like there's a glass wall dividing us from them.

Are we safe here? I don't know. But where *is* safe? So far – nowhere. This is the best I could come up with. My hand

133

instinctively moves to the bag, feeling for the heavy bulk of the guns. Maybe I should sneak one out and hide it under the sweater. But then the sound of children's squealing laughter drifts past and I realise that that's a dumb idea. It's too dangerous.

After I finish programming both the phones I hand one to Jay. 'You should call your mum. She'll be worried,' I say.

He takes the phone and slips it into his back pocket. 'Yeah,' he mumbles.

I frown at him. For someone who was so keen to have me – a complete stranger – break the news to his mother about his arrest, he's acting kind of strange.

'You still want me to do it?' I ask.

His eyes fly to mine and my pulse quickens.

'No,' he says and a dark look crosses his face.

I lie back on the sun lounger, my knees drawn up to my chest and the sweater stuffed behind my head as a makeshift pillow. 'Do you think the police will have tried to find you? Maybe gone to your house to look for you?' I ask.

Jay's glaring at the horizon, squinting at the Statue of Liberty in the distance. His expression is so black that I expect to see a bank of storm clouds rolling in across the horizon ready to swallow the city.

'I don't know,' he says in a neutral voice, but I can tell that he's been considering this very thing. 'It's possible.'

My stomach muscles are tense and I wait a few seconds before I ask the question that's been burning on the tip of my tongue for the last few hours. 'Why'd you steal the car?'

Jay breathes in deeply before turning his head in my direction. 'I had to.'

I try to control my facial expression – keep a poker face – but the cynic in me rears up and my eyebrow shoots up of its own accord. 'You *had* to? What? You had a gun held to your head?'

His look darkens even more and my stomach flinches in response. 'No,' he says before looking away, shaking his head. 'It's complicated,' he murmurs. Then adds, 'But I didn't steal it.'

I can't help smirking. 'So you weren't driving a car that didn't belong to you, without the owner's permission?'

Jay turns his head slowly back, observing me through half-lowered lashes, and I think he's angry and I instantly regret my tone, but then I see the small twitch at the corner of his mouth. 'No,' he admits. 'I was.'

'Unless they changed the meaning of stealing without me knowing,' I say, unable to drag my eyes off his mouth and that smile pulling at the edge of it, 'I think that qualifies as stealing.'

I might be mistaken but it seems like Jay can't take his eyes off my lips either and my pulse irritatingly accelerates.

'I was going to take it back at the end of the night,' he says. 'Technically, I think you'll find that counts as borrowing, not stealing.'

'Technically,' I say, my heart doing a *grand jeté* in my throat, 'I don't think NY state law accepts borrowing as a statement of defence.'

'Wow,' he says, 'you know your stuff.'

'My mother is a lawyer. *Was* a lawyer,' I correct myself.

'What does she do now?'

I shrug. 'Holds dinner parties, keeps up with the Joneses. Actually she overthrew the Joneses. She trampled the Joneses into oblivion.'

Jay smiles. 'Well, if she's anything like you, I imagine she had an unfair advantage over the Joneses.'

'Hold up,' I say. 'How are we talking about me again? This is about you. Why did you steal that car?'

'I *borrowed* the car because I had to. Because I thought it was the right thing to do and there weren't any other options.'

I purse my lips but figure that I'm not going to get any more detail out of him. 'Is that why you're helping me now?' I ask. 'Is that what you meant when you mentioned repaying a karmic debt? Is this your way of making it right?'

'Yeah, something along those lines,' he mumbles, looking away and scowling once again at the horizon, summoning those clouds.

I ponder letting things lie but there's something I really want to know. 'What's the deal with not wanting to call your mum?' I ask.

He tips his head to one side and considers me carefully, and once again my pulse decides to behave like it's on a trampoline. 'I like your accent,' he says, 'the way you say *mum*.'

And he sidesteps it yet again. I sigh. 'It's the English in me,' I tell him. 'My mum hates me saying *mom*. And I went to the English International School in Oman. And anyway you can't talk, *Jaime*.' I try my best to imitate his Spanish inflection but it sounds like I'm hacking up a lungful of phlegm. Jay starts laughing, actually clutching his sides. I reach over and thump him on the leg, except I manage to miss and almost hit him in the balls. He catches my fist in his hand.

'Woah, Rambo, watch it. I want to be able to use that again.'

That? Oh God. Without warning, the image of Jay pulling his jeans on – the full frontal view I got – leaps into my mind in IMAX Technicolor glory.

'Save the death blows for the people trying to kill us, would you?' he jokes.

'Sorry,' I mumble, my cheeks throbbing.

He lets go of my hand and closes his eyes. 'I think it's nap time,' he says, and he yawns.

I rearrange my sweater pillow once again and hug the bag close to my chest, finding small comfort in the butt of the gun digging into my ribs. Though I try to fight it, after a few minutes my eyes slide of their own accord across to Jay, lying less than a foot away, his chest rising and falling in a slow, steady rhythm. Is he already asleep? Is it safe for me to sleep too? I wonder. Shouldn't one of us keep watch?

I sit up and look around, uncertainly trying to figure it out, and then I stay sitting up, letting my eyes linger on Jay's face. He looks so defenceless, and I feel a sudden surge of protectiveness towards him and also guilt that I've dragged him into this. He looks so young lying there and, ironically, so innocent. But then I notice the stubble starting to darken his jaw and the broad lines of his shoulders filling my dad's T-shirt and once again the image of him naked flashes with immaculate timing into my mind and I breathe out long and slow, reminding myself he's anything but a boy. I wonder how old he actually is? Nineteen? Twenty?

My eyes flit over the rest of his face, pausing on his lips. The smile I've come to look for, to rely on as a marker of his mood, has vanished. His lips are parted and suddenly I can't help wondering what it would be like to kiss him. I picture him pulling me against his body and holding me like he just did and . . .

'I can feel you staring at me.'

I freeze. Jay's eyes remain shut.

'I'm not,' I stammer as every capillary in my body dilates in order to force every ounce of blood in my body towards my face.

With his eyes still closed Jay reaches his hand towards me and circles my wrist. I wonder what he's doing but then he gives a gentle tug and suddenly I'm toppling forwards and my head collides with his shoulder. His face stays smooth and expressionless, as though he's sleeping, but his arm pulls me tighter against his side as naturally as if he's done it a thousand times before.

I'm paralysed. My muscles lock and my breathing hikes to the point that Jay must be able to feel my ribs rapidly expanding and contracting. I stare at the smooth tanned skin running to stubble across his jaw and take a deep breath in, feeling myself relaxing ever so slightly against his side, my stomach pressing automatically closer against his hip. I have a sudden urge to fold my leg over his waist and press even closer. OK. I'll admit it. I am attracted to him. Even if I didn't admit it, my body wouldn't let me deny it. But I am not falling for him. This is some kind of survivor guilt syndrome. I've seen it in the movies. It's just the pressure of the situation we're in. I am thoroughly in control still.

22

I wake with a start, my eyes flying open and my heart exploding like an IED in my chest. It takes several seconds for me to get my bearings and to realise that the sound that woke me was just a kid screaming for an ice-cream and not someone screaming in terror.

Then I realise where I'm lying. Or rather how I'm lying. I am still pressed against Jay's side. His arm is still around my waist, his hand resting loosely on my hip, and in my sleep I've shifted so my cheek is now pressed against his chest and my leg is bent, my knee wantonly thrown across his thigh. A half second after I process this I bolt upright, disentangling myself.

'Morning,' Jay says with a grin. He's already awake. God. How long has he been awake for?

I squint up at the sky. It's not morning. It's mid-afternoon, judging from the position of the sun and the shadows stretching across the sun loungers. I brush my hair out of my face and rub a hand over my eyes. I'm groggy and oh my God, my body feels like it's been run through a mangle. I try to stand and almost fall, having to balance myself against the seat as the muscles in my legs seize up. My knees start smarting from the grazes on them and my shoulder throbs violently. I feel like a walking headache.

Jay hops up next to me, sprightly as a mountain goat, damn him. 'You OK?' he asks me, looking concerned.

139

I nod blearily, glancing around, still trying to get my bearings. The High Line is even busier, crowded with people, and it's seriously hot out. We were asleep in the shade thankfully, but standing in the sunlight I can feel my skin starting to sear. Jay looks fine. The circles under his eyes have faded a little, though the stubble is giving him the look of a vagrant and his T-shirt is rumpled.

'Did you sleep?' I ask him, embarrassed.

'Yeah, though I got woken up by a mouthful of hair.'

I squirm inwardly, but notice that among the squirming worms of embarrassment currently writhing in my stomach, a few butterflies are also beating their wings. So not the time for this, I think, rolling my eyes at myself in frustration.

'You hungry?' Jay asks.

I consider the question briefly. But my stomach answers first, growling loudly. Jay nods at some food carts lined up in the distance under an overhang. The smells are wafting this way; vanilla and sugar and chilli and onions combining in a way that's making my mouth water.

'You stay here,' Jay says. 'I'll get us something.'

I hand him some of the money from the bag and watch him walk off, rolling his shoulders as he goes. For the first time I properly take note of the catlike grace with which he moves, with a strut that's just this side of a prison swagger. The thing that saves him from looking like a douche is that it's completely unconscious. He's not posing. That's just the way he moves. As though he feels me watching him, Jay suddenly spins around. He catches me in the act of gawping and even from this distance I see the glimmer of triumph in his eyes and the dimple in his cheek as he shoots me a grin. Goddamn. I turn away and rummage in the bag for the phones, mumbling a string of curses

140

under my breath. *Really, Liva? You're choosing now of all times to fall for a guy?*

I never fall for guys. Ever. I didn't even fall for Sebastian, the one guy brave enough to approach me. I dated him because I was so amazed he had dared ask, and because I felt like bravery like that deserved reward. And, well, with Sebastian, it was also easy to manage the situation. There were no feelings involved. I mean, I liked him. He was fairly good-looking and made me laugh, occasionally. We went to the same school. Our parents approved. It was easy to date him, to go through the motions, without having to worry about doing something as utterly stupid and teenage as falling in love. I don't fall for guys. I don't fall. Period. Which is why I have to ignore these really unhelpful and distracting thoughts I'm having about Jay and focus on the situation before we both end up dead.

I check the time on the phone. It's 3.46. We slept for almost five hours. That's pretty impressive, given our beds were basically two uncomfortable slats of wood, though admittedly I had Jay's shoulder as a pillow. No wonder my body feels as stiff as the boards we were lying on. I'm kind of amazed too that the volunteers working along the High Line didn't move us on. At that I start thinking about where we should head to next. We can't stay here all night. For one thing the High Line closes at eleven.

I'm still trying to think of where we might spend the night that isn't a park bench, when Jay returns a few minutes later. In one hand he holds two melting ice-pops and in the other a greasy brown bag. He passes me one of the ice-pops.

'There weren't any bacon caramel flavoured ones so I got you Strawberry Rhubarb Rain.'

141

I take it, staring at him in bemusement.

'We're doing dessert first otherwise it will melt,' Jay explains.

He sits beside me and starts enthusiastically licking his ice-pop, and I try very hard not to stare at his mouth.

'Wanna try mine?' Jay asks, offering it to me. 'It's Lemon Basil. I think Felix would have liked it.'

I smile at him.

'Don't smile,' he warns, 'I used up half our money on these. You would not believe how much they are charging for what's basically frozen water on a stick.'

I lean towards him, holding my hair out of my face, and he pulls his hand away at the last second so I almost topple forwards into his lap. He laughs as I scowl at him, then brings the ice-pop back and holds it close to my lips, staring at me the whole time with a half-taunting, half-curious look on his face. I find myself holding his gaze as I take a bite out of his ice-pop.

I offer him a taste of mine in return and he leans close, his fingers circling my wrist to hold it steady.

'I could go for that,' he says, his eyes locked on mine.

'It's mine, hands off,' I tell him, my pulse leaping. He must have felt it – his thumb being pressed to my wrist – because his eyes narrow at me slightly and a strange expression crosses his face before he looks quickly away.

When we're done I hold up my sticky hands. Jay is busy licking his fingers clean. He looks at me. 'What?' he asks innocently, then rolls his eyes.

'Do you have a tissue?'

He shakes his head, more in disgust than denial. 'Man,' he says. 'Here.' He pulls his bandana out of his back pocket and hands it to me.

I take it, trying to hide my distaste, but he's like a hawk sighting a mouse from a mile away. 'What?' he asks.

I blank my face, cursing silently. 'Nothing.'

He shrugs and gets busy opening up the brown bag. The smell of Mexican food rushes out and smacks me in the nose.

'These look good,' Jay says, pulling out two well-stuffed, foil-wrapped burritos spewing black beans and sour cream down their sides.

Jay bites into his with relish but I just stare at mine, calculating the calories.

'Is it the ballet?' Jay suddenly asks.

'What?' I ask, my head jerking up.

'Is that what the whole *I can't eat anything with a calorie in* is all about?'

'How'd you know I do ballet?' I ask, startled, trying to shake off the calorie comment, but how the hell did he guess that was exactly what I was thinking?

'I saw the certificates in your bedroom. And you look like a dancer. I mean, the way you hold yourself. You got what my mum would call good posture. And your legs. You have a dancer's legs.'

I flush involuntarily. I can feel his gaze on my thighs and I cross them and uncross them self-consciously. No one – not even my mother – has ever called me on my calorie counting before. I'm not anorexic, not by a long shot, but I do have to watch my weight – I don't naturally have a ballet dancer's build. I've got boobs and hips for a start, long legs but also a long torso. When I meet Jay's gaze he's giving me that disarming searching look. I've never known anyone so astute, so able to read me, and I squirm under the attention.

'You like it?' he asks me, taking another bite.

I stare at the burrito, confused. He can see I haven't touched it.

'Ballet,' he says, seeing my bewilderment.

I shrug at him. 'I've done it my whole life.'

'That's not what I asked.'

I pause, playing with the foil wrapper on my burrito. 'I like dancing,' I say.

'Why?' he shoots back.

Like before, I have this sudden desire to share with him, to try to make him understand. 'I like the perfection of it,' I say in a rush. 'You know?' I look at him and see that he's nodding. He's with me. 'The steps are all there, laid out,' I continue, 'choreographed by experts, and if you follow them right, you make something beautiful, exquisite even.'

He nods some more. 'That's your problem right there.'

'What?' I ask, confused.

'You think that if you follow the rules everything's always gonna be perfect?' He shakes his head, smiling ruefully at me. 'Life doesn't work like that. If you follow the rules it doesn't mean bad shit's not going to happen to you or the people around you. I think that's been proved.'

I open my mouth to protest and then shut it again. Is he right?

'What about contemporary dance? What about improv? That can be beautiful,' he says.

I stare at him, trying to process his previous comments and then getting confused because now he's talking about dance? *What?*

'What do you know about dance?' I ask.

He grins at me, his eyes sparking, 'Hey, I'm half Cuban. We know all about dance.'

144

I bite my lip, trying to imagine Jay dancing. I have to admit that that's something I would like to see. He certainly has the grace of a dancer, and he moves like he has rhythm, but the thought of him in tights and a leotard makes me want to grin ear to ear.

He keeps his gaze fixed firmly on me as he finishes his burrito with a final bite, then he scrunches the foil up and tosses it into a nearby trash can, before picking up the bandana lying beside me to wipe his hands.

'You not going to eat that then?' he asks, pointing at the untouched burrito in my hand.

I peel away the foil and nibble at it.

He purses his lips in disapproval.

'Are those gang colours?' I ask him, pointing at the bandana, trying to distract him from my calorie intake, which frankly, is none of his goddamn business.

Jay looks at the bandana and then gives me a long, cold stare.

'You are nothing if not direct, anyone ever tell you that?' he says.

I give him a vague shrug.

'Is that why you went all weird when I gave it to you?'

I shrug again, noncommittally.

'Do you even know anything about the gangs in this city?' he asks.

'Only what I've heard from my father. Which isn't much,' I admit.

'It's just a bandana. It doesn't mean anything.' He turns away and glowers at the horizon, still shaking his head.

'I'm sorry,' I say quietly, regretting having mentioned it at all.

He wheels around. 'I'm not in a gang,' he says, barely reining in the anger. 'Never have been. Never will be.' His jaw is clenched and his hands are fisted at his side. The abrupt change in mood has thrown me for a loop. But I guess I only have myself to blame for having brought it up.

'I'm sorry,' I say again, swallowing the knife blade lodged in my throat. 'I made an assumption.' Stupid. I'd already agreed not to do that.

'Yeah,' he mutters.

'Let's just agree no more assumptions, OK?' I say.

He laughs then, unexpectedly, 'Sure thing, Moneypenny.'

I pull a face at him, but I'm smiling.

'Look,' he says, his tone softening, 'my older brother – Luis – is in a gang. The Latin Blades.'

He has a brother. I lean forwards, alert. I want to hear this. I *really* want to hear this, to find out more about him. So far, I feel like the exchange has only been one way. Jay's watching me, though, like an examiner determined to find fault, so I make sure my face stays neutral. 'He's in prison,' he goes on. 'Been there the last two years. Got another six to go.'

I keep my gaze fixed on Jay. I can tell he's reading my every look, waiting to pounce at any sign of judgement on my part. I want to ask what he's in prison for but decide not to.

'My middle brother too – Teo – he's getting mixed up in the same gang.' He presses his lips together so they turn white. 'My mom's only got me to rely on. I'm the one that she was proud of, the one she could boast about.' He blows out a loud breath and rests his head in his hands. 'Now I've messed it all up.'

I don't move for a while. I just watch him, feeling like a massive wall has fallen between us. I know nothing about his world. But then again, he knew nothing of mine either, but he still tried to understand. His shoulders are tensed and he looks ready to spring like an attack dog if anyone comes too close, but I move to sit beside him anyway, my thigh brushing against his. I put my arm tentatively around his shoulders. 'After we get through this I'll help you fix it,' I say.

He stiffens under my touch and then tilts his head slightly towards me.

'There's no fixing this,' he says.

'But if it's the police, we can tell them that you saved my life. They'll have to take that into consideration.' I can hear my voice rising in pitch. 'My dad's got influence. He knows people. He can do something. I'll make him.'

Jay shakes his head and smiles softly at me. 'It's not the police I'm scared of.'

He's scared?

'Not them I gotta *worry* about,' he quickly corrects.

'Then who? Who are you worried about?' I ask, my arm falling away.

He grimaces, rubbing a hand over his head. 'I was doing a favour for my brother Teo. He's on parole.'

I frown.

'He was done for possession. Mota. Marijuana.' He grimaces as he speaks, glancing at me warily. 'He's an idiot. But he's my brother. And if he got caught this time then he'd be facing time. Ten or twenty years even.'

'Hold up,' I say, the pieces falling into place. 'Is that what happened? Was he supposed to steal the car and you did it for him?'

He nods and I see the anger flashing in his eyes, and something else – something close to despair.

'They needed him to drive,' he says now, pressing his knuckles to his forehead. 'The Blades. And he owed them. They called in the debt. That's how it works. And when they call in a debt there's no way out of it. There was something big going down. They needed a driver. But he turned up at my place, wigging out, begging me to do it for him.' He shrugs as though embarrassed. 'I've never stolen a car before though,' he says, his eyes flying to mine. 'I was telling the truth. Someone else jimmied it. I was just doing the driving. But the car they chose had one of those tracking devices in it. I didn't make it six blocks.'

'So now you think that the Latin Blades are going to be pissed at you?' I ask.

'No,' Jay answers grimly. 'I *know* they're going to be pissed at me. And pissed doesn't even cover it. These people don't do pissed. That's for polite rich people. They do vengeful fury. Usually involving hollow-point bullets.'

'Is your mum going to be OK?' I ask, feeling the blood start to flow a little faster, my brain shifting back into gear as I try to figure out what all this means for Jay – for us. 'I mean, would they do anything to her in retaliation?'

Jay shakes his head and looks away, embarrassed. 'No. Look,' he says with a sigh, 'I already called her.'

I sit bolt upright. 'What? When?'

'When you were in the shower. I didn't want to tell you as I figured you'd be pissed. I used the phone in your dad's study.'

I stare at him as what he's just said sinks in.

'You used the phone?'

He nods. Then his face pales as he sees the look on my face. 'What?' he asks.

'Jay, they'll have traced it for sure. The people chasing me. I mean, think about it, they traced that call I made to my dad's cell. These guys are good. If they hadn't figured out who you were already, they will have by now.'

23

We jump in the first cab we can find. The driver grumbles when Jay gives him the address.

'How long's it going to take?' Jay asks, leaning forwards.

The driver mutters something about rush-hour traffic and the Queens Tunnel and that it'll take as long as it takes.

'You want to take the subway instead?' I ask Jay, who's practically bouncing off the sides of the car.

'No,' Jay says, shaking his head. 'Too many police.'

'You should try calling her again,' I say. 'Just make sure you keep the call under thirty seconds in case they're putting a trace on it.'

Jay nods at me, already pulling out his phone, his fingers flying over the keypad. He lifts it to his ear and I watch, holding my breath.

After a minute he cuts the call. 'No answer,' he says, his leg jittering up and down beside me.

'What did you tell her earlier, when you spoke to her?'

He stares at me blankly for several seconds, then shakes his head. 'No. I didn't speak to her,' he says. 'I left an answerphone message. She wasn't in.'

He rocks forward and puts his head in his hands.

'What did you say on the message?' I ask, putting my hand on his back, between his shoulder blades.

'Just that I was fine. That she shouldn't worry.'

I swallow down my own worry. 'It's going to be OK,' I murmur.

He sits upright. 'I swear to God, they do anything to my mom,' he growls, 'I'm going to kill them.'

I take hold of his hand and squeeze. 'It's going to be OK. I'm sure she's fine.' I wonder if Jay can hear how hollow my words sound.

'She should be at work,' Jay suddenly says, brightening. 'Maybe she's not answering because her phone's in her bag or something.' He looks at me, desperate for agreement. I nod, giving him an overly enthusiastic smile.

'Where does she work?' I ask.

'She's a receptionist at a medical centre.'

'Do you know the number by heart?'

He shakes his head. I grab the phone and switch it to internet mode. We Google search and Jay places the call. This time he grips my hand tight. My bones crunch but I don't say a word. Someone picks up but I can tell from the look on Jay's face it's not his mum.

'Hey, I'm looking for Lucia Moreno,' he says to whoever is on the other end. 'Is she there?'

Silence.

Jay swallows, his grip relaxes a notch. 'OK, thanks anyway.'

He hangs up. 'She's not there. Never showed up for work today.'

'Could she have gone somewhere? Taken a day off?' I ask, clutching at straws. 'Maybe she's sick.'

'No. She only takes off holidays and birthdays. And she's never sick.'

Jay lets go of my hand and leans forwards to tap on the Plexiglas. 'Hey, any chance you could step on it?' he asks the driver.

151

The driver doesn't answer. He doesn't seem to have heard. I lean forwards. 'I'll double the fare if you make it there in twenty,' I tell him.

The driver puts his foot to the floor. People are right. In this city, money talks.

I make the cab drop us a few blocks from where Jay lives in Jackson Heights.

'You think this is wise?' I ask as we duck inside a convenience store.

Jay just stares at me. 'I gotta know if she's OK.'

I nod. He's stuck by me all this time. I'm not going to leave him now.

'OK,' I say, swinging the bag on to my back. 'Let's go then.'

Jay knows how to get into his apartment building the back way, via a series of alleyways and then a basement service entrance. He wears his hooded sweater, pulling it up to shield his face.

In just one block we walk from an area that looks like Mumbai – with women on the street wearing saris and shops selling gold jewellery and life-size Ganesha statues – and cross into what appears to be a suburb of Mexico City. The contrasting smells and bright colours and all the different sounds and languages being spoken make my head spin. We walk past a food cart. A short, squat woman is busy cooking tamales, a man stands beside her keeping one eye out for the police or whoever it is that cracks down on unlicensed food sellers. Two guys with shaved heads wearing red-and-black bandanas walk out of a liquor store a few feet ahead of us and Jay turns his face away from them on the pretext of looking back at me.

"Are we in Latin Blade territory?' I ask, once they've passed.

'Not right now. But one block east, yeah.' Jay's nervous as hell, keeping his chin tucked in close to his chest and his shoulders hunched. He moves fast, dodging in and out of people on the sidewalk before disappearing down a narrow alley between two shops.

I follow behind him, my fingers gripping my dad's Smith & Wesson, which I've taken out of the bag and stuffed down the waistband of my jeans and covered with the sweater which I've wrapped around my waist. It's still in flagrant disregard of all Felix's lessons on gun safety. But I don't have a holster or anywhere else to hide it and, in the event that we do run into trouble, I'm not going to be able to hold up a hand and ask for time out while I rummage for my weapon in my bag. All this talk of gangs is making me nervous. So nervous in fact that for the last twenty minutes at least, I've forgotten all about the cop who's after us and Agent Kassel and her partner.

At the end of the alleyway Jay stops and does a quick scan behind us. When he's sure no one's following, he beckons me over, cupping his hands together and holding them out to me. I stare at the wall he's braced in front of and sigh, before putting one foot into his hands and letting him boost me over.

With no one to boost him, Jay has to take a running leap to reach the top. I sit straddling the wall, watching for any witnesses as he scrabbles up and hauls himself over, dropping silently down on the other side. He catches me for a third time and then leads the way quickly across a scrappy dirt yard backing on to a dilapidated apartment block. I glance upwards. Six storeys, one rusting fire escape, a flat roof with guttering that looks ancient and rickety. I hope to God we don't have to flee via the roof again. There's

153

a locked rusting gate at the side of the yard which I guess leads through to the street we were just on and, up some steps, there's a door with a boarded-up glass panel. Jay takes us down some dingy concrete steps towards a solid metal door that's coated in orange rust.

He runs his hand across the top of the doorjamb, finds what he's looking for – a key – and fits it into the lock, then he pulls me inside into a gloomy basement.

We tiptoe past some wire cages filled with boxes, rusting bicycles and broken sports equipment. My dad's apartment building has the same storage facility, except in his building the cages are filled with top-of-the-line skis and snowboards and even a kayak – still wearing its Christmas bow.

Just as we reach a doorway that must lead to the stairwell Jay suddenly stops and turns to me. 'I think you should stay here,' he says, worry furrowing lines between his eyes.

'No way,' I answer. Where he goes, I'm going too. We stick together. There's no debate on that any more.

He chews his bottom lip but decides not to press it, I guess figuring that there's no way of making me stay put. 'There's only one way up,' he says. 'We're on the fourth floor.'

I push past him, pulling the gun out of my waistband. 'Follow me. We'll move fast. Any sign of trouble we turn around and get out of here. Agreed?'

Jay blocks my way with his arm. 'Give me the other gun,' he demands.

I stare at him, surprised that he even knew there was a second gun. I had kept the one I took from my dad's safe hidden.

'That's not the one I took from the cop,' he says, nodding at the one in my hand.

I scowl at him but he refuses to budge. 'Fine,' I huff, digging the other gun out of the bag. 'But do you even know how to fire one of these things?'

Jay takes it from me. 'I'm sure I can figure it out,' he says, slipping off the safety and smirking at me. 'I'm a quick learner,' he adds when he sees my surprise.

'You're going in front though,' I tell him. 'I don't want my head blown off.'

'Afraid of a little friendly fire?' he asks me.

'Hold it in both hands and aim low, for the chest area,' I tell him, positioning the gun in his hands. 'The Glock's not got much recoil but it's easy to aim too high, especially on a second shot.'

Jay nods at me, all traces of humour gone.

'Are there any other exits?' I ask him, turning back to the door.

'Front and back doors only,' he says. 'And the fire exit. But please, no more roofs.'

I grin at him briefly and then I move. Although I told him to go in front of me, now I don't want to let him. Adrenaline scores lightning tracks through my body, pushing me to go faster. I let it carry me all the way to the second floor and then the fear cuts like a razor blade through the adrenaline, severing it at its source, and I stumble. What the hell are we doing? But Jay's right behind me, urging me onwards, trying to overtake me, so I push on, fighting down Felix's voice in my head, which is telling me that we could be walking straight into a trap.

And then we hit the landing to the fourth floor and Jay is suddenly ahead of me, blocking my way. I move to his side and it's only then that I realise why he's come to a sudden halt. The door to his apartment is hanging wide open.

155

Jay takes a step forward and every instinct in my body screams at me to turn and run. I take hold of Jay's arm and start pulling him back towards the stairs. It's not safe. We should never have come.

But Jay shrugs me off and walks inside. I hover in the doorway on the balls of my feet, glancing once over my shoulder back down the stairwell, before I push my instinct down and follow him inside, bringing the gun up to shoulder height.

The apartment is eerily silent. I can just hear the sound of a TV in an adjacent apartment blasting a Spanish soap opera through the walls and, somewhere in the distance, on the street below, the sound of rap music thumping.

The kitchen is tidy but a glass of water sits on the table and there's a plate with a half-eaten piece of toast sitting on the side. We edge along the hallway towards a small living room. I take in the religious pictures on the wall and the gilt-framed photographs of three dark-haired, smiling children at various ages and breathe out a sigh of relief that there are no signs of a struggle. And no body either.

When I turn around Jay has vanished. I head back into the hallway, the hairs on the back of my neck rising. I can't shake the sense I'm being watched, but that could just be the doleful eyes of Jesus on the wall. Jay walks out of one of the rooms off the hallway.

'She's not here,' he says.

'Why was the front door open?' I ask in a whisper.

Just then we hear a creak and both of us fall silent. My stomach clenches and I grab Jay's arm. With a finger to his lips, Jay gestures behind the living-room door and as silently as possible we ease ourselves behind it, sucking in our stomachs to fit. He positions himself in front of me, so my cheek is pressed against his shoulder blade.

A footstep, heavy and slow, heads in our direction. I close my eyes and lift the gun, my palms sweating, my heart slamming against my ribs. I try to picture Felix beside me, coaching me, telling me to brace, to check the safety, to take aim.

Someone stops behind the door. I can feel Jay in front of me, so tense he's practically vibrating. He's holding his gun by his shoulder, like I'm holding mine. Neither of us dares take a breath. Whoever is on the other side of the door isn't moving. Do they know we're here?

Shit. I glance at Jay and he glances at me. The meaning in both our eyes is clear. We can't just stand here. I nod. He nods back and then we both leap from behind the door, guns aimed.

It's only down to sheer luck that we don't fire ten bullets through the woman standing there. I smack Jay's shooting arm down even as he smacks down mine, yelling, 'Don't shoot!'

The lady standing in front of us – a tall, robust woman in her seventies, with greying cornrows, wearing a floral summer dress and big woollen slippers that at first glance look like bedraggled cats – lets out a scream. Her hand flies to her chest. 'Dear Lord! Mary, mother of Jesus! Don't you dare be shooting me.'

'Mrs Francis?'

Jay runs to her side and puts his hand on her arm, guiding her towards one of the sofas. She collapses into it, fanning herself, still clutching a hand to her heart. I'm fairly sure that however hard her heart is beating, my heart is beating fifty times harder.

'You almost killed me,' she screeches. 'What you trying to do? Give an old lady a heart attack? What you doing with a gun?'

'Sorry, Mrs Francis. Sorry,' says Jay, kneeling at her side, 'I'm looking for my mom.' He glances at me. 'She's a neighbour,' he explains, before turning back to the woman. 'Have you seen her?'

Mrs Francis straightens up, pulling her dress tighter at the throat. 'Sure I seen her,' she says. 'She went off this morning with those two police.'

'Police?' Jay interrupts, undisguised terror in his voice. 'Mrs Francis, what do you mean, police?'

'Of course,' she says, ignoring him, 'I was thinking it was Teo. What with the crowd he's running with these days.'

The tendons in Jay's neck are stretched so taut they look like they might be about to snap, but Mrs Francis seems oblivious. 'And now I see it's you she's got to be worried about, as well as him. And you being the one boy your mama's always so proud of.' She shakes her head at the gun still in his hand, her lips pursing in disgust. 'You should be ashamed of yourself.'

'Mrs Francis, what about the police?' I interrupt, before Jay loses the plot completely.

'It's none of my business of course,' Mrs Francis says, her eyes landing on me and narrowing like pincers. 'I was just going about my day but they were so noisy, bang bang banging away on the door to get Lucia to open it.'

'What did they look like? This is important,' Jay asks through gritted teeth. 'Do you remember?'

'It was two police.' She says it *po-leece,* and at the same time her nose wrinkles. She's clearly no fan either of the men in blue. 'They took her with them this morning.'

'What did they look like?' I repeat, almost about ready to start threatening her with the gun if she doesn't hurry up and tell us.

Mrs Francis gives me a look that would knock a man dead at fifty paces. But, after the day I've had, I'm hardened. I just smile sweetly back, trying not to bare my teeth.

'There were two of them, like I said,' she says. 'A man and a woman.'

My gut tightens. 'A woman?'

'Mmm-hmmm,' Mrs Francis says. 'Not that I was listening, mind, but they was talking so loud you could have heard them all the way over in Jersey. She said she was an agent. Looked like that Jennifer Lopez girl. Pretty. About thirty. And the other was a black man. Handsome as Sydney Poitier.'

Jay's staring at me.

'It's her,' I say. 'It sounds like Agent Kassel. The woman who tried to get me into the car. And Agent Parker. The guy who was driving.'

Jay's brow furrows in confusion.

'My mom went with them?' Jay asks, turning back to Mrs Francis.

'Mmmm-hmmmmm, yes she did.' Mrs Francis nods.

'And they didn't force her?'

'Nope, she went placid as a lamb.'

To the slaughter? The thought pops into my head before I can stop it.

'And then about an hour later those other police came knocking,' Mrs Francis adds, turning her steely eyes on Jay.

'What other police?' Jay and I both ask at the same time.

'Two men in real police uniforms showed up – not plainclothes like the others – and let themselves in. I spied on them through my little peephole. Them two police, they went in, had a look around, left. I was just coming by now, because I saw they left the

159

door hanging wide open. And I wanted to see if that good-for-nothing brother of yours was home.'

'Did one of them have blond hair and blue eyes?' I ask, gripping Jay by the shoulder.

Mrs Francis sucks her teeth loudly. 'Yes, that's right. He turned in the hallway, looked right at my door. I swear it was like looking the devil right in the eye. I'll remember that face until the day I die.'

24

We stumble out of the apartment, ushering Mrs Francis ahead of us. My mind is whirring, frantically trying to process everything. Nothing is making any sense and I can tell from Jay's brooding silence that he can't make sense of it either but that he's assuming the worst. I want to take his hand, tell him it's going to be OK and that we'll figure it out, but we're both holding guns and Mrs Francis is staring at us like we've got horns growing out of our heads.

'We've got to get out of here,' I tell Jay. 'You never know, they may come back. They might be watching the place.'

Jay barely responds. He looks utterly defeated, so I grab him by the arm and start yanking him down the stairs. Mrs Francis stands at the top, holding on to the banister, making that sucking noise through her teeth and muttering something about the youth of today.

Halfway down the stairs I think to ask Jay whether he wants to get anything while we're here – clothes or money – but he just shakes his head dumbly at me.

I lead him back into the basement and find a dark, dusty corner that stinks of mildew. I pull up two old boxes and Jay slumps down on to one.

'Who do you think they are?' he asks in a voice that makes me want to lean across the darkness and take his hand.

'I don't know,' I answer. 'But let's not jump to conclusions. At least it wasn't the others. If they'd got there first, well . . .' I break off. I don't need to spell it out to him, he's already seen what would have happened.

'What if those agents – Agent Kassel and the other one – *were* sent by your dad? You ever think of that?' Jay asks. 'What if you were wrong and your instinct was off? I mean who else could they be? They knew your name. They turned up on the street corner you told your dad you'd be waiting at.'

'They pulled a gun on me.'

'Yeah, there is that,' Jay admits, frowning at the ground.

'Look, I'm still wondering about them too,' I admit. I mean, while she did try to force me into the car at gunpoint, they did also come to my rescue and ram that cop's car.

'She said she was an agent. What does that mean? Are they FBI, do you think?' Jay asks.

'I don't know.'

'But why would they come here?' Jay asks. 'To where I live?'

'They must have figured out that we were together – maybe from the phone call you made from my dad's or maybe they have CCTV footage from the police station? Who knows.'

'But what would they want with my mom?'

I shake my head. Nothing makes sense and sitting here in the dark is only making me feel more lost and confused. I have a sudden urge to be outside, to be back on the High Line again in the sunlight, licking ice-pops, lying next to Jay, not having to think about any of this or deal with any of it. Jay's mother is in trouble because of me. I don't know what to say so I turn away, my hands fisting. I feel like punching the wire cage in front of me.

'And what about Teo?'

162

'What about him?' I ask, turning around but unable to look Jay in the eye.

'Where is he?' Jay continues. 'He's usually at home most the day. He never gets up before noon.'

'Why don't you try calling him?' I suggest.

Jay already has his phone in his hand and is tapping in the number. The light from the handset illuminates his face, throwing a ghostly pall over his features. He stands up and starts pacing and I watch, wishing there was something I could do and feeling like I want to throw my head back and howl. My insides are frayed and my emotions swinging all over the place. I'm the one who got Jay messed up in all this and now his mum has disappeared and his brother's God knows where. I stare at the gun in my hand. How the hell did I get here? And more to the point, how do we fix it? I don't know what to do any more. I wish Felix was here to tell me.

Jay hangs up, slamming the phone into his palm. 'No answer,' he says.

Just then I have an idea. It's a stupid one but it might be worth trying. 'Give it here,' I say, holding my hand out. Jay passes me the phone.

I switch it to internet mode and type in *FBI Bureau New York* and then hit the switchboard number. After a few seconds the phone connects and it starts ringing.

'Who are you calling?' Jay asks.

'The FBI,' I say.

'What?' he asks, jumping up from his box.

Just then the operator picks up.

'I need to talk to Agent Kassel,' I hear myself say.

There's a silence on the other end before I hear, 'Just putting you through.'

My heart dives to the bottom of my chest and stays there. I hadn't actually expected that to be the response. I thought that I'd get a *I'm sorry we don't have anyone of that name working here.* Not that it's necessarily the same agent, I tell myself as I wait on hold to be transferred. I mean there might be someone else called Kassel who works for FBI. It's possible.

A man picks up – gruff, tired-sounding. 'COU,' he says.

'Um, I'm looking for Agent Kassel,' I say.

'She's not in the office. Can I help?' the man asks, and maybe I'm imagining it but he suddenly seems to sound less tired and way more alert.

'Um . . .' I say, thinking on my feet. 'How about Agent Parker?'

'He's not here either.'

My heart's now beating a hundred times a minute. Jay's crouched beside me, one hand gripping my knee, his head pressed against mine, trying to listen in on the conversation.

'What's COU stand for?' I ask, my mouth suddenly drier than the desert.

'Criminal Organisation Unit,' the man says, then, 'Can I help at all?'

'No, no, it's OK,' I stammer and then I hang up. With a shaking hand I break the phone apart and slide out the SIM, then crush it beneath my heel.

Jay stares at me in the gloom. 'I thought your dad worked for a gang task force.'

'Yeah, he does.'

There's a long silence, and then he says, 'Now I'm confused.'

'Me too,' I tell him. 'He said it was the Criminal Organisation Unit.'

'What does that mean?'

'I don't know.'

'You think they have my mom?' he asks me, a glimmer of hope in his voice.

'Yeah, I'm guessing.'

'But why?'

'I don't know,' I say again, feeling even more helpless and lost than I did a few minutes ago. Knowing that they are FBI makes me feel better – but then again, does that mean I can trust them?

'Maybe it's for her own protection,' I tell Jay, not wanting to worry him. 'Maybe they knew those guys would come here looking for you or me and so they took her into protective custody?' It certainly makes sense as hypotheses go and Jay seems to brighten at the thought. But if they're FBI agents why'd they pull a gun on me? And what were they doing there in the first place?

'We could go there,' I say, my gut lurching even as I say it because it's the last thing I want to do. 'If you wanted. We could find out for sure.'

Jay shakes his head, grim-faced. 'I can't go. Besides I need to find Teo. And I promised you I'd stick with you until you got back to your dad.'

Of course, Jay's still a wanted man. I rub my eyes. What do we do? I don't want to leave him. And I don't trust the police, or necessarily the FBI either. Felix and my dad always said that there was more corruption and more criminals inside the police force and government institutions than there was on the outside – it's part of the reason the task force my dad works on is made up mainly of civilian and NGO experts. And even if we could trust them, it's not like they can even protect us from these people who are after me. An entire police department couldn't keep me safe.

I look up at Jay. His eyes glimmer in the darkness as he waits for me to answer. Trust is as rare as unicorn horns, but I've found it. I haven't trusted anyone in a long time, but I trust Jay.

We've been doing fine on our own so far, I decide. We can last until morning, until I meet up with my dad. And then he can get us all the answers we need. And, more to the point, he can protect Jay.

'OK,' I say, standing up. 'We stick together. We try to find Teo. And then tomorrow we meet my dad and let him take it from there.'

25

I pull down the Yankees cap that I just bought from a guy selling fake Chanel handbags and baseball paraphernalia from a stall on the street and glance over my shoulder. I don't like this. Nerves take a hold of me and my teeth start chattering. I realise that I'm feeling this way because I'm suddenly on my own. There's no Jay by my side, shooting me that easy grin, or relaxing me with a sarcastic comment.

I take a deep, steadying breath and keep walking. I can see the place up ahead; the neon sign – a pair of flashing scissors – is obvious as signs go. Darting another glance over my shoulder, I hope that Jay is OK and that he's staying well hidden. We figured that it was too dangerous letting him show his face. So he's hiding behind a dumpster down an alleyway a few blocks back.

I push open the door to the hair salon and the noise of gabbling women, clicking scissors and Jessie J's vocals blast me. The women instantly stop talking. There are three women having their hair and nails done at a row of chairs facing along one wall. They all lift their eyes and stare at me over the tops of magazines, gazes flickering head to toe, taking in my scabby knees, beat-up Toms and messy hair.

'Can I help you?'

A woman with a really bad perm and red-painted talons stands eyeing me from her position in the centre of the salon. She's holding a hairdryer in one hand and a brush in the other. People let this woman loose on their hair? For a moment I lose track of why I'm there as I catch sight of the frazzled bleached mop atop the woman she's currently working on.

'Um,' I say, wishing that I could speak Spanish, or that I looked a little more like I belonged in this part of town. 'I was wondering if Marisa was available.'

'What? You want a manicure?' the woman says, scrunching her nose at me in suspicion. Her hand goes to her hip as she takes in my appearance. Admittedly I don't look like someone who goes to nail bars regularly, and my hair, stuffed under the cap, doesn't look like it's seen sight of a brush for well over a day. Not that I'd ever let her near it, however.

A girl a little older than myself, seated at a manicure table behind the scary talon lady, stands up. 'I'm Marisa,' she says, eyeing me warily. She's about five foot and voluptuous as can be, with a cleavage so eye-popping it momentarily renders me speechless.

'Can I speak to you?' I ask, feeling all eyes still glued to me. The chatter has fallen away completely and only Jesse J can be heard, singing about bling and wanting to make the world dance.

Marisa looks to the woman, her boss I assume, for permission. The woman gives me a look that could relax a perm and says, 'Yeah, you can take five. But only five, mind.' Marisa switches a little fan on and places her client's wet nails beneath it, then indicates with a nod of her head for me to follow her through a beaded curtain and towards a back door.

We step into a tiny bereft courtyard littered with cigarette butts and torn chocolate wrappers. There's a flaking wooden chair propping open the door and through it I can hear the noises from the salon wafting in our direction as all the women start nattering away again in Spanish at ninety miles an hour.

Marisa turns to face me with her arms crossed over her chest and stares at me, and for a second I'm completely taken aback by the similarity between her and Jay. They're cousins, but they could be siblings. OK, so she's about a foot shorter and a whole lot rounder, but they have the same beautiful skin and, though she has brown eyes, they're framed by the same thick dark lashes. She also has that exact same arched eyebrow thing going on.

'So, you wanted to talk to me?' she asks, her curiosity obviously piqued, even though her posture is weary, bordering on defensive. I notice her nails are painted with a complicated tropical flower pattern that must have taken hours to do.

'It's about Jay,' I tell her, looking up.

Instantly her expression switches, her arms drop to her sides and she steps closer. 'Where is he?' she says, breathlessly. 'Is he OK?'

I nod again and the relief that floods across her face makes something in my gut twist painfully. She has no idea what danger he's still in.

'He's nearby,' I say. 'But he's in trouble. *We're* in trouble.'

'Hang on,' she says, suspicion saturating her voice. 'Who are you?'

'My name's Liva, I'm a friend of his.'

Her eyebrows shoot up at that and I suppress a silent growl. Why's it so inconceivable Jay and I could be friends?

'What happened? Where is he?' she demands.

'We need your help.' I realise how desperate I sound and try to rein it in. Jay had seemed confident that she would help, but

169

now I'm standing here in front of her, bracing myself against her suspicious gaze, I'm not so sure.

'Well, why isn't he asking himself?' she asks me.

'He tried calling the salon but when he asked to talk to you your boss hung up on him.'

'That was him?' Marisa asks. 'Gloria thought it was my boyfriend. She doesn't allow us to take personal calls.'

'He couldn't come himself because we were worried someone might recognise him.'

Her jaw tightens and I take that as a sign she knows something about last night and the trouble he's in with this gang.

'I am going to kill Teo when I get my hands on him,' she spits.

'So you know what happened then?' I say, relieved that I don't have to explain it all.

'No. I just heard that Teo was messed up in something and got Jay involved, the idiot.' I'm not sure if she's referring to Jay or to Teo as the idiot, but she carries on. 'Then I heard Jay got arrested – is it true he stole a car?'

I nod.

She rolls her eyes heavenward and says something in Spanish, which it's easy to guess the meaning of.

'And is it true he escaped from the police?'

'Well, yeah, we did. But only because the choice was that or staying around and getting killed.'

Her eyes go wide and her hand flies to her mouth. '*Mio Dio!*' she whispers. 'It's true then, he was at the police station last night. The one in Brooklyn that got hit?'

I nod.

She swallows rapidly, her eyes darting across the courtyard. 'I tried calling Tia Lucia this morning after I couldn't get hold of

Teo but she wasn't answering her phone. I was going to go over there straight after work.'

'No, don't do that. Stay away,' I tell her, thanking God she didn't go there this morning.

She glares at me, her lips pursed together. 'What *is* going on?'

'We were both at the police station last night when it got hit. We made it out of there, thanks to Jay.' I close my eyes as a wave of nausea hits me. 'But now we're in trouble. Big trouble.'

Her face darkens. 'What kind of trouble? What's all this about? Is it that gang Teo's involved with?'

I shake my head. 'No. Look, I can't explain. We're not entirely sure what's going on but we didn't have anywhere else to go.'

'What do you need?' she asks immediately and I see the fire in her eyes, the fierce pride that I saw in Jay's when I first met him.

'A place to stay. Just until tomorrow morning,' I tell her quickly.

'Marisa!' The boss lady with the Edward Scissorhand nails sticks her head around the door. 'Five minutes is up.'

Marisa nods at her and moves towards the door. As she passes, she presses something into my hand. 'Here, give these to Jay.' She looks at her watch. 'It's almost six. I'll be home as soon as I finish work, around seven. But tell him I want to talk to him.'

I glance down at the keys she's given me. 'Thank you,' I say.

She pauses in the doorway to look back at me, her brow furrowing. 'Be careful.'

26

I duck into the alleyway where Jay is hiding out and slam straight into someone. I'm about to let out a scream when familiar hands squeeze me by the arms.

'Woah, Moneypenny, it's only me.'

'Jesus, you scared me,' I say, looking up at Jay. 'What were you doing?'

'I was coming looking for you,' he says, letting me go. 'You were ages.'

'We were talking. Here.' I show him the keys. 'She gave me these.'

Jay takes the keys from me, his face brightening. 'Come on,' he says, 'let's go.'

'Is it far?' I ask.

'About four blocks.'

'Wait,' I say, and I pull the cap from my head and stick it on his, pulling it down low over his face so his eyes are in shadow.

'Thanks,' he says, and for a moment it seems like he's going to say something else but then he thinks better of it.

We walk straight on to the street and Jay suddenly takes my hand. Instantly I feel that connection, my body relaxes. I feel stronger with him at my side. He's holding the go-bag in his other hand and I take a surreptitious glance behind him and spy the shape of the Glock tucked against the small of his back. He's lucky the T-shirt is loose enough that it's not obvious to anyone unless they're looking. I have wrapped the NYPD sweatshirt around my waist to hide mine because my tank top clings too tight to disguise much of anything.

Jay takes us a back route to Marisa's apartment, which is a tiny one-bedroom place above a pizza delivery restaurant. The smell of peperoni and garlic follows us up the stairs and into the living room and makes my stomach growl.

Jay bolts the door behind us and puts the chain on. I take the bag from him and root through it for the doorstopper and then slide that beneath the gap at the bottom. We both stand back and observe our security measures. The door doesn't look that sturdy and the doorstopper looks like a comical afterthought, like trying to stop a bullet with a tray. We've seen that those guys will stop at nothing. But they'd have to find us here first. Is that likely? We seem to have shaken them off our tail – maybe the credit card trick worked – and they'd probably not expect us to come near Jay's neighbourhood either. I think we're safe for the moment. I hope so, as I really don't want Marisa dragged into anything bad.

Jay seems familiar with Marisa's place, helping himself to glasses from the cupboard over the sink and filling them with water before raiding another cupboard above the fridge, opening an old ice-cream container and finding a clearly meant-to-be-secret stash of chocolate.

He breaks the bar in two and hands it to me. I take it and break off a square, realising I'm famished.

Jay drops down on to the sofa beside me. He leans forward and rests his head in his hands.

'Are you OK?' I ask. It's a dumb question and as soon as it's out of my mouth I regret it.

'Yeah, I'm just worried about my mom,' he says. His foot beats an angry rhythm against the floor. 'And Teo.'

'I'm sure your mum's OK,' I say. 'We could try calling Agent Kassel again if you think that would help.'

'I want to find Teo. He might know something. Maybe my mom's called him. And I need to find out what went down with the Blades.'

I can't help feeling a spurt of anger towards Teo, even though I've never met him. He's dragged his brother into this shit storm and has now bailed on him, leaving him to handle the flack alone.

'So you're the youngest, huh?' I ask, trying to get him to focus on something else.

'Yeah,' Jay says, settling back into the sofa. 'Luis is twenty-three. Teo is twenty-one.'

'How old are you?' I ask.

'About to turn twenty.'

'Wow, your poor mum had her work cut out for her when you were little.'

'Nothing like she has now,' Jay answers grimly. 'You know, after my dad left, my mom never complained. She just went out and got a job and made it work. She busted her ass every day so she could make sure we never wanted for anything, and they repay her by joining the Blades and getting mixed up in all this shit.'

I put a hand on his forearm, feeling the hardness of muscle, rigid with anger.

'But you were the good one, huh?' I ask, remembering what Mrs Francis said, and wanting to distract him from his anger.

Jay laughs under his breath, 'Yeah, really good. I'm the one who just got busted for car theft.'

'I told you, we'll sort that out. I promise you, there are ways.' I know this from my mother who once defended oil corporations when they were accused of things like illegal drilling. There are always ways. Bad guys walk free all the time. Not that Jay is a bad guy, but the principle still applies.

'Yeah, there are ways if you have money and a good lawyer,' Jay snaps.

'We'll get you one. Stop worrying about that.'

His eyes blaze for a second at me and I know I've hit him in his Achilles heel – his pride.

'So, what makes you the good one?' I ask, trying to break the tension.

He glances sideways at me and then throws his head back against the sofa.

'I'm the one who got straight As all through school, got a place at college,' he sighs.

'You're going to college?' Again I want to smack myself for not disguising the surprise in my voice.

I catch the look he gives me and my insides shrivel. 'Yeah,' he says, 'I got a scholarship to study automotive design at the University of Michigan.'

'Wow,' I say, impressed. 'Car design?'

His face lights up. 'Yeah. All my life I've been obsessed with cars. And then Father Gomez got me into racing. I started off on dirt bikes and—'

'Father Gomez?' I ask.

'The local priest. He likes to make projects out of some of the boys in the neighbourhood, the ones he thinks have potential to make something more out of their lives, you know? Be role models for the others.'

His face has transformed as he speaks, fire burning in his eyes, passion filling his voice, and something catches in my throat as I watch him.

'It's kind of an anti-gang project. Not that he calls it that. But it works. There was a boy in Teo's class at school – used to be a choirboy alongside him – and now he's working as an architect. Another one who's an NFL coach. I was going to college this fall . . .'

Suddenly he breaks off and the brightness vanishes. '*Was*,' he says. 'Guess I can kiss that dream goodbye now. I'm not even going to be here in the fall.'

I don't know what to say to that. I want to ask him what he means. Is he referring to the fact he might be behind bars by then, or is he planning on trying to run? I want to tell him again that it will be OK, that my father will help, that we'll figure something out, but I remember the look of wounded pride he shot my way when I suggested it before, and the scepticism behind it too. And he's right. We don't even know where we'll be this time tomorrow, let alone in a couple of months. But as I sit here, beside this boy I hardly know, I'm aware that the thought of not seeing him again makes panic shoot acid through my veins.

Jay runs his hands through his cropped hair and then stands up, shaking out his shoulders. 'Back in a minute,' he says and he walks off, disappearing into what I assume is the bathroom. I hear the tap running and take the opportunity to wander through the apartment. I am guessing Marisa lives here alone because it feels very much like a girl's apartment – stacks of gossip magazines sit on the coffee table, a vase filled with flowers perches on top of the television, a shopping list is tacked to the fridge. On the wall there's a framed photograph of Marisa with her arm around an enormous boy. Both of them are wearing high school graduation gowns and are grinning with delight at the camera. And then there's another one of Marisa with an older woman who I'm guessing is her mother and another girl, a little older and a lot bigger – maybe it's Jay's other cousin, Maria – the one he said liked donuts.

Out the window I watch the busy street below, but when I realise that I'm scanning it, on alert for any sign of police, I draw the curtains. Am I always going to be like this? Running scared? Suspicious of anyone in a uniform? I push the thought away. Along with every other thought. I'm acutely aware that I've been forcing myself all day not to think about what happened to the Goldmans or what happened at the police station. Every time my mind wanders there, I shut it down. I keep pacing the apartment, trying to distract myself, trying to find other things to focus on.

I peer into Marisa's bedroom. There's a double bed made up with a patchwork quilt and a mountain of pillows which siren-calls my name. But I turn away from it. The tiredness I felt earlier is back, as is the headache pulling behind my eyes, setting up a gentle throbbing beat, but Marisa is going to be home soon and wouldn't much appreciate finding me in her bed, I doubt. And I'm not sure I could sleep anyway.

I notice the dressing table bowing under the weight of about fifty bottles of nail polish and a metal make-up box so big it looks like it could be used to transport nuclear warheads. I'm half tempted to walk over and take a look in her mirror and maybe borrow the hairbrush I can see sitting on the side, but I'm too scared of what I might see staring back at me in the mirror, so instead I walk into the little kitchenette and idly start opening cupboards.

They're full of ingredients I hardly recognise – cooking not being my strong point thanks to having grown up in a house with a cook. The refrigerator is loaded with fresh fruit and vegetables, a half-eaten lasagne, cans of Diet Coke and more chocolate. My mouth waters. Man, I'm so sick of having to watch what I eat. What was it Jay said to me about not having to worry about counting calories? I smile a little to myself as I remember his eyes tracing their way down my body, the trail of warmth they left.

Just then the front door rattles and I almost jump out of my skin.

'Hey, let me in!'

I recognise Marisa's voice. The surge of adrenaline evaporates, leaving me shaky as I run to the door, remove the doorstopper and slip off the chain. She bustles in, looking me over warily before scanning the apartment.

'Where's Jay?' she asks, dropping her handbag on to the floor.

The bathroom door opens bang on cue and Jay appears. He's stripped off his T-shirt and is standing there in just his jeans, with a towel thrown over one shoulder. He's shaved and he looks younger as a result, not that my attention is on his face for long because it's quickly diverted by his chest. I properly look this time – I can't help myself – drawing in a breath that I hope isn't audible. I was right about him having the upper body strength of a dancer or at the very least, an athlete. His shoulders and pecs are exceedingly well defined and the lines of his stomach traceable. Not that I'm thinking about tracing them. Then my view is blocked, as Marisa throws herself into his arms and I have to mentally remind myself that she's just his cousin.

Jay holds her tight as she clings to him and another pang hits that I fight to stifle. She barely comes up to his collarbone, but when she pulls away eventually she keeps hold of him by the tops of his arms. I notice her bottom lip is trembling and her chest is heaving up and down. Then, without warning she smashes Jay in the arm and he lets her go.

'Ow! What was that for?'

Tears pour down her face. 'For being an idiot. What were you thinking? You know what this is going to do to your mom? To all of us?'

'You don't need to remind me, OK?' he answers tersely.

'The whole neighbourhood is talking about it. They're saying you took a job that Teo was meant to do and you got arrested. Are you crazy? You got the Blades looking for you *and* the police?' To her credit she doesn't finish that sentence with *and you came here?*

'I didn't know what else to do,' Jay says, and for a moment they just stand there, eyes locked. Marisa with her hands on her hips and Jay, shoulders slumped.

'Where's Teo?' Marisa demands finally. 'Where's your mom? I can't get hold of either of them.'

Jay glances at me over her head. 'She's, um . . . we think maybe the FBI has her.'

Marisa blinks at him and doesn't say anything for about ten seconds straight. Then her legs give out and she collapses down on to the sofa, making the cushions bounce. 'The FBI?' she asks, starting to rock back and forth.

Jay nods, sitting beside her. She turns towards him and clutches his knees. 'What do you mean, the FBI? Is this something about Teo? Is it something to do with the Blades? What's going on?'

Jay gestures with his hands for her to calm down. 'We don't know for sure,' he says. 'We think it's something to do with Liva.'

179

Marisa turns to me and shoots me with a gaze so lethal I feel as if she's bolt-gunned me to the wall.

'With her?' she spits, staring at him like he's lost his mind. 'Then why are you mixed up in it? Or your mom? What's the FBI got to do with any of it?'

I glare at Jay – couldn't he have found a better way to explain things to her than making me the scapegoat?

Jay catches my glare and gives me an apologetic look in response.

'We think maybe they took her into custody for her own protection.'

'Protection from what?' Marisa screeches.

'You saw the news, right? You saw the police station that got hit?'

Marisa nods, her lip starting to tremble again. 'That was just some crazy ex-cop, wasn't it? That's what I heard.'

'No. We think they were coming after Liva,' he says. 'She witnessed a murder last night. She was in the police station giving a statement. And then, later, after we escaped, the same guys who shot out the police station found us again.'

Marisa is now staring at me as though I'm the grim reaper standing in her front room waving a scythe. The horror isn't even masked. 'Why?' she asks Jay. 'What do they want from her?'

I force myself to stand there even though I can hear the blood pounding in my temples and want nothing more than to run from the room. I shouldn't be here. We shouldn't have brought anyone into this. We made a promise about no communication. We were stupid to break it. I steal a glance at the door.

'We're not sure,' says Jay quietly, 'but possibly it has something to do with her father and his line of work.'

180

'Who's your father?' Marisa asks, her attention flying to me.

'He works for the government on a human trafficking task force,' I tell her, wishing Jay had just kept his mouth shut.

'Trafficking?' she asks, frowning. And then it dawns. 'People?' Her voice rises and her eyes grow round.

'Yeah,' says Jay, and I can tell he's finally having second thoughts about coming here too, or the wisdom of telling her any of this.

Marisa sinks back against the sofa cushions and takes us both in with a slow shake of her head. '*Mierda*,' she says.

'Yeah,' says Jay, smiling wryly. 'You can say that again.'

She leaps suddenly to her feet. 'How do you know they didn't follow you here?' Her eyes fly to the door as though fully expecting someone to come bursting through it.

Jay stands up and puts a hand on her shoulder. 'It's OK, Marisa, we shook them off this morning. They don't know where we are. We're not being tailed. We made sure.'

Marisa studies him, her shoulders rising and falling fast before she takes a deep breath. She closes her eyes and when she opens them again she nods. 'OK. Of course you can stay here. As long as you need.' But her gaze slips to the door again and I can tell from the nervous swallow that her feelings for Jay are fighting her better instincts. If the real police find Jay here then she could be charged with harbouring a felon. And if the other people find us, well, that thought's probably scaring her a whole lot more. I shoot a glance in Jay's direction, hoping he's realising that coming here was a stupid idea and that he'll suggest we leave, but he's not looking at me. He's grinning at Marisa.

'Thanks, Risa,' he says. 'It's just till the morning. I promise.'

Marisa shakes her head ruefully at Jay, then throws back her shoulders and marches into the kitchen. 'Who's hungry?' she asks.

'Yeah, we could eat,' Jay answers for us both. We hear the sound of cupboards opening and then a sudden torrent of Spanish hits us.

'What?' I ask Jay, alarmed.

Jay winces. 'She just found out we ate her secret chocolate stash.'

'Oh.'

Pots and pans start clanging.

'Are you sure she's OK with us staying?' I ask in a whisper.

Jay steps closer, 'Yeah, don't worry. She's cool. She never stays mad for long. And she's not mad at you anyway, just worried.' So he *did* notice.

'Do you think it's a good idea that we came here?'

'Where else we going to go? You want to sleep rough in Prospect Park?'

Though the idea doesn't appeal that much, yeah, I think I would. At least we wouldn't be putting anyone in danger. And at least we'd be moving again. Staying still, stopping in one place, is making me antsy. It's giving me time to think and I don't want to think.

Just then Marisa sticks her head around the door. 'You like spicy?' she asks me.

'Um, yeah,' I say.

She smiles slyly and I wonder how many chillies that just earned me.

'Don't worry,' Jay says, behind me, close to my ear. 'She's always a little like this whenever I bring a girl home.'

A sharp stab of what feels disturbingly like envy spears its way through my gut. How many girls does he bring home? But at the same time I feel a surge of warmth because his breath is still against the nape of my neck, causing goosebumps to travel the entire length of my spine.

'Not that I bring home a lot of girls,' he adds quickly. 'You know, there have only been a couple.'

He's rambling. I have never heard Jay ramble. I turn slowly around to face him, noticing his cheeks are infused with colour. Is he embarrassed?

'Liva, you want to freshen up? Be my guest,' Marisa says, sticking her head back around the doorway, an onion and a bag of chillies in her hand.

'Yeah, sure,' I say, glancing between her and Jay. I'm getting a very strong hint that she wants me out the way so she can talk to Jay, so I back off and head towards the bathroom, wondering if she's about to start lecturing him on his sanity. When you think about what we just dumped on her – that Jay has been arrested and is currently evading custody, that we're being hunted by the police, the FBI and what we think is a human trafficking gang, as well as the Latin Blades – I would understand if she wanted us to leave. Or if she thought Jay needed his head read.

'There are spare towels in the cupboard in there and help yourself to whatever you need,' Marisa tells me with a forced smile.

I close the bathroom door, glancing once more at Jay before I do. He give me a reassuring smile. The kind an executioner might before he throws the switch.

27

As I turn the lock I hear the first angry hiss of rapid-fire Spanish. I twist the faucet so it's on full and tiptoe back to the door, hoping the sound of the water rushing down the plughole will cover me. Once I'm there though, with my ear pressed to the wood, I realise that my three years of high school Spanish qualifies me to answer questions about the weather and ask the way to the beach, but doesn't qualify me for listening in on a conversation this fast or this furious. Jay's voice is a low and steady murmur against Marisa's machine-gun rattle. I have no clue what they are talking about. But I do hear my name mentioned several times in the midst of a torrent of colourful-sounding adjectives and after a while I begin to feel grateful that I can't understand what's being said.

I head back towards the sink, forcing myself to ignore the argument and focus instead on sorting myself out, if not emotionally, then at least physically. I throw cold water over my face to try to wake myself up a bit and only then do I gather the courage to look at my reflection. My hair is tied back in a ponytail but strands have fallen loose, framing my face, which looks pale and washed out. My eyes look grey rather than blue and *haunted* is the word that springs to mind as I consider the shadows etched beneath them. Marisa has a pharmacy's worth of cleansers, moisturisers and other lotions arranged around the sink and in the cabinet, so

I help myself, in the hope that if I can make myself more present-able then maybe Marisa might feel warmer towards me, though even as I dab on some moisturiser that says its going to soothe, illuminate and hydrate me to the max I know I'm lying to myself. It's not Marisa I want to look good for. It's Jay.

Five minutes later, with hair brushed and teeth finger-brushed, with some colour returned to my cheeks and the dirt scrubbed away, I look more human. Though I certainly don't feel the same way on the inside. Now we've stopped to draw breath and I have room to start thinking again, my emotions have started to seesaw madly. The knot in my stomach is pulled so tight that I feel nauseous as the smells from the kitchen start to seep through the door. Briefly, my mind wanders to my dad. Is he back yet? Will he find the note I left him in the safe? Will he be there tomorrow? Does my mum have any idea what's happening? Is she going out of her mind with worry? I picture her pacing the marble-floored hallways of our house in Oman with Sven trying ineffectually to calm her down. Should I call? I press my hands to my head, trying to rub away the tiredness so I can think clearly, but then my thoughts turn, as they've been threatening to all day, to the rela-tives of all the people killed today in the police station. What must they be going through right now – knowing what's happened to their husbands, wives . . . their children? I think about the woman pushing the pram who rammed me from behind on the street and the look of sheer terror on her face, and I think about Jay's mother and where she might be right now and what she must be thinking. And I think of the Goldmans being carried out of their house in black body bags.

I think of everyone who's fallen into the path of these men who are trying to find me. *Me.* And I wonder how it can be possible that so many people have paid with their lives while I'm still standing here, still breathing. It's not fair. I try to remember what Jay said about it not being my fault, about not being responsible for all the shit that happens in the world, but I'm not sure how to reconcile that. I stare at myself hard in the mirror, blinking through a film of tears. Wasn't Felix enough? How can I live with all these other people on my conscience too?

An insidious thought slides through all the others, worming its way to the forefront of my mind. Maybe I should let them take me. That way, I start to reason, at least no one else would get hurt. But the thought makes a cold, solid lump form in my gut. Could I just do that? Hand myself over to them? The lump rises up my throat. I could make a phone call they could trace. I could wait for them to find me. Is that what I should have done from the start? Could I have stopped all this from happening? If I hadn't climbed on to the roof at the Goldmans', would everyone else still be alive?

I realise I'm clutching the edge of the sink and that I'm shaking hard. My legs are rubbery, and it's my arms that are doing the work to hold me up. My lips are tingling and I realise that's because I'm hyperventilating, the air going no further than the back of my throat.

I close my eyes and the room spins wildly. The taste of the chocolate I ate earlier fills my mouth, cloying and acidic, and I think I'm going to be sick. Bending over the sink, I practise the breathing and visualisation technique that Felix taught me to help me get over my fear of the dark.

He sat with me in the dripping dank basement of our house in Nigeria, where rats the size of cats used to hang out and play, and he talked me through the fear that had me paralysed and sobbing. He showed me that fear was nothing but a product of my imagination and that I could make it go away by changing my thoughts, taking control of them, and showing the fear who was boss. Fear became an animal that I could put on a leash and lock away in a cage.

I need to use that same technique now, trap the fear like an animal, and keep it locked away. I need to be able to think clearly if I'm to have any chance of making it through this. Of helping Jay. After a few seconds I'm able to get hold of my breathing and bring it back under control, and then the nausea ebbs. My mind is still flying in a million different directions, battling panic and trying to sweep frantically at the fear, but I make myself move towards the door. I've been in here too long. Jay's going to come looking. And also, a part of me recognises that being close to him helps in its own way to keep the fear at bay.

I reach for the lock and that's when I hear Jay and Marisa talking in low voices, only now they're talking in English.

'I've got to find him,' I hear Jay saying. 'Where do you think he is?'

'I don't know,' Marisa answers, 'probably with a girl somewhere, getting wasted. Why do you need to find him anyways?' she asks, and I hear the hiss of a hot pan hitting water. They must be talking about Teo.

'I need to know what went down with the Blades after I got busted, find out what the score is.'

I miss the next part because something starts sizzling loudly. The smell of cooking meat hits me through the door.

'What are you going to do?' I hear Marisa ask.

'I'll take the rap,' Jay answers. 'Keep my mouth shut. If they can guarantee they won't come after Teo or my mom.'

Marisa's sigh is audible. 'Jay—'

'Jay nothing.' He cuts her off. 'What other choice have I got? If I run, they'll catch me sooner or later and then it'll be worse. I need to find Teo, though. Talk to him. He's gotta get his ass clean and start being responsible. Mom's gonna need him when I'm not there. Someone's gonna have to look after her.'

I hear Marisa sobbing.

Jay's voice softens. 'You gotta promise me that you'll take care of her too, Risa. She's gonna need you.'

'I promise,' Marisa says through her tears. 'You don't need to ask me that. You know I will.'

A drawer opens and crashes shut. The sound of cutlery being dumped on a hard surface follows.

'What was the job? Why did you do it?'

'Because I'm an idiot, like you said. They needed a driver. Gave me an address. Told me to be there, to ask no questions and just to drive wherever they told me to drive.'

'And you did it?' Marisa asks incredulous. In the bathroom, I rest my forehead against the cool wood of the door.

'What choice did I have?' Jay spits. 'Teo was in no state to drive anywhere. And he's on parole anyway.'

'And now you're going to go to prison in his place. What about college?'

'It was just a dream,' Jay says bitterly. 'It was never going to happen.'

'Don't you dare say that,' Marisa hisses. 'It was never just a dream. You were going to go. You *deserve* to go.'

'No. I don't,' Jay says firmly.

There's a pause. The sound of someone setting the table. Then: 'When are you going to hand yourself in?'

I hold my breath. 'When Liva's safe. Tomorrow morning, I guess.'

'What?' Marisa's voice rises almost to a shout.

'I promised. And I just need to, OK?' Jay sighs, his tone telling her to drop it.

She doesn't. 'Why you care so much what happens to this girl?' she demands. 'You don't even know her.'

I hold my breath, my hands falling to my sides.

Jay pauses. 'She did me a favour. I'd be dead if she hadn't helped me get out of that police station. Simple as that. I'm not gonna abandon her now.'

I exhale under my breath.

'But these people—' Marisa begins.

'It's OK, I promise.' Jay cuts her off. 'It's just a few more hours and then . . .' He stops and I realise he had been going to say *it'll be over*. It hangs there, in the silence, the ominous knowledge that it isn't going to be over for Jay. Not by a long shot.

I realise then that I've been in the bathroom way too long and that if I stay here much longer it'll be obvious that I'm eavesdropping so, plastering a smile on my face, I open the door and walk out.

'Smells good,' I say even as my stomach rolls over at the sight of the food.

Marisa's smile tightens on her face. She quickly turns her back and starts serving up whatever she has cooking in the pans on the stove. Jay carries the plates to the table without a word, and then pulls out a chair for me. I drop down into it, my legs still not feeling strong enough to hold me up.

'You want something to drink?' he asks me.

'Just water,' I say and I watch him fill a glass at the sink and bring it to me. He has the gun still tucked into his waistband

and I realise that I do too. I figure that taking it out in front of Marisa isn't a good move so I just leave it there, checking quickly that the go-bag is still over by the door.

Marisa sits down and picks up her knife and fork. Jay sits opposite me and seems to be waiting for me to start, so I pick up my fork with a shaky hand and stab a piece of chicken with it. It looks like she's made some kind of chicken stir fry. I take a bite. Yeah, she didn't scrimp on the chillies either. I chew and swallow as the roof of my mouth ignites.

'Too spicy?' Marisa asks.

'No, it's great,' I say, smiling weakly and swallowing. I can actually deal with chillies. I spent a few years in Pakistan when I was a child and the food there isn't exactly bland.

'Jay says you saved his life,' Marisa says, after a heavily weighted silence.

I glance up. She's watching me carefully over a glass of water.

'He saved mine too,' I say.

'We're a good team,' Jay adds, catching my eye. He's trying to lighten the mood, make me smile, but I can't smile back. I drop my gaze to my plate. Even eating is hard. I focus on the burning sensation in my mouth to try to distract me from the thoughts whirring around my head.

We fall into silence, everyone wrapped up in their own thoughts. I spy Marisa wiping away a tear and Jay drops his fork and squeezes her hand under the table. I watch him, wondering if he's thinking like I am, that this will be the last time he has dinner with his cousin in a long time.

28

I eat as much as I can, but judging from the others' barely touched plates no one is much in the mood for food. I start clearing the table and carrying everything through to the kitchen. When I turn around to go back for more, Jay is standing in the doorway blocking my way.

'How are you holding up?' he asks.

I shrug, keeping my gaze fixed on his chest. 'How 'bout you?' I ask, risking a quick glance at his face.

He gives me a sad smile, which says it all. Then he lifts his hand and almost absently strokes my hair behind my ear, his fingertips gently sweeping the skin beneath my ear lobe, and an arrow of heat shoots all the way to my fingertips.

'Not long now,' he whispers.

I close my eyes and feel myself swaying towards him. I want to press my forehead against his sternum. I want to rest there, and I want him to hold me. I have this idea that Jay might be able to help me wrestle the fear back into its cage, though rationally I know that I need to do it alone. There's no point ever relying on anyone for something like that. You can only rely on yourself.

His hand curls then around the nape of my neck, slowly, tentatively, and my breathing stills for a beat before abruptly speeding up. When I make no move to pull away, he draws me against his chest and my body responds instantaneously, everything inside coming undone. All those things I've been keeping caged in the dark come tumbling free, rising up inside me, frantically scrabbling for an exit point, and for one hideous moment I think I might collapse to the floor and start sobbing, or worse, screaming. My fingers curl into Jay's T-shirt, bunching it tight, desperately clutching at him – at something solid to hold on to.

'It's OK,' Jay whispers, his voice trailing soft against my skin, making it even harder to keep everything contained.

His lips press down on the top of my head and stay there. And there's that connection I keep feeling between us again – something magnetic, not just electric – holding me to him. And suddenly I'm not thinking about anything any more. My head empties of every single thought. His thumb traces a line down my neck and all I'm aware of are the sensations taking over my body, raiding every cell. Fire flies through my veins, burning through my bones, searing the underside of my skin. And with it comes a barely controlled desire to slide my hands under Jay's T-shirt and press my palms against his stomach, to trace the lines of muscle with my fingertips.

I fight the urge to loop my arms around his neck and pull his head down so I can feel his lips against mine. Jay's arms tighten fractionally around me and I feel him take a breath. He holds it and one of his hands slides down to my waist, comes to rest on my hip. I grip his T-shirt tighter and hear the sigh that falls from my lips. And that's all it takes. Jay's hands move quickly, and suddenly he's holding my head, tipping my face up to his, his thumbs stroking along my jaw. I glance at his face and see the light in his eyes – the intensity of his stare, like I'm the only thing that matters right now to him. And I'm staring back at him, unblinking, my breathing coming faster and faster. His lips part and he leans down. I close my eyes.

But then Marisa clears her throat behind Jay and my eyes flash open. I dance out of Jay's arms and the white heat dissipates, leaving me reeling and unsteady on my feet. My heart is still fluttering and I'm breathing like I just ran a marathon. Marisa bustles past us, carrying the rest of the things from the table, giving Jay an unmistakeable glare as she passes.

'I'll make up the sofa in the living room. It turns into a bed,' Marisa says over her shoulder. 'You can take that. Liva, you can sleep on the floor in my room.' She gives Jay another pointed look and I turn away, my cheeks throbbing. Now Jay's no longer touching me my brain has switched back on and started processing what just almost happened. Were we really about to kiss? My stomach flips over at the thought. I can still feel the ghost pressure from his fingers against my jaw, can remember the look in his eyes as he leaned down to kiss me – the fire in his eyes, like he needed me as much as I need him right now. And God, how much I wanted to kiss him too. *Still* want to kiss him.

Jay starts to say something about helping Marisa, but he's interrupted by the sound of someone pummelling their fist against the door. I jump and my hand moves instantly to my gun. I glance at Jay as I step into the living room. He's beside me, his gun already in his hand. But then Marisa barges past us both, screaming, and stands blocking the door with her hands on her hips, looking like she might be about to breathe fire.

'*¿Qué coño?* What do you think you're doing?' she demands. 'It's only Yoyo! Put the gun away,' she yells at Jay.

Through the door we hear a guy shout, 'Risa? Open up! What's going on?'

Marisa yanks open the door.

'What the hell's going on?'

A guy in his early twenties, built like a refrigerator, fills the doorway. Marisa tugs him into the apartment and slams the door behind him, bolting it. The guy's face lights up the instant he sees Jay and he crosses the room in two big strides and pulls him into a massive man-hug. Jay's shoulders relax. The guy Yoyo is at least six four and almost as broad across, and from the way Marisa is staring at him with a mixture of fondness and annoyance, I'm guessing that he's her boyfriend.

Yoyo (is that really his name?) pulls back and slaps Jay on the back. 'Man, where you been? We're hearing all sorts of shit.'

Jay glances at me quickly over Yoyo's shoulder. 'It's a long story.'

'He's in trouble, Yo,' Marisa says, coming to stand beside him.

His eyes flash to Jay. 'Popo?' he asks.

'Yeah, the police. But that's not the half of it,' Marisa answers, clutching his arm.

'You don't want to know the other half,' Jay interrupts, before Marisa can get started. I'm grateful because I'm pretty certain that in her version I'd be the one shouldering all the blame, never mind the fact Jay got caught behind the wheel of a stolen car, and never mind the other fact that we're the ones being chased by stone-cold killers.

'This is Liva,' Jay says, nodding at me.

'Hey,' I say as Yoyo's gaze travels the length of me.

He turns to Jay and smiles slyly. 'Only you, Moreno.'

Jay gives him an almost imperceptible shake of the head, warning him not to go there, though I see the smile twitching at the corner of his mouth.

194

'Where'd he find you?' Yoyo asks, offering me his hand, which is the size of a small ham.

'In a police station,' I say.

'What were you being booked for?' Yoyo asks, appraising me anew.

'She was a witness to something,' Jay answers for me.

Yoyo steps away, still considering me. 'Well, nice to meet you. Any friend of Jay's . . .' He lets the sentence trail off and I note the inflection on the word *friend*.

'Did you find him?' Marisa suddenly interrupts.

Yoyo turns to her. 'Yeah. Someone's seen him at a party.'

'Who?' Jay asks, his head jerking up. 'Teo?'

'Yeah,' says Yoyo, his brow creasing. 'Risa asked me to keep an eye out for him after we heard what happened. I've been all around the neighbourhood trying to find him.'

'Where is he?' Jay asks, impatient.

'My friend Mike's seen him at a club on Roosevelt. He just called.'

'Well, what are we waiting for? Let's go,' Jay says and moves straight towards the door.

Marisa scoots in front of the door, resting her hands on her hips. 'Jay, you can't go out there,' she says. 'Not with everyone looking for you.'

'It's all the way up on Roosevelt. No one from the Blades will dare step foot in Kings territory,' Yoyo says, putting his hand on her shoulder and trying to move her aside.

'Well, what's Teo doing up there then?' Marisa shoots back, shrugging off his hand. I can't see even Yoyo managing to get past a stance that firm.

'He's hiding,' Yoyo answers. 'Look,' he says, 'I'll go with Jay. You two girls stay here.'

My eyes fly to Jay. I'm not staying here without him.

'We'll be fine,' Yoyo continues. 'Anyway, I see he's packing these days.' He nods at the gun sticking out of Jay's waistband. 'Where'd you get that thing?' he asks.

'Stole it from a cop,' Jay answers, leaving out the *dead* part.

Yoyo's eyebrows rise up comically in his head, almost meeting his hairline and then he shakes his head. 'You're right. I don't want to know the half of it.' He grimaces at Marisa. 'You going to move out the way?'

'Nope,' she answers, tilting one hip and pursing her lips. 'Why doesn't Yo go on his own and find Teo and bring him back here?' she asks Jay.

'He's not going to come if Yoyo asks him,' Jay fires back. 'I know him. I've got to speak to him face to face. After tomorrow, I'm not going to have another chance.'

Marisa's face crumples at that. Yoyo looks between them both confused.

'OK,' Marisa says, moving aside.

Jay moves to unbolt the door.

'I'm coming too.' The words are out of my mouth before I can stop them.

Jay looks at me. He opens his mouth but then shuts it and nods.

'You sure?' Yoyo asks him, his brow darkening.

'Yeah,' Jay says, without taking his eyes from mine. 'She's coming with me.' A buzz sweeps through me at his tone – there's no debate on this one. He feels it too then – that unspoken agreement between us – where one of us goes, so does the other. And maybe there's something more too in his tone, in his expression. After what just happened in the kitchen, I can't tell. I'm not sure

196

I trust my own feelings or intuition any more. I'm not sure that I want to either.

'Well then,' Marisa says, looking annoyed, 'I'm coming as well.' She narrows her eyes at Yoyo, 'And don't you even think about trying to stop me.'

Yoyo and Jay exchange a look and then Yoyo shrugs at her. 'Woman, you want to zip my balls in your purse too?'

'They're there already, aren't they?' Jay asks, before dancing out the way of one of Yoyo's fists.

'Give me five minutes,' Marisa says, 'I just have to get ready.'

'Oh man,' Yoyo says, tipping his head back to the ceiling, 'Mami, we're going to find Teo, what you need to get dressed and put on make-up for?'

'I'll be five minutes,' Marisa says, ignoring him and closing herself in her room.

Yoyo rolls his eyes heavenward. It's clear he's been here many times before. Jay's eyeing the door anxiously. I head to the go-bag and root through it, wondering what I should take with me. I pocket the credit card and some more cash, but leave everything else. Is it safe to take the gun? But the thought of detaching myself from it is not an option, so I just make sure it's well hidden beneath the sweater wrapped around my waist.

I stash the bag underneath a sofa cushion and when I turn back I find Jay watching me. 'You sure you want to come?' he asks. He's giving me an out, just like the one I gave him, but I hear the slight waver in his voice.

Yoyo looks once between us and then makes a beeline for the kitchen, clearly thinking we need some space to talk.

'I'm not staying here by myself,' I tell Jay, when he's gone. 'I need to get out. Sitting around here's . . .' I break off. What

197

I want to say is that if I stay here, locked in this apartment, then there's nothing to distract me from the contents of my head. And I'm not ready to deal with that. I can't. So I need to keep moving. And, I think to myself, as I register Jay's relief, I need to be near him too.

'Yeah,' Jay says, nodding, 'I hear you.'

Suddenly Marisa appears in her bedroom doorway. She's wearing a blue dress that's cut so low over her boobs that from the kitchen I hear Yoyo start choking on the leftover chicken stir fry. Marisa ignores him and arches an eyebrow at me. 'Get over here,' she orders.

I don't move.

'Listen, I'm not going out with you looking like that,' she says, her nostrils flaring. She has a look of distaste on her face that's normally reserved for when meat's gone bad. 'You want people to stare at you, then at least have them stare for the right reasons.'

'Marisa,' Jay says, 'give her a break. She looks fine.'

'Did you see what she's wearing?' Marisa asks. 'We're going to a club.'

'On Roosevelt,' Jay points out, rolling his eyes at her. 'I don't think there's a dress code.'

'She'll stand out like a habanero chilli in an ice-cream store if she goes dressed like that,' Marissa snaps back. Then, resting one hand on her hip in a posture I'm beginning to understand is the equivalent of a judge slamming a gavel, she says, 'Look at it this way. Everyone will be so busy looking at us girls, nobody will notice you.'

Jay considers that and then looks at me grinning, 'You know, she does have a point.'

I doubt that very much, considering that Jay could probably wear a paper bag over his head and still turn most heads in a six-block radius. But I acknowledge that Marissa does have a point. Standing out isn't a good idea.

29

Marisa has her head buried in her wardrobe. I stand in the doorway, glancing nervously around and over my shoulder at Jay, who
gives me an apologetic shrug. I can tell he's thinking rather me
than him.

Marisa straightens up and tosses something towards me before
marching to the door and slamming it in Jay's face. I shake out the
thing she threw at me and discover it's a little black dress.

'That should fit,' she says, scrunching up her nose as she sizes
me up. 'Even though you're what I would call *sardina*.'

'A sardine?' I ask, put out.

'Skinny,' she answers, not bothering to hide her distaste for my
lack of fat cells.

'I'm not skinny,' I answer, annoyed. I'm lean.

'Just put it on,' she says, already moving to her dressing table
and starting to sort through a pile of make-up.

I turn my back, pull the gun from my waistband and place it
on the bed, and then start easing off my shorts and tank top.

'Ahh,' Marisa hisses. 'What did you do?'

I realise she's staring at the bruise on my shoulder.

'I fell,' I tell her, reaching quickly for the dress as I feel her eyes
raking the rest of my body. I tug the dress down over my hips and
twist to face her. I catch her wincing and hope it's not the sight of
what I look like in her dress.

'I'm sorry,' she says, surprising me. 'Jay told me what you went through.' She shakes her head. 'It's awful,' she whispers. 'I can't even imagine.'

'Yeah,' I say, dropping my eyes to my feet. Awful doesn't quite cover it and I wouldn't want her to imagine any of it.

'What size are you?' she asks me suddenly, forcing a smile, maybe sensing I don't want to talk about it. 'I can lend you some heels.'

'I can't walk in heels,' I tell her. Let alone run in them.

'Well, what about sandals then? I've got these.' She rummages in the bottom of her wardrobe and comes up with a pair of tan leather sandals. 'Will these fit?'

I take them and hold them against my soles. 'Yeah,' I say, sitting to put them on. Really I feel stupid, and more than a little guilty, dressing up to go out to a club. It seems wrong. But it's not like we're going out to have fun. We're going to find Jay's brother. Marisa comes over and starts brushing my hair and pinning it up without even asking me if I mind. I don't have the energy to argue so I just let her.

'Listen,' she says to me, her fingers busy pulling and yanking at my hair, 'I didn't mean to be rude earlier. It's just – I'm worried about Jay. He's always helping people out and it only ever seems to get him into trouble.'

I don't know what to say to that, so I don't say anything.

'He's a good guy, you know. He doesn't deserve to take the rap for Teo.'

'I'm going to get him as much help as I can,' I tell her. 'I promise. My father knows people. We can argue his case. I don't want to see him go to prison any more than you do.'

Marisa's hands stop whatever they're doing to my hair. I glance up and see myself reflected in the mirror opposite. Marisa nods at

201

me. 'There,' she says, smiling weakly. 'All done. Let me just . . .' she grabs hold of my chin and sweeps a brush over my cheekbones before dapping something on my lips and swiping some concealer over the cut on my cheek. Then she stands back to appraise her handiwork. 'Yeah, you'll do,' she says.

I stand up and take a quick look in the mirror. I don't look like me. The dress is not something I would ever wear. It's short, showing off my grazed knees, and though it covers the top of my arms it reveals a length of collarbone and a shadow of cleavage. She's done something to my hair, sweeping it up off my neck and pinning it in a loose fifties-style chignon. The make-up is barely there but the spots of colour on my cheeks and lips do more to make me look alert and alive than my previous attempts in the bathroom managed to.

I contemplate the gun lying on the bed. The dress has no pockets.

'Do you have a purse I could borrow?' I ask Marisa.

Marisa flips through several hanging off the back of the door and hands me a black leather one with a gold chain for a strap. It's way more bling than I'd normally go for, but I can sling it over one shoulder. I take it and shove my money and the credit card into it. Marisa makes a disapproving grunting sound when I pick up the gun and slide that in too, but I choose to ignore it. She's not the one who has people chasing after her, trying to kill her.

Yoyo pounds on the door. 'Y'all coming or not?' he asks.

Marisa rolls her eyes as she pulls on her shoes. '*Si*, we're coming,' she yells back, opening the door.

I catch Jay's expression as I walk out into the living room, the quick once-over he gives me, and the way his eyebrows shoot up in surprise and then darken with a look I can't read – irritation, anger, or something else maybe? I look away and catch Yoyo winking at Jay.

It's only then that I notice the tension, a thin, prickly layer, which has settled over the room. It's almost palpable, and I take a guess that Jay has told Yoyo about the situation he's in and how he's going to hand himself in to the police tomorrow. As I glance at Jay again, who's looking tense and wired, I realise that this is his last night of freedom for what could be a very long time. Is that what he's thinking too? Or, like me, is he just focussed on getting through every second as it occurs and not dwelling too much on what comes after?

'We ready then?' Yoyo asks.

Jay's already by the door.

I walk over and join him.

30

We take Yoyo's beat-up old Ford. Jay climbs in the back with me, not even trying to call shotgun, and I breathe a sigh of relief. His hand rests a few inches away from mine and I'm intensely aware of his thigh stretched across the seat, his knee almost touching mine. Is he as aware of me as I am of him? Of every movement and every breath?

I glance sideways at him. He's busy staring out the window, glowering. Does he feel the same way that I feel when I'm around him? He can't. Because, right now, all I want to do is cling to him, crawl under his skin and lay myself bare, both literally and figuratively. And the thought that I might do so – might act on any of these feelings – utterly terrifies me. As if I didn't have enough fear to deal with right now.

The rational part of my brain, the part that seems to be shrinking by the minute, wonders if I'm just trying to find a way of avoiding dealing with the images in my head. Is focussing on Jay simply a way of blocking out the screams of dying men and the sound of bullets pinging off metal? Is that what it's about? Psychologists would probably call it transference. It's what happens to kidnap victims when they fall in love with their kidnapper. I guess the same rules could apply to shooting victims and their co-escapee.

I turn to stare out the window. It's all too much to process. I try to focus on what's around me instead of what's inside me. That seems easier to do. It's dark out and I glance at the clock on the dash. It's almost ten. The streets are still busy, crowded with food carts and vans, people buying fake handbags from makeshift stalls, and bars and restaurants luring customers with their bright neon signs.

Jay's foot jitters as Yoyo drives carefully, keeping well under the speed limit. He slides down in the seat at one point, keeping his head low, and his knee touches mine and stays there – a point of contact which I fixate on, no longer able to focus on anything outside the car, because it's as if I can suddenly feel Jay's pulse alive inside of me, beating time with my own erratic heart.

'So, Liva,' Yoyo says from up front. 'You from round here?'

Marisa whacks him across the handbrake. 'Does she look like she's from round here?' she hisses. 'Does she *sound* like she's from round here?'

'No,' I say over the top of her. 'I'm not from round here. I grew up overseas. I just moved to New York.'

'Oh yeah? Where were you living before?'

'Oman,' I say.

'Where's that?' Yoyo asks.

'It's in the Middle East, bro,' Jay says, smirking.

'The Middle East?' Yoyo asks, frowning as he glances back at me over his shoulder. I guess he's wondering where my burqa is or something like that. It's what some people immediately assume or joke about when I tell them where I grew up. 'You like it there?'

'Yeah,' I say. Briefly, I try to picture my house and my friends, but they seem so far away, like characters from a book I once read. I wonder if I'll ever see the place again.

'So, why'd you leave?'

I ponder my answer.

'Boyfriend troubles?' Yoyo asks, in an obvious attempt to pry into my romantic status. No doubt on Jay's behalf.

I realise that I don't want Jay thinking that I have a boyfriend, so I answer quickly. Too quickly – without thinking. 'No. I got expelled.'

Jay's jaw drops. He shifts in his seat so he can to look at me face on. '*You* got expelled?'

'Yeah, why's that so hard to believe?' I say, kind of insulted.

He shakes his head at me in wonder. 'You're just full of surprises, Moneypenny.'

That buzz hits me in the solar plexus again. I'm even starting to not mind the Moneypenny name-calling.

'What did you do? Skip cheerleading practice one too many times?' This from Marisa.

'I don't cheerlead. And no.'

'Drugs?' Yoyo asks.

'No. I don't do drugs either.'

'Drink?'

'No.'

'You found a really straight one here, Jay,' Yoyo laughs.

'Oh, I wouldn't say that,' Jay answers, smiling at me knowingly across the gloom of the back seat.

'So what was it for then?' Marisa asks, turning around. Even her interest has been piqued.

'I was somewhere I shouldn't have been,' I say, glancing sideways at Jay, who's still watching me hawk-eyed.

'Like where?' Yoyo asks. 'Wait! With who? Were you having an affair with a teacher?'

206

'No. God!' I say.

'Let me guess,' says Jay, grinning at me. 'You climbed on to the roof of your school?'

'No,' I say, leaving a long pause before I say, 'the clock tower.'

'With a gun?' Yoyo asks. ''Cause you know, I can see why they might have expelled you for that.'

'No, not with a gun.'

'Then what were you doing up there?'

'I just wanted to see what the view was like,' I say, leaving out the part about the rush I got from climbing out on to that ledge – the real reason I was up there. I can't explain to him the sense of victory I had standing on the lip of the roof, my arms and legs burning with the effort it had taken to climb, looking down at the tiny square of grass beneath. Or the way my blood ran like quicksilver through my veins, as fast as it's doing now, with Jay's knee pressed to mine. I steal a quick look at Jay and see that he gets it. He knows exactly why I climbed on to that roof, what it was that I was searching for – and maybe he also gets what it felt like too.

'How high was it?' Yoyo asks.

'Four storeys,' I say.

'Shit. But why'd they expel you for that?'

'Rules are rules. And they thought that—' I stop abruptly.

'What?' he presses.

I take a deep breath. 'They thought that I was going to jump,' I say. The idea still smarts. That's what all my friends in Oman think too – that I was suicidal. I wonder if that's why none of them have bothered to email me or post a message on my Facebook wall since I left. If I *was* suicidal I'd probably be pretty pissed at their lack of giving a damn.

'*Were* you trying to top yourself?' Yoyo asks.

I stiffen at his bluntness, then realise he's the first person other than my parents to actually bother asking. 'No,' I say. *You'd have to actually feel something to be suicidal*, I add silently. And I'd made a good job of learning how to switch off my emotions.

'So what were you doing up there then?'

'Hey, don't you need to take the next right?' Jay cuts in, leaning between the two front seats. I stare at his shoulder blades, his arms hanging loosely over the back of the headrests. He's deliberately cutting off the conversation, trying to protect me. My heart aches at the gesture and my instinct is to lean forwards and press my cheek against his shoulder.

But then that annoying rational part of my brain butts in. Clearly it's done with shrinking and is putting up a fight. I don't want anyone to protect me. Do I? *Look what happened last time*, it says. And it's true. I need to listen to that voice. The last time I let someone else protect me, step in front of me and shield me, they died. And the thought of anything happening to Jay because of me makes my blood run cold.

I can't go through what I went through with Felix again. I just can't. I'm already feeling too much and it's complicating things – interfering with my judgement.

There's only one option that will keep Jay safe – and I should have done it long ago. I was just being too much of a coward. I didn't want to do this alone – but I realise now that I have to.

For the final minutes of the car ride I shift so my knee is no longer touching Jay's and I concentrate on the air freshener shaped like a lemon dangling from the ceiling of the car, focussing my attention on it until my heartbeat returns to normal. Then I make a decision; I will wait until Jay's found Teo, when we're back at Marisa's, and then I'll leave. I'll finish this thing by myself.

And, I make one last decision, though it's more of a promise to myself – that I'll keep my word to Jay and to Marisa. I'll make sure that my father gets him the best lawyer. I'll tell them this whole story. I'll tell them all about Jay, and all the ways he's saved my life.

31

As soon as I step foot inside the club I am grateful that Marisa insisted on making me dress up. If I'd turned up in my jean shorts and tank top combo I doubt the doorman would have let me in. Having said that, he may not have noticed. He certainly didn't bother carding us or checking our bags . . . he was too busy staring mesmerised as a king cobra at Marisa's cleavage. Yoyo is still grumbling about it as we wind our way through the packed dance floor towards the bar.

Most the guys in the club are all wearing what I presume is wannabe gangsta fashion – low-rise baggy jeans, Nikes, snapback caps, T-shirts stamped with logos – or maybe it's not even wannabe gangsta fashion. What do I know? I spent my teenage years in Oman, surrounded by wealthy private-school kids whose wardrobes bowed under the weight of all the polo player and crocodile logos. A quick glimpse of the girls pushing against the bar and gyrating on the dance floor reveals hair extensions are big news, as are skyscraper heels and dresses that cling like sandwich wrap to every curve.

Jay is anxiously scanning over the top of the crowd, as is Marisa. Yoyo is on his phone, plugging his other ear with his finger as he tries to talk to whoever is on the other end. The music is brain-damagingly loud, but the beat's good. I glance around. I don't know what Teo looks like so I'm not much help.

Yoyo hangs up. 'He was here half an hour ago. Mike's not seen him since.'

'*Mierda*,' Jay mutters, scowling.

'There are a few girls over there I recognise, let me go ask them if they've seen him,' Marisa says, pointing to a small table on the other side of the bar, around which are six or seven girls who look like they've spent the day having their hair teased by Marisa's boss Gloria. Before Yoyo or Jay can say anything she's off, barging through the crowd at the bar to reach them.

'I'm going to go ask around. See if anyone has seen him,' Jay says. Then he turns to me, scowling. 'Stay here with Yo. Don't go anywhere OK?'

I just nod even though I don't need or want Yoyo to protect me. I think of the gun in my bag. Not that I'd ever think about pulling it out in a crowded club. But still it makes me feel better knowing it's there.

Jay disappears into the crowd and my stomach knots with anxiety. I don't like not being able to see him.

'So,' Yoyo says, rocking on the balls of his feet, 'you want a drink or something?'

'No, thanks. I'm good,' I tell him, standing on my tiptoes to try to see where Jay went.

'Wanna dance?' Yoyo asks.

My head spins back to him. 'What here? Now? To this music?' I ask him. Is he crazy?

He shrugs his big shoulders at me. 'Yeah, why not? Jay told me you're a dancer.'

'He did?' I ask, surprised.

He grins at me, 'Yeah.' I wonder from the smile what else Jay

211

told Yoyo. 'What's the matter, scared I'll show you up on the dance floor?' he asks, putting on a pretend pout.

I cut him a look. Is he seriously offering me a line straight out of *Step Up 2: The Streets*?

I take a leaf out of the Marisa handbook on putting men in their place. I put my hand on my hip and I offer him a sardonic eyebrow raise.

It doesn't work. Yoyo takes a step back on to the dance floor then wriggles his backside provocatively, and I actually laugh. Because the guy is huge. He's the human equivalent of a super-tanker. His biceps are the width of my torso. The dance floor clears around him, like a shoal of fish sighting the shadow of a trawler looming above. But then he actually starts moving and my jaw does a cartoon drop to the floor. Holy shit. Yoyo can actually dance. The space around him opens up, not because people are rushing to give the big guy room and to avoid being trampled, but because people are staring at him. He has every hip-hop move known to man down pat, and then some. Then he throws in some body-popping until I'm having to clutch my sides, I'm laughing so hard.

When he finishes, he rolls back his shoulders, cracks his knuckles and swaggers towards me as the dance floor explodes, clapping and cheering around him. 'You were saying?' he asks, sweeping one hand across his sweat-drenched brow.

I am too speechless to answer. Things just took a turn for the even more surreal. It's like my life is being directed by David Lynch.

'Over to you,' Yoyo says, gesturing at the dance floor.

I shake my head quickly. No way. But Yoyo places his dinner-plate-sized hand on my back and shoves me forward.

'What you afraid of?' he whispers in my ear.

'Fine,' I say, tearing my bag off my shoulder and shoving it at him. 'Hold this.'

He grins at me, showing all his teeth, including one that's capped with gold. He's like a giant man-child, but he looks kind of comical standing there holding my handbag clutched in his arms, so I can't help but smile back. What was it that Jay said about me? That I had heart? I get what he meant now – because that's the first thing that springs to mind when I look at Yoyo. He has heart.

I turn my back on Yoyo and close my eyes, trying to listen to the music, to get a feel for the beat. This is as far from classical ballet music as you can get but I've taken contemporary dance too and a few hip-hop classes on the side.

When I dance it's one of the only times I'm not aware of what's going on around me and when I can turn off whatever chatter is inside my head. That's one of the reasons I'm so happy to spend three to four hours a day inside a ballet studio. I'm one hundred per cent in my body for that time. It's similar to being up on a roof looking down, I guess, the same kind of explosion of light and air charging my blood, the same kind of high, only more muted. It's a physical reaction, not a mental or emotional one.

As I move to the music, I'm only slightly aware that people have moved back. I glimpse Yoyo's face for a brief moment and see that his eyes are bulging in surprise. When I stop, sweat pouring down my back and panting for breath, he's the one clapping the loudest.

'Damn straight, he wasn't lying. You can dance.'

I wipe a hand across my brow, slicking back some hair that's

213

come loose. God, that felt good, like I was burning some of the excess emotions. I feel calmer now, less panicked.

Yoyo suddenly glances over my head and scowls at something. 'Be right back,' he growls, ploughing straight through the crowd, still clutching my handbag. I try to see where he's going and catch sight of the back of Marisa's head. She's talking to three guys. I guess Yoyo has a possessive streak.

'Hey, nice dancing.'

I spin around. A guy with carefully crafted facial hair and a diamond stud in his ear is standing in front of me. He's sporting the baggy jean look and has full tattoo sleeves.

'Thanks,' I say, crossing my arms over my chest and looking around for an exit.

My crossed arms don't appear to be putting him off. He takes a step closer and I catch a waft of cigarette smoke and alcohol. 'Want a drink?' he asks.

A hand slides firmly around my waist and someone presses themselves close behind me. 'Actually,' I hear Jay say, 'we were just leaving.'

I draw in a breath at the feeling of his hand, which now lies possessively across my stomach, and without thinking I press back against him.

The guy scowls at Jay. 'He your boyfriend?' he asks me.

'Er, no,' I admit.

'Well then,' the guy says to Jay, 'what's your problem?'

'There's no problem,' I say loudly, feeling Jay's body tensing against me. I turn around and take hold of Jay's hand. 'Let's go,' I tell him.

Jay stands there glaring at the guy until I drag him away towards the bar.

'Did you find Teo?' I shout over the music when we're clear.

His attention comes back to me. He shakes his head. 'No.' He casts a glance around. 'Where's Yoyo? I asked him to take care of you.'

'I can take care of myself,' I tell him, annoyed. 'He went to find Marisa. He's over there,' I say, pointing. It's hard to miss someone the size of Yoyo.

Jay seems to relax. 'Nice moves, by the way,' he says, smiling a smile that tugs at my heart and makes my earlier decision to leave him once we get back to Marisa's seem both absurd and impossible.

'Yo, *cabron*.'

Both of us jerk around. The guy with the diamond stud is standing behind Jay and this time he has company. Two other guys flank him on either side, like pet Rottweilers.

Jay immediately blocks me with his body and I see his hands crunching into fists at his sides. Shit, I think, what is it with us and trouble? I move around him and position myself at his side.

'What's your problem?' Jay asks them calmly.

'We heard you been dissin our bro,' the guy on the right says.

Jay laughs under his breath and I cut a look at him. Laughing doesn't seem like a wise plan, given there are three of them and two of us, and Yoyo has handily disappeared with the bag containing the gun.

'I wasn't *dissin* anybody,' Jay says almost wearily, his arm coming up to press me back behind him again. It's then I remember the gun stuck down the back of his jeans. My eyes slide towards it. Should I make a grab for it? But how stupid would that be? To wave a gun around in a crowded club? If I do that we'll end up arrested, which is not how we need the night to end.

215

'*Te voy a matar!*' the main guy says, cricking his neck to one side and cracking his knuckles.

I don't speak Spanish but even I can understand the gist of his words, and I grip Jay's arm and squeeze hard, but Jay ignores me. He takes a step forwards so he's almost banging chests with the guy.

'Listen,' he says softly. 'Me and my girl here,' he jerks his head in my direction, 'we've had a really shit day. Truly *mierda*. Like you would not believe.' He starts ticking off on his fingers. 'We've been shot at, we've been chased, we've had to climb out the window of a twentieth-storey apartment and free-climb our way up on to the goddamn roof. We have two guys dressed like cops trying to kill us,' he smiles and leans in closer, dropping his voice to a conspiratorial whisper, 'and let me tell you something, these guys, they make you three look like total pussies.'

I squeeze Jay's arm harder. *What is he doing?* Is he out of his freaking mind? They do not look like pussies. But he doesn't stop. No he's just hitting his stride. He keeps going, ticking off even more things on his fingers.

'My mom's being held somewhere by the FBI for reasons neither of us can figure out. I can't find my brother –' he draws a deep breath '– and on top of all this I had to pay a really crazy amount of money for two sticks of frozen water, though admittedly it wasn't my money.' He exhales in a rush. 'So we could really do without you and your fellow *amigos* giving us more shit, *me entiendes?*'

The guy with the diamond stud stares at Jay like he's speaking in tongues, a purple worm of a vein pulsing violently in his neck. I glance nervously at the other two guys. I'm not sure Jay's little speech did us any favours. I'm not sure they even understood it. I think he lost them at the ice-pops.

The guy on the left, who has a shaved head and is missing part of an ear, crunches his knuckles together loudly, and the one on the right, who is wearing a thick gold chain and a black bandana over his head, reaches into his back pocket. I glance around for Yoyo, but I can't see him or Marisa anywhere. Where's a guy built like a refrigerator or an Israeli killer robot bodyguard when you need one? Jay and I are plain out of luck today.

'Listen,' I say, before anyone can make a move or Jay can say another word.

All three of them turn to me in surprise. I'm guessing because girls probably never speak back to them. The one on the right's hand freezes halfway to pulling out whatever it is he has in his back pocket.

'I'm giving you two choices,' I say, shouting to be heard over the hardcore rap that's started playing. 'You can back the hell off right now or—'

'Or what?' sneers the guy with his hand behind his back, looking amused.

I shrug. 'Or you can regret it,' I say with a smile.

The one with the stud stares at me as though I just made fun of his facial hair. And then he bursts out laughing.

'I wouldn't laugh, man,' Jay warns him, shaking his head solemnly. 'I've seen her in action. She could take Rambo.'

The guy stops laughing and stares at me in confusion, unsure if Jay is jerking him around. Then, clearly deciding that Jay is still spouting crap, his top lip curls upwards in a sneer. He makes some sign to his buddies and the one on the right flicks a knife open right in front of us. I move in the same heartbeat, shoving

217

Jay with my left shoulder while simultaneously grabbing the diamond-stud guy by his collar and pulling him in front of the guy with the blade. In almost the same movement I bring my knee up and slam it straight into his crotch. The high-pitched scream that explodes out of him is drowned out by the sound of a glass smashing and the screams of people on the dance floor who've caught sight of the knife and are now pushing and shoving towards the exits.

As the guy with the stud doubles over, clutching his crotch, his eyes bulging like they're about to pop, I look up and see the other two glance at each other briefly and then spring at us, snarling.

32

We run, Jay clearing a path with his free arm and shouting at people to get out the way. We slam through a fire escape by the toilets, ricochet off the brick wall in front of us and then hurdle a couple of stunned people sitting on the ground outside having a smoke. Behind us I can hear yelling and doors bashing against concrete. We hit the street, the noise of the club blazing around us. The security guy on the door frowns at us as we go steaming past him and I feel the familiar spurt of adrenaline pushing me on, pounding through my veins, making my legs feel like they're made of air. Jay's hand is tight around my wrist and he yanks me hard around a corner and down another alleyway.

He pushes me behind an enormous dumpster that offers us some cover from the street and crushes his chest against mine as he presses us both back further into the shadow. His forearms come up on either side of my head, as though he's bracing us for a crash, and he ducks his own head so I can feel his breath hot and fast against my cheek. My heart is hammering hard and sweat trickles down my back. I strain to listen. Are they following?

Just then we hear footsteps pounding the sidewalk. They come to a halt right by the entrance to the alleyway and Jay presses further against me, the buttons of his jeans cutting into my waist, my forehead against his collarbone. Neither of us breathes. My hand slides down Jay's back and closes around the butt of the gun. He hadn't thought to draw it. I ease it out as he tenses and pulls back enough that I can see the whites of his eyes. He gives a tiny shake of his head and puts a finger to his lips.

I stare up at him and we wait, listening, me with the gun still in my hand, my finger sliding the safety free, Jay still pressing me tight up against the wall. The voices start arguing about which direction we've gone in. Someone takes a few steps into the alleyway but stops just an inch or so shy of seeing us. I hear the sound of a zipper and then the sprinkle of urine spraying against metal. I wrinkle my nose and press my face into Jay's T-shirt.

If he takes one more step he'll see us. I picture what I'll need to do. If I can push Jay aside I can aim the gun and we can hopefully hold them off until we're far enough away to make a run for it.

We listen in absolute silence as the guy re-zips himself and heads back out towards the street. The three of them talk some more – though I can't make out what they're saying – and then finally, after what feels like an eternity, they walk away. Jay's shoulders drop fractionally, but he doesn't take a step back. No, he keeps me pressed up against the wall. And I notice that we're both breathing fast again – as though we're still sprinting. I tip my head back against the brick behind me so I can see his face. He's looking down at me, and in the shadow all I can make out is the strong line of his jaw, the soft curve of his lips. I can't read his expression. But I can guess at it.

He shifts his weight slightly and his thigh presses against my hip. I draw in a breath. My free hand – the one not holding the gun – rests on his upper chest. I slide it up and over his shoulder and with my eyes still on him I pull him even closer, until he's pressed completely against me and I can feel the hardness of muscle through his T-shirt and his jeans. My heart explodes in my chest as I tilt my head back further, reaching on tiptoe, and his mouth finds mine in the darkness.

His kiss is hard, full of heat, uncontrolled.

The earth doesn't just spin, it shatters into a million pieces. Lights burst lightning bright behind my eyes as Jay's hands run the length of me, and I have to grip hold of his shoulder to keep from sliding down the wall.

His hand settles behind my waist, pinning me to him, and the other holds the back of my head. And I don't fight it because I want him to hold me tighter, to kiss me deeper. I want to melt into him and I'm grasping at him even more frantically than he is at me. It's as though all the pent-up energy and frustration and emotion of the day is spilling out of one and into the other, and the desperation in our kisses becomes a wild hunger for more, for touch, for connection, for closeness stripped bare.

I start tearing at Jay's T-shirt, wanting to finally feel his skin, needing to touch every part of him, and then I am, my fingers tracing the taut lines of muscle running up his stomach and chest. He murmurs something against my neck as his lips trace the curve of my shoulder and then run back up again to meet my mouth and his hands drop at the same time to my waist.

God, I want him. I've never wanted anyone in this way before. 'Jay!'

My breathing is so loud that at first I don't hear Marisa, and it's only when Jay stops kissing me that my senses tune back into the outside world and I hear her shouting.

My knees are shaking. My heart feels fragile, like it's no longer inside my ribcage, but hurtling through space. I grip hold of Jay by the shoulders and lower my leg, which somehow has wrapped itself around Jay's hip. Jay takes a deep breath, lowering his chin to his chest to breathe out slowly, even as his hands fall away from my waist and he steps away from me. I nearly collapse without his arms holding me up.

He runs a hand through his hair and waits as I steady myself, reaching out and pulling the sleeve of my dress up where it's slipped. The touch of his fingers on my bare shoulder is enough to make me jump, fire licking ribbons across my skin. He feels it. I know he feels it because his hand hovers just an inch above me as though feeding on the flames. I feel the temptation he has to take one step closer, enfold me in his arms again and just keep kissing me, ignoring Marisa altogether. I will him to with every fibre of my being.

'Jay!'

He clenches his jaw and takes another step back, 'Here!' he yells, his voice hoarse, his gaze not straying from my face.

Marisa and Yoyo appear in the next second, bursting breathless around the trash container.

'What the hell you doing back here?' Marisa asks.

'What happened?' Yoyo asks simultaneously and stops short the second he sees us. Jay's still trying to block me from view. Do I look that disarrayed? I guess so, judging from the expressions on Yoyo and Marisa's faces. Marisa tilts her head at Jay and purses her lips with a glare that could stop a man at fifty paces and make him collapse to his knees confessing to any crime. Yoyo just grins and pulls Marisa back out of the alley, winking at Jay as he goes. *I totally saw that*, I feel like yelling at him, but I'm too embarrassed.

Jay clears his throat and gestures for me to go ahead of him. I do, tugging at my dress and trying to tidy my hair, tripping on my giddy legs over a pile of trash at the entrance. My lips are throbbing so hard I feel like it must be obvious to other people.

'I think he's lying in an alleyway bleeding out, but no, he's just *making* out,' Marisa is ranting when we stumble back on the street. 'What are you? Fifteen?' she asks, rounding on Jay.

'What is it with you and trouble?' Yoyo asks us, shaking his head.

'I told you it was a stupid idea,' Marisa adds. 'You should have sent me. How do you manage to get on the wrong side of so many people, Jay? You're a trouble beacon. We stand here any longer we'll probably have Al Qaeda try to bomb us.'

'Did you find out where Teo is?' Jay interrupts, obviously not wanting to argue.

'No sign of him anywhere,' Yoyo answers.

'And I'm done with looking,' Marisa says angrily. 'It's late.' She rummages in her bag. 'Here,' she says, thrusting something at Jay, 'take my keys. You can stay at mine. Liva can have my bed. Jay, you can sleep on the couch. I'm staying at Yoyo's.'

Jay takes the keys as Yoyo hands me my handbag, still grinning. He slaps Jay on the shoulder, winking so obviously that again I want to yell at him *I'm right here*. I turn away and pretend not to notice, though my stomach is doing a prize-winning gymnastic routine at the thought of being alone with Jay.

'Thanks, Risa,' Jay says.

'Yeah,' she sighs. 'Thank me in the morning.' She glowers at him. 'You're not going anywhere, right? Not until we get there, at least. Promise me.'

'Yeah, OK. I promise.'

But his jaw tenses and a muscle tweaks at the edge of his eye, and I wonder if Marisa knows she's just been lied to.

33

We take a cab back to Marisa's and Jay hops in the front beside the driver, leaving me alone in the back, where confusion wraps itself around me like tentacles. My nerve endings are frayed electric cords, my lips still throb, and my skin feels raw.

I keep casting glances in Jay's direction, wondering what he's thinking, whether he regrets what just happened. But he's staring straight ahead and I can't see his face. I try to get a handle on my own feelings. What do I want exactly? I ask myself.

I want him.

I want him completely. I want his touch and his breath on my skin and his hands running over my body like they want to own me. Just imagining him touching me makes my whole body shiver and burn like I have a fever. It's better than any high I could get from climbing on to a roof. Way better than an entire factory of Ben & Jerry's ice-cream.

Rationally, I know this is a physiological response to almost dying, to the litres of adrenaline still running through my body and the dormant effects of shock. But I don't care. I have never, in all my life, felt this way, and I can't just switch it off. Even if I knew how, I'm not sure I'd want to. Because it makes all the other things I'm feeling – the guilt, despair, and the anger – all fade into the background. And OK, that might just be temporary, but I feel like they might be worth facing if I can also have this – this feeling of being totally, one hundred per cent alive, and ferociously strong, and desperately needed.

I slept with Sebastian in the hope that it would make me feel something, but I felt nothing – not before, during or afterwards – except maybe a slight feeling of disappointment and boredom. I never wanted to repeat the experience. Which is why he dumped me and called me frigid (on Facebook no less). And I thought that he must be right, because I couldn't imagine ever wanting to do it again with him or anybody. But all that's changed in an instant.

I've only kissed Jay, but I feel like I have a narcotic running through my veins. Jay's given me a glimpse of what it's like to feel again. And now I'm an addict wanting another fix. Everything is brighter, more vivid, more real. My heart beats stronger. My blood moves faster, rushing in my veins like a flash flood. My senses are better tuned. Not even in my wildest imaginings could I have imagined desire to feel anything like this.

After this night I won't see him again, I remind myself angrily. But I don't want to think about that. I want to stay in this moment, in this night that's entirely divorced from reality.

When we pull up to Marisa's, I open my door before Jay can, and without a word he leads the way into the apartment, double bolting the door behind us and then heading to the kitchen for a drink. I wade through the atmosphere which is thick as an oil slick – as though neither of us wants to move too fast or say a single word, for fear of creating a spark that might ignite it. Jay won't even look my way.

I duck into the bathroom so I can get my head together. A shower doesn't help. I have to stand in front of the mirror, a towel wrapped around myself, and take several deep breaths before I can head back into the living room.

Jay is lying on the sofa, his legs hanging over the arm. His eyes are shut and he looks like he's sleeping. But his lips are pursed and his jaw tense. He's faking sleep. Numbness starts to creep up my limbs.

'I'm done in the bathroom,' I say.

One eye opens but he barely looks in my direction. 'Cool,' he murmurs.

I hover by the sofa, unsure of what to say or do. Something has obviously shifted between us. The connection has been severed. Even the atmosphere has changed – it's not charged any more. It's become a vacuum instead. Nothing exists in it.

Dignity scraps with all my other emotions, eventually winning out and forcing me to walk to the bedroom with my head held high, not that he's even looking. He's closed his eyes again. Damn him. What's changed? What is he thinking?

Standing in the doorway to Marisa's room, I glance back a final time over my shoulder. He's still lying there feigning sleep. Is this it? Is this the last time I'll ever see him or speak to him? I realise it is. I'm leaving here before dawn. I'd planned on sneaking right by him. It's only then that I remember the small matter of the go-bag, which is right at this moment conveniently located right behind Jay's head.

I walk to the sofa, clutching my towel, as well as my dignity.

Jay opens one eye and looks up at me standing over him. Before he can stop himself his gaze slides down my body and I feel as if he's just stripped me bare.

'I need the go-bag,' I tell him, blood starting to pound in my temples.

Jay looks at me blankly.

'It's behind your head.'

He sits up, swinging his legs over the side of the sofa, and digs it out from under the cushion. When he hands it to me our fingers brush.

My pulse quickens. His hand suddenly circles my wrist. His breathing is shallow, his gaze pinned to my waist, which is level with his eyes. He makes no other move and we just stay like that. My skin sparks from just that small bit of contact. I lift my other hand slowly and place it gently against Jay's cheek – feeling the softness and warmth of his skin. Jay's grip on my wrist tightens and I feel the tension in him, the fight he's having with himself even as the heat between us builds and builds. But then he's on his feet, pushing past me. He strides to the far side of the room and stands with his back to me by the window.

'You better go to bed,' he says.

I pause, taking that in. 'No.'

He spins around, angry. 'Liva,' he says, 'don't you get it?'

'Get what?' I ask, feeling anger spurting hot inside my veins.

'All I want to do is rip that towel off you and—' he breaks off abruptly and stares at me, his eyes blazing, his breathing fast, and he doesn't need to finish the sentence for me to understand, in exquisite, intimate detail, exactly what it is he wants to do.

'Do it,' I say.

Jay blinks at me. Then he gathers himself and shakes his head, angrily. 'No,' he says. 'I'm not going to take advantage of you. I'm not going to treat you like a cheap one-night stand, which is all it would be. Just *one* night.' He glares at me as though he's won the debate based on this point alone. 'Is that what you want?'

I keep my chin up, my back straight and I take a step towards him. 'No. But if it can only be one night then that's what I'll take.

And besides, who says you're the one taking advantage of *me*? Who says I'm not the one taking advantage of you?'

Jay stares at me, stunned, and I see him struggle between what he feels is right and what he wants. He wants *me*. And the knowledge elates me, gives me another hit of that dangerous narcotic high. I take another step, closing the distance between us. Water drips down my back from my wet hair, and I'm still clutching the towel as I look up at him, daring him, inviting him.

I watch him wrestle with whatever remnants of self-control he has left and perhaps it isn't fair, but I don't care – it's not a one-night stand if you know you'll hold that person in your heart for the rest of your life – I lean into him and, rising on tiptoe, I kiss him.

He resists for about two seconds but then his lips part and his arms come around my waist, drawing me against him and holding me fast, and the energy in the room ignites in a blaze. When I stand on the edge of a roof, stars shoot through my veins. But that has nothing on this. This is comets and meteors.

We're on the sofa before I'm even aware of having moved. Jay must have carried me. His hands push back my wet hair and he holds my face as he lays kisses across my eyelids and jaw and down my neck to my shoulder, where he pulls back, frowning in anger at my bruise. I shake my head at him – I don't want him to get distracted – and pull him back down to kiss me, pausing only to tear at his T-shirt, pulling it over his head so I can run my hands over his bare skin, feeling his skin contract in a shiver.

Our kisses are frantic, laced with urgency and a million things I can't even name, can't even catch hold of before another sensation takes over. It's like an overwhelming, all-consuming need to own the other person completely, to come undone at their hands.

And I realise that the thing that makes this different is not just about the circumstances we're in, the adrenaline we're both drenched with, it's trust. I trust Jay. Which is why I can let the barriers down. All of them.

'Are you sure?' Jay asks me, when I don't feel like my body can contain me any more and I'm going to burst out my skin.

'Yes,' I say, my eyes locked on his.

He releases the knot of my towel and slides it open, drawing in a breath. I watch the expression on his face, as it slides from wonder to something darker, altogether hungrier.

'You're beautiful,' he says, as his hand traces a path over my hip and down the length of my thigh.

I shiver and he pulls me closer against his chest and he kisses me, and the rush is so intense that it drowns every other feeling and every thought. I'm wrestling with the buttons on Jay's jeans when a knock on the door tears us apart. Jay leaps to his feet and I instantly pull the towel around myself. My heart is beating wildly and I stagger up on to my knees, reaching for my clothes, for the gun, but my fingers are clumsy as panic takes flight in my chest.

'Jay?' a guy yells.

Jay moves like lightning to the door and I have to shout at him to stop as he draws back the bolts. I'm naked, save the towel I have pressed to myself.

He waits for me to pull on the little black dress before he draws back the bolt and opens the door.

A guy who looks like Jay, only taller and skinnier with longer hair, bursts past him into the apartment. One look tells me what I already had guessed. It's Teo. He stops short when he sees me and turns back to Jay, a look of surprise on his face.

'Teo, where the hell you been, man? We were looking all over for you,' Jay asks.

'Where have *you* been?' Teo shouts back defensively. His eyes, which are bloodshot and ringed with dark circles, dart in my direction. 'And who's she?' he asks.

'This is Liva,' Jay says as he pulls on his T-shirt. He shoots me a look I can't quite read. Apologetic, regretful, sad? 'Liva, this is Teo.' Definitely not happy.

'Hey,' I say, equally unhappy.

'We gotta talk,' Teo says to Jay, turning his back on me. He's bouncing on the balls of his feet, agitated and on edge, and I wonder if he's high.

'Yeah, tell me about it,' mutters Jay. 'That's why I've been looking for you all night. I called and called. You weren't picking up.'

'Well, I'm here now,' Teo answers, his voice rising defensively. 'Someone told me you were trying to find me. I was lying low.' He pauses, flicking a look my way before dropping his voice. 'What happened last night?' he asks.

I move quietly towards the window. He's making me nervous with all his jerky movements, and I want to check that he came alone. I pull the curtain aside, but apart from a few parked cars the street is empty. It must be nearly two a.m. Maybe later.

'I got busted,' Jay tells Teo.

'I heard. So what you doing out?'

'We were in the police station that got shot up last night.'

Teo's face pales. 'Oh, man . . .' he says.

'It's OK,' Jay cuts him off. 'But the police are looking for me. I'm going to hand myself in tomorrow.'

'Woah, woah . . .' Teo starts pacing the small apartment,

clutching his head in his hands. 'No, man, we can figure something out.'

'Teo, I did the crime . . . you know how it goes.'

Teo comes to a sudden halt in front of Jay. 'No,' he says, his eyes frighteningly big in his head. 'You don't get it. The Blades – they say I need to pay for fucking up.'

'What?' Jay says, instantly alert.

'They're blaming me, you know?' Teo rattles on. 'Say these guys had paid them already for the job and because you messed it up we gotta pay. *I* gotta pay.'

'Teo, Teo,' Jay says, putting his hands on Teo's shoulders and trying to calm him down, 'you're not making any sense. What guys are you talking about? Who paid them for the job?'

Teo's eyes are almost rolling in his head now. 'The *guys*. These Russian guys – gangsters. I don't know who they are. They paid the Blades – for the Willow Place job. You were supposed to be there to pick up a package. One a.m. You didn't show. Now they're pissed.'

'Willow Place?'

They both turn to me.

My body has gone numb, ice runs through my veins. I'm amazed that my voice sounds so steady and calm because I can hardly breathe. 'Willow Place?' I say again. 'That was the address?' I stare straight at Jay. 'That was where you supposed to be the other night?'

They both nod and I see the line of confusion running like a fault line between Jay's eyes.

'What was the package?' I ask, my voice firmer now.

Teo glances at Jay, trying to figure out who I am and why I'm asking.

I see the crease of confusion smooth away as Jay figures it out. A look of pure horror crosses his face. 'Willow Place? Was that the place you were staying?' he asks, his voice a rasp.

I nod slowly.

'It was you,' he says, reeling back as though I've dropkicked him.

I think my knees are going to give way.

Jay suddenly slams Teo against the wall. 'What was the goddamn package?' he yells at him. 'What were you supposed to pick up?'

Teo doesn't bother fighting back. He has a couple of inches on Jay but he's no match in terms of strength. 'I don't know, bro,' he says, his voice high-pitched as a girl's. 'They didn't say. Just told me to be there at one a.m. And that I had to drive wherever they told me to go.'

'Was it a person? Did they say that you'd be picking up a person?'

'I don't know!' Teo screams.

The muscles in Jay's neck are thick as ropes and his teeth are bared.

'But I heard them say something,' Teo says, his eyes darting wildly about the room as he struggles for breath.

Jay releases his hold just enough to let Teo speak. 'What?' he growls.

'They said something about keeping our hands off the package because it was valuable.'

My legs buckle and I fall to my knees. Jay stares at Teo for several seconds before he releases him, taking several steps back, still staring at him like he's fighting the urge to smash him into the wall again. He walks to me and puts his hand under my arm to help me to my feet, but I smack it away and lurch to my feet. 'Get off me!' I yell.

'Liva,' he says, jerking back in surprise.

I back away, putting distance between us, trying to think, trying to figure out what it all means.

'What's going on?' Teo asks, hugging his arms around his skinny torso. It sounds like he's about to burst into tears, and I have an overwhelming urge to smack him in the face.

Jay acts like Teo isn't even in the room. He takes a step towards me, fully focussed only on me. 'Liva,' he says again, in a low voice, 'I didn't know.'

'What?' Teo asks again then he stops, his arms falling to his sides. 'Woah,' he says. 'Are you saying *she's* the girl? She's the one they want? *She's* the package?'

'I trusted you,' I say to Jay, ignoring Teo.

Jay's expression is one part fear and three parts despair.

I keep my gaze fixed on him as I reach to the floor and pick up Marisa's sandals and my gun, which lies on the table by the sofa. My hands are shaking so hard I can barely keep hold of it. I stretch over the sofa and grab the go-bag and I start edging towards the door. Jay follows me the whole time, at a distance, his face pleading, desperate.

'Liva,' Jay says one last time, his voice barely above a whisper.

As I reach the door, Teo darts in front of it.

'Get out of my way,' I tell Teo, through a film of tears.

'No way,' he says. His body is jerking with adrenaline and nerves and possibly withdrawal. He looks at Jay. 'We could take her now. Take her straight to them. Get them off our backs.'

I stare at Teo, wondering for a brief moment if he's joking, before realising he actually means it. He means to stop me from leaving. And not just that, he's *wanting* to hand me over to the same people who just murdered a dozen people in cold blood. I look over my shoulder at Jay and for one incredible second I actually think he might be about to side with Teo, but then his face transforms, despair giving way to blind fury.

'Get out the way, Teo,' he snarls.

'No way, man,' Teo says, shaking his head. He grabs hold of the top of my arm and shoves me back into the room. I stumble against the table and let out a cry.

Everything that happens next is a blur. Jay moves fast, ramming his fist into Teo's gut, slamming him against the wall. Teo grunts and starts trying to kick out, but Jay has him pinned there and is yelling at him.

I don't wait to see what happens next or to listen to what he's saying. I just reach for the door, pull it open and dive down the stairs.

34

I slam into the door at the bottom and yank it open, falling on to the street in a tumult of tears and adrenaline. I'm barefoot, in Queens, all alone, and it's the middle of the night. All I can think is that I need to move. I need to get out of here. But where? And how?

An arm suddenly comes around my waist, another around the top of my arms, pinning them to my sides. I let out a scream which becomes a cry as a sharp pain shoots up my wrist. I drop the gun I had been holding. It clatters to the sidewalk. I buck and try to kick backwards at whoever has me.

'Woah, calm down. It's me. It's only me.'

The hand around my chest loosens. I jerk my head hard around and in the harsh green light from the neon pizza sign in the window behind, I see that it's Agent Kassel.

She lets me go and I scrabble backwards, eyes darting left and right. 'What do you want?' I choke out. I'm hunched forward, as though on a starting block, my knees bent, ready to run.

I register the click of a car door behind me and then footsteps. I turn. It's Agent Parker. He isn't wearing his shades and I see a deep scratch across his forehead. Probably from the car crash earlier. His face remains blank as he strolls up behind me, cutting off my retreat. He shoves his hands deep into his pockets and I wonder at the gesture, what it's designed to do, because though on the one hand it seems to suggest that he's not going to hurt me, the gesture also offers me a good look at the leather gun holster under his arm.

'What are you doing here?' I ask them, my heart still pounding.

'You're a hard person to trace, Olivia,' Agent Kassel answers, reaching to pick my gun up off the sidewalk.

'Get in the car,' Agent Parker says, opening the rear door of their black sedan. 'And we'll explain.'

I take one last glance up the street. Then back at the door leading up to Marisa's apartment.

'Come on, Olivia.'

I stare into the darkened interior of the car and then I glance at the gun in Agent Kassel's hand. What choice do I have? I can't run. I'm barefoot. I sure as hell can't go back inside. I'll lead them straight to Jay. So I do their bidding. I slide across the cool leather seat and hear the solid click of the door as they shut it behind me and the lock thumps into place.

Agent Kassel has joined me in the back. As Agent Parker puts the car in gear and starts driving she turns to me. 'Where's Jaime Moreno?' she asks. 'That's who you were with, right? You escaped with him from the police station. We have the CCTV footage.'

I don't say anything. Silence is my only weapon right now. And despite everything, I'm not about to rat Jay out. Also I don't want to talk, I want to try to process everything that's just happened with Teo and what it might mean. Felix always said you had to gather as many facts as you could before you made your move. So that's what I need to do.

'Look, we know that was Jaime's cousin's place,' Agent Kassel continues. 'And we followed his brother Teodoro there.'

I say nothing. If they found me here, does that mean the Russians will too? Is Jay safe? They're not after him, I remind myself. They want *me*. And what do I care about Jay any more anyway?

'Liva, we're not interested in Jaime,' Agent Kassel says, almost echoing my own thoughts. 'We'll leave that to the police. Right now we're just interested in you. And in keeping you safe,' she adds.

I turn to face her at that. The safety part seemed to be very much an afterthought. And what does she mean about leaving it to the police? Are they coming for Jay even as we speak? I realise that I'm hoping that they are. Because better the police than the Russians. And even though I'm telling myself I don't care what happens to him, of course I do.

'Jay,' I say, his name bitter on my lips. The lips that still throb and burn from his kisses. 'I need to know he's going to be safe.' I look at Agent Kassel, ready to read it if she lies to me.

'The police are on their way. They're probably there already.'

I nod, taking that in. 'I want to get him a lawyer,' I say.

'We can talk about that later,' Agent Kassel counters without missing a beat.

Irritation swells inside me but I rein it in, gritting my teeth behind as cool an exterior as I can manage. I have to keep the upper hand here.

'Who are you?' I demand. 'You're FBI, I know that. But what's COU? What do you do?'

Agent Kassel smiles wryly. She must have heard about the phone call earlier.

'We'll explain when we get to where we're going.'

I glare at her, but she just gives me a steely smile. 'And Jaime's mother? You have her?' I ask.

238

She blinks at me in surprise. 'Yes,' she says finally, weighing her answer. 'We took her into custody for her own protection as soon as we realised you were with Jaime.'

'Is she safe?' I ask. Protective custody isn't all it's cracked up to be, in my humble opinion.

'She's safe,' Agent Kassel says. She pauses. 'Why'd you run before?' she asks me, her tone softening. 'Could have saved us a whole lot of bother, you know, if you'd just come with us in the first place.'

I frown at her. Is she seriously asking me that question? 'A man in a police uniform is trying to kill me,' I say as evenly as I can. 'I'm having some issues with trust right now. Also,' I add, 'my father told me there was no FBI involved in the task force he works on. He was relieved about it. Said you guys were a pain in the ass when it came down to jurisdiction and getting stuff done. It's mainly civilians, he said.' Agent Kassel's jaw locks. 'You introduced yourself to me as an agent,' I say with a light shrug. 'I did the math.'

Agent Kassel opens her mouth to speak, but I continue before she can get a word in. 'Thirdly, you pulled a gun on me. Word of advice: if you want people to trust you in future, don't point a gun at them.'

From up front Agent Parker clears his throat, stifling a laugh.

'I'm sorry about that,' says Agent Kassel, squaring her shoulders. 'My priority was to get you somewhere safe. And you weren't complying. Force was necessary.'

I give her a look that makes her stop talking.

'How did you find me on that street corner?' I ask.

'We're tapping your father's phone. We wanted to get to you before he sent one of his team to collect you.'

I ponder that. I think of Jay. How he waited to see if I was OK. How different everything could have played out if he hadn't. Then I try to push him out of my mind again. Goddamn him. I can't believe I ever let my guard down enough to trust him, to start feeling something for him. God. I was that close to sleeping with him. I can still feel the trail of heat from his lips – a brand across my stomach, the ghost pressure of his weight pressing down on me. I shake my head, so angry I can barely see straight. Felix was right about trust and unicorn's horns. I will never trust anyone again as long as I live.

'We didn't know that they were tapping your father's phone too.'

'Who? The guy dressed as a cop?'

Agent Kassel nods.

'Who is he? There's two of them. They're not police, are they?'

'No. They're not police. We'll explain it all in due course.'

'Due course?' I shout making Agent Kassel flinch. 'With respect, I've been shot at, chased and hunted by two men dressed as cops for the last twenty-four hours. Screw your due course. I want to know.' I tip my chin towards the window. 'Or I'll take my chances out there, on my own.'

She considers me. I can tell I've surprised her with how much I know and it's put her on the back foot. 'It's complicated,' she finally says. 'And classified. But we need your help, Olivia.'

'Well, unclassify it and maybe I'll think about helping you.'

She gives me a stare that I assume is something she learned at Quantico or wherever the hell they train FBI agents, a look that's designed to intimidate me into rolling over and complying, but after the day I've just had, after the events of the last half hour in particular, I don't give a damn what she thinks. I don't care what anyone thinks.

Agent Parker smirks at her in the rear-view mirror.

We ride the rest of the way in silence.

35

We weave through the streets of Manhattan and finally pull into an underground parking lot, beneath a nondescript, sturdy skyscraper in mid-town. There are several security checks along the way. IDs are held out for inspection and faces pressed against the window to verify the contents of the car – i.e. me.

We're waved through and finally make it into a service elevator that drops us into the bowels of the building. They march me along a tiled corridor that reminds me of a morgue and usher me into a small room with a bolted-down table and four white plastic chairs. There are no windows and it has the heavy, echoey feel of a bunker. The air is stale and the carpet muffles the sound so it's like being held in an underground cave with artificial lights frying my eyes. I can't help but stare at the door they close behind me. It's reinforced steel and mutes any noise from outside. It looks like it could withstand an explosion. But even so I can't relax. Every single muscle in my body is primed for flight. I perch on the edge of one of the plastic chairs and scan the walls and ceiling for cameras. There's an air-conditioning vent silently blowing air into the room and in the top right-hand corner a small hole has been drilled in the ceiling, through which I'm guessing a lens is trained on me.

I pick up the go-bag, which is by my feet, and pull out my phone. There's no reception this far underground but I'm only checking the time. It's nearly two a.m. Which means I have just five hours before I'm due to meet my father. My foot starts tapping as I start working out a plan.

I toss the phone back in the bag and rezip it, thanking my lucky stars that they didn't take it from me. Agent Kassel seemed to be debating it, before deciding to let it go. She did make me pass it through a security check though, which resulted in a few raised eyebrows and the confiscation of the switchblade. They left everything else though, including the roll of dollars, and they didn't find the envelope hidden beneath the false bottom either.

I guess they're treading lightly, not wanting to annoy me unduly, which is why they've left me the bag. It makes me think they're eager to keep me onside, which then makes me think they want something from me. But what?

At just that point Agent Kassel and Agent Parker enter the room. I wonder if they took these last five minutes to figure out their good cop/bad cop roles because for the first time Agent Parker looks friendly – he smiles warmly at me as he drops down into the seat opposite mine. He's taken off his jacket too and rolled up his sleeves. He even tears open a packet of M&Ms and offers them to me.

Agent Kassel, meanwhile, keeps a stony face. She drops a manila folder down heavily on to the table in front of me.

'Coffee?' she asks, holding a Styrofoam cup out to me. For a minute I'm flung back to the police station and Detective Owens asking me the exact same question just minutes before the shoot-out occurred. What happened to him? I wonder . . . I want to ask, but I'm afraid to know.

I shake my head at the proffered coffee. My brain is firing too fast – coffee will only spin me out more. I'll end up like Teo – jittery and unable to think clearly. For a second my mind flips to Jay. Did the cops arrest him yet? Is he safe?

No. Forget him. He betrayed you, I tell myself. Except he didn't. Not really. He didn't know that it was me. And he was only doing the job to protect his brother. Maybe I should tell Agent Kassel about the link between the Blades and the people chasing me. But is it important? Won't it get Jay in even more trouble? And besides, I'm not giving them any information. I'll trade it, but I won't give it.

'So, is it all still classified?' I ask, sarcasm drenching my words.

Agent Kassel shakes a sugar packet into her coffee.

'Olivia,' she says, and she sounds even more tired than I feel. I guess she's been up for over twenty-four hours too. But my sympathy quota is exhausted. 'What I'm about to tell you is going to be hard to hear.'

I open my mouth to fire back some razor-sharp retort but the look on her face silences me. She looks deeply sad, can barely hold my gaze. The air leaves my lungs in a blast. She has the expression of a doctor before they give you a fatal diagnosis.

'Agent Parker and myself are seconded to the Criminal Organisation Unit here at the FBI,' she says, holding my gaze firmly. 'But in actuality, we're both with Internal Affairs.'

I blink up at her. 'Internal Affairs?'

'Yes. Do you know what Internal Affairs does?' she asks.

'Don't you investigate the police and government departments for corruption?'

'Yes. Exactly. We investigate crimes and corruption being committed by government employees.'

'I don't get it.'

244

She takes a deep breath then exhales sharply. 'We're investigating your father.'

'My father?'

'Yes.'

'I still don't get it.' My mind whirs. *What?* I look at Agent Parker hoping he'll be able to provide clarification. But he just gives me that perfect blank stare of his. The smile has gone AWOL I note though.

'We have substantial evidence and reason to believe that your father is behind one of the biggest trafficking rings seen this decade,' Agent Kassel says. And while I sit there feeling the room start to spin, she starts reeling off numbers and facts from a sheet of paper. I don't hear her. I don't compute a single word because I'm struggling to understand what she just said. My father? As in MY father? The guy running the task force to try to stop trafficking is actually the one behind the trafficking?

I burst out laughing. Then I stand up and walk to the door. 'Let me out,' I say tiredly. 'I want to go.' There isn't enough air in the room. It feels as though they're pumping poison gas through the vents. My legs feel leaden all of a sudden and my head all woozy.

'Olivia, sit back down,' Agent Kassel barks.

'Open the door,' I say, starting to pound on it.

'Even if I wanted to open the door, I wouldn't,' she says evenly. 'It's not safe for you outside. The people who are after you have still not been apprehended.'

I spin around. They're both just sitting at the table, impassively observing me like a pair of scientists watching an atom bomb explode from a safe distance. 'Well, maybe you should be out there now trying to apprehend them,' I shout. 'Rather than in here spinning me a bunch of lies about my father.'

Agent Kassel presses her lips together. Her hands are clasped on the table top as though she's praying.

'A bunch of lies? Let's see.' She spreads the papers from the manila folder across the table and picks out a sheet. 'A six-million-dollar transfer into a bank account with your father's name on it, by way of the Caymans, just last month. And another here. His name on the company accounts of the shipping container firm used to traffic girls as young as six into this country from Pakistan, Oman, Nigeria. Ring any bells to you, Olivia? Sound familiar? Your father's contacts and his network make him the perfect man for the job.'

'Yes, for the *task force* job,' I hurl back.

'No, Liva. For the job of running a trafficking business.'

I stare her down, my arms crossed over my chest. 'No.'

'There are other bank accounts. All offshore. Linking him to contacts we already have under surveillance in Nigeria and Thailand. Middlemen who cut the deals. Who buy the girls. And the boys. It's not all girls. Want to see the pictures?' She tosses some photographs across the table towards me, but I refuse to look. 'We're working with Interpol and various police forces around the world to apprehend them, and chasing down the money trail, because that's the rule of thumb in all this. Follow the paper trail, find your man. Your father has offshore accounts containing hundreds of millions of dollars, Liva. Where do you think he's getting money like that from?'

The piece of paper in the go-bag – the one with all the numbers on – flashes into my mind.

'His job,' I say, a seed of doubt germinating in my stomach. There's no way my father earns that much from his job. Not even factoring in the payments from oil companies, and rich Arabs

246

needing bodyguards, and insurance payouts from shipping companies who sail into trouble in the Gulf of Aden and need his help getting out of it.

Agent Kassel shakes her head at me.

'The men who are after you, Olivia. Why would they come after you so relentlessly if all they believed you were was the daughter of the head of a task force? A task force with no more authority to stop them than a Girl Scout troop. It's a task force of civilians.' The word *civilians* drops with scorn.

'They write a few reports with lots of big words in,' she scoffs. 'Someone in the White House might read it one day, probably an intern, and if they're lucky it might get fed into some policy that may or not get passed on to the statute books but which will never, ever do anything to actually stop a single girl or woman or child from being trafficked into this country.'

'Shut up.'

'No,' she says, her voice angry now. 'You're a bright girl, Liva. Does it make sense to you?' She leans across the table. 'Or does it make more sense that they might come after the daughter of the man who's threatening to kill their business – a business worth billions of dollars a year? A rival businessman?'

'No!' I shout. 'None of it makes sense.'

I want Jay. I want him so badly I feel like I'm going to lose my mind. I want to cling on to him. I want him to help me figure it out. Then I remind myself I'm on my own. I bang on the door again, uselessly, feebly. 'Let me out.'

'We need your help, Olivia.'

I turn around. 'My help?' I ask, dumbfounded. 'For what?'

'To bring your father down.'

36

They leave me in the room alone with the now-cold coffee and a desk strewn with papers. I stand in the corner of the windowless box, staring at the table and not moving. They locked the door behind them. I heard the bolt sliding across. My fingers bite into the flesh of my arms. I glance up into the corner of the room at the camera, knowing that they are right this moment watching my every move.

I drop my arms and try to take stock. I need to get it together. But it's difficult in here. I hate this feeling of being caged. Of being observed by unseen eyes. I want to be outside. I want to be up high. I need air.

What would be the purpose of lying to me? I ponder.

I can't think of any reason. What Agent Kassel said about the relentlessness of the pursuit struck a chord. It didn't make sense. Not until she put it the way she did. Why would they come after the daughter of the boss of a task force with no power?

The papers on the desk are beckoning me, but I fight the urge to step closer. I question why that is.

The answer is obvious. Because I'm scared.

Why am I scared?

Because I think she might be telling the truth.

I close my eyes. The walls shrink nearer, squeezing the air out of the room.

I stride to the desk, the camera feeling like a laser burning a hole in the back of my skull. Let's see what proof they have.

Agent Kassel has left a sheet with the facts on the very top of the pile, clearly a deliberate move on her part. I pick it up though, holding it in both hands, trying not to let them shake. It's similar to the UN Report summary I read at my dad's.

Two point four million people across the globe are victims of human trafficking at any one time.

Only one in every hundred victims of trafficking is ever rescued.

My muscles feel as though they've been injected with a neuro-toxin; they contract sharply, refusing to relax, and it's getting hard to breathe. I collapse down heavily on to one of the plastic chairs and rifle through the rest of the papers. There's a whole folder of surveillance notes – detailed ones – covering the last six months. I scan them and realise it's a detailed list of every move my father has made, from taking his suits to the dry cleaner's to the size of the coffee he bought at Starbucks. I flick forwards and find the date I arrived in the States. It's there. My name. My flight time. There's even a photograph of me walking through the arrivals hall. Another one, shot through a haze of people, of me hugging my dad. We're both sharply in focus. My dad is almost picking me up off the ground and he is grinning, his face half buried in my hair. My throat squeezes closed, my eyes burn.

I toss the papers aside. Several of the sheets go floating off the table.

I grab something called a witness statement and I start to read.

By the time I finish reading, I'm sick to my stomach. Paperclipped to the back of the statement is a small photograph – a headshot of a woman. A girl, in fact. Not much older than me. It's colour. All the better to showcase the split lip, puffy eye and look of hopeless defeat on her face. She was the one in a hundred. The girl who escaped and who managed to tell her story. The report says she's from Oman. I stare at her photograph for several minutes absorbing the final sentence of her statement.

Witness identified Daniel Harvey from a photograph.

Daniel Harvey. My father. The room pulses, the walls pressing close. I have to force myself to breathe in, though it hurts so much I think I might suffocate.

Stapled together in a pile are close to thirty more witness statements. With shaking fingers I pick up the pile and read one more, but then I set the pile down. I can't read on. The details are horrific. But even without them all you need to do is look at the photographs to get an idea of what these girls and women – and in some cases, boys – have been through. The lights have gone out in their eyes. They look unseeing into the camera in most cases, though some glare with defiance, some seem to burn with shame, others with anger. And even though they've been rescued, are considered the *lucky ones*, their expressions tell otherwise.

I move the statements to one side, my heart a ticking bomb.

At the bottom, just peeking out of the manila folder is a stack of photographs – black-and-whites mainly, glossy as varnished tiles, white bordered. Some are blurry and pixellated, like they've been taken through a blizzard, others are crisp as wedding shots.

Even in the out-of-focus shots I recognise my father. He's a big man, hard to miss, his bearing military and upright. He has a thick head of dark hair that in the pictures shows not a trace of grey. In one shot, the biggest, he is standing alongside another man in what looks like a warehouse. There are massive containers in the background. A dock of some sort? I lean closer over the picture and then hold it up to the light, my heart beating faster and faster until it feels like it's going to burst. It's the cop. The other man is the cop who's chasing us.

And my father is shaking hands with him.

I sit there for what feels like hours and I don't move. I push all the paper to the edge of the table and I just stare at the wall opposite and try to keep my face impassive. But behind the façade I'm in a thousand jagged pieces. There will never be a way of putting them back together again. Numbness fights shock, fights anger, fights despair, fights disbelief. And rage threatens to overcome all of it. And I don't want to feel any of this. I don't want to feel anything. It's too much.

I close my eyes and I picture myself in that basement with Felix. He's holding my hand, murmuring softly, telling me how to grapple with my fear and lock it away. To survive that's what you need to do, take control of all your emotions – not just fear – and lock them away. I have to think my way through this – and the only way to do that is by locking all emotions down. Switching them off and using reason. Only, Felix morphs in my head into Jay. And he strokes the inside of my palm with his thumb and in the darkness I know he is shaking his head at me.

I hear the lock click in the door and my eyes flash open.

Agent Kassel is alone this time. I notice the badge on her belt, and the gun in its waist holster. I notice the tight-fitting white shirt tucked into her navy pants and I notice that Mrs Francis was right – she does look a bit like Jennifer Lopez. She sits down in the seat opposite me but I stand up.

'No,' I say. 'If you want my help then I want to talk outside.'

37

I can tell they're nervous because as well as Agent Kassel and Agent Parker, there are two other agents stationed by the stairs at the entrance to the High Line. The upside to them being FBI agents is that despite the fact the High Line is closed to the public until seven a.m., they've somehow managed to get access. It's not yet four a.m. and the sky is velvet dark, with no sign yet of the approaching dawn.

I told them I would only talk up here, out in the open. They complied, but from the steel glares and unsmiling faces I can tell I've pushed the limits of their patience. It's strange being here so early. The streets are almost quiet below. I can even hear birdsong. The rumble of traffic is replaced by the occasional rise and fall of a siren in the distance. I can pinpoint the sound of someone whistling on the sidewalk below us and the clanking sound of containers being unloaded at the wharf a few blocks over.

Agent Kassel keeps checking her watch. She looks like the consummate FBI agent from the movies, hands on her hips, scowling at me as though I'm Hannibal Lecter. I feel like I'm tainted by association with my father and a part of me realises that from now on every time I say my name I'm going to be hit with a wave of shame.

'Your father stepped off a plane at JFK two hours ago,' she tells me. 'He's just made it back to his apartment. Where's he expecting to meet you? Here?'

I refuse to answer her. Because, the truth is, I didn't really come here to talk. And I'm already busy calculating, calibrating distance and footholds. I'm wearing Marisa's sandals, which doesn't help, but I know for a fact I'm more nimble than any of them. I just have to time it right. And also rely on my intuition, which is telling me that they won't shoot me. I hope to God I'm right about that.

I stroll towards the railing, remembering walking this same route with Jay. It feels so long ago already. Like it happened a hundred years in the past, not just yesterday.

Agent Kassel keeps pace with me. 'Olivia, I know this is a lot to have to deal with. I understand your instinct is to protect your father,' she says, 'but think of all the people who are being hurt because of what he's doing. You can help us.'

'How?' I ask, rounding on her.

'You could help us capture his testimony.'

'You mean wear a wire? Get him to admit it all on tape?'

'That's one way, yes,' she answers.

'And the others? The Russians? What about them?'

'We've got that situation handled.'

'Oh really?' I ask. 'Like they had it handled in the police station?'

A flicker. A muscle close to her eye twitches. 'We're closing in on them. Once they realise that we have you, then they'll quit trying to get to you.'

'That photograph,' I say. 'The one of my father shaking hands with a man. It's the same man who's trying to kidnap me.'

'Yes.'

'Who is he?'

'His name is Vladimir Demitri Bezrukov.'

'If he's an enemy of my father's, why were they shaking hands?'

'They had a deal. Your father arranges the supply, they feed the demand.'

My teeth grind together as I fight to keep my face impassive at the terms she's using to describe the sale of human beings.

'And your father's now decided to cut them out of the supply chain,' she carries on. 'He wants to control it completely.'

'And so they thought if they had me as collateral, they could get him to change his mind?'

'Couldn't they?' she asks.

I consider that for barely a moment. Yes. I feel many things towards my father right now, but one thing I do know is that he would kill any man who ever hurt me. He's already shown that with the third kidnapper in Nigeria.

'Why haven't they just tried to kill my father?' I ask. That makes more sense to me. Why come after me? Why not just kill him?

'Because your father controls supply. If they remove him, they shoot themselves in the foot. It will take them months, maybe years, to build the supply chain again. Time that can be measured in tens of millions of dollars of lost revenue.'

'Right,' I say. The sky feels suddenly like it's weighing down on me heavy as chain mail. I need to get away. I need to be by myself so I can think.

Just then, Agent Parker shouts something. He's holding up his phone. Kassel walks over to him and they start conferring. It's the moment I've been waiting for. I put a hand on the railing and jump up on to it. It's narrow, about four feet high and two inches across, but I keep my balance. I can stay *en pointe* for minutes at a time, so this is easy.

I hear all the agents yelling at me and for a brief second I catch sight of their faces – eyes round with shock, mouths tumbling open, hands diving into jackets for their guns – and I know that what I'm doing is the wrong thing. I should stay. I should help them. I know this. But I just can't.

I jump. And as the wind rushes in my ears I hear Kassel scream my name. I bring my knees up and ready myself to land. It's jarring, sending shock waves rolling through me and jolting my bones hard enough that I worry for a second that my ankle's broken. I stand up dizzily. My ankle hurts but I test my weight on it. It's just a strain. About twenty feet above me I see the agents standing peering over the railing. They expected to see me splattered all over the sidewalk below. They hadn't counted on the fact there was a stairwell just beneath this part of the High Line. And I'm already swinging down the last flight as they're all running to the top.

I have a good head start and I sprint towards Chelsea Market, a block away. There has got to be a cab somewhere around here. I'm praying there is because it's four blocks to the nearest metro and no way I'm going to outpace them over that distance. And then, with all the luck in the world seemingly on my side for once, a yellow taxi pulls across the street right in front of me, as though it was waiting right there, just for me to run past. I race into the road with my arm in the air and it brakes with a squeal. I fling open the door and throw myself inside even as I catch sight of Agent Kassel in the distance sprinting towards me.

'Brooklyn Bridge,' I pant.

38

The driver pulls over and taps on his meter. I hand over a few notes and get out of the car, lead-limbed and aching inside and out. Staring up at the thick cables of Brooklyn Bridge and the two massive solid stone arches that mark the entrance, I wonder what on earth I am doing here. I just chose the first place I could think of. A place I didn't think anyone would look to find me. Somewhere outdoors, somewhere I could be alone so I could figure out what to do. I couldn't do that in a windowless box or surrounded by federal agents all glancing at their watches and flashing their guns and badges at me.

That girl's face – the one from the file – is all I can think about. The statement she gave detailing everything she had endured in the six months she was held captive runs on an endless loop in my head. Despite the dry, official language her statement was written in, I can picture it all – and it carves something out of my heart, something I don't think I'll ever get back. Some remnant of innocence maybe? Whatever it is, it makes me feel heavy and sad beyond all measure.

My mind feels like it's crumbling under all the information that's been forced on it. I have to find a way of getting control again, of pushing all these feelings back into their boxes. Because there is no way of dealing with them that won't destroy me in the process. Is that self-preservation? Is it selfish? I guess so. But isn't that what Felix was trying to teach me? How to get through life without succumbing to fear and despair? Wasn't that basement lesson really about how to survive in the world?

And the only sure way I know to survive everything – the shooting, what I know about Jay, all the deaths that lie heavy on my conscience and this sickening truth about my father – is to turn off the emotion like a faucet, to block it all out. I was doing it so well before. Until I met Jay.

Before I let my guard down.

I walk out along the pedestrian walkway that's suspended over the roaring lanes of traffic. At this time of the morning, pre-dawn, the walkway is empty. In the distance I see a few people walking and, down below on the expressway, I see the flashing red and white lights of a police cruiser. It's just sitting there, its engine idling, and I walk overhead quickly, hoping the officers inside don't notice a lone girl out for a walk in the early hours of the morning and wonder what I'm doing. I surreptitiously scan the towers as I pass. They're like fortresses, ladderless, smooth, with no footholds. I keep on walking, eyeing the cables as thick as my thighs, pulled taut as guy-ropes and stretching at least a mile across the East River.

It takes just over ten minutes to make it to the middle of the bridge. As I get there I slow my pace, checking in both direc- tions to make sure there's no one nearby. Casting a brief glance down at the unceasing traffic flying over the bridge beneath me, I leap over the railing that divides the walkway from the cables. It's high and takes all my upper body strength, but when I'm over an exhilarating jolt of freedom runs through me. My mind shuts down almost instantly, focussing only on what's keeping me alive – my balance. I step lightly on to one of the steel cables

257

that slopes steeply upwards towards the tower on the Brooklyn side. It vibrates slightly under my hand, feeling as though it's alive, or is carrying a low electric current. Underfoot, though, it feels steady as a rock face.

'You're not really going to climb that, are you?'

I almost lose my footing and have to clutch hold of the cable above me with both hands. I peer over my shoulder, my heart full in my mouth. Jay is standing on the walkway below me, and for a moment I cannot believe what I'm seeing, and wonder if my exhaustion has finally caught up with me and is making me hallucinate. But then he hauls himself over the barrier, up on to the cable I'm balancing on and it sways with his weight, and the realisation he's here literally vibrates through me. He has a bruise starting to burst purple and blue across his cheekbone – from Teo?

'What are you doing here?' I ask, my voice a rasp carried away by the roar of traffic and the scream of wind.

'Narrowed it down,' Jay says, glancing down nervously at the cars flying across the bridge not twenty feet below us.

'What do you mean?'

'It was either the High Line or here, but I figured you wouldn't choose the High Line because it would remind you of me. Guess I figured right.'

'But how did you know I'd come here?'

'You said before that the Brooklyn Bridge would be an amazing climb. And I figured that if you were going to go anywhere in the mood you were in, you'd go somewhere outdoors, up high, away from people.'

I stare at him incredulous. Why isn't he in police custody? Agent Kassel said the cops were on the way to Marisa's. 'Why are you here?' I ask, still reeling from shock but trying not to show it.

Seeing him again has sent my pulse rate rocketing, even as my stomach folds over on itself. It's not just the surprise of seeing him, it's the fact that I wanted to be mad at him, expecting to be, but I find I'm not. I'm relieved. So relieved I could cry.

'I'm here to say sorry. Teo . . .' He shakes his head, squints into the distance before turning back to me. 'I didn't know,' he says softly. 'Honest to God, Liva. If I had known it was a person, that was it *you* . . . I – I don't know what I can say to you, but I'm sorry.'

He looks up at me, half pleading and swallows nervously. 'And I also wanted to keep my promise to you. I told you I wasn't going to leave you until you were safe with your father. I want to see this through.'

My hands, gripping the cable, are shaking and tears have started to slip silently down my cheeks. Jay tilts his head to one side and looks at me with an expression that still begs me to forgive him. Then he stares at the bridge, taking in its height and then the drop to the water.

'What are you doing?' he asks.

'I needed somewhere to think and . . .' I stop. Why am I explaining this to him? He should be the one explaining things to me.

'You don't need to climb up a freaking bridge to feel like you're in control of the situation, Liva.'

I glower at him, but he doesn't notice. He's too busy staring down still at the churning brown mess of water beneath the bridge, as though he's only just realised how far and how fatal a fall would be. The knuckles of his fists bleach through the skin and beads of sweat appear on his temples. He swallows and looks up at me, several shades paler.

'But if that's what you need to do,' he says, pressing his lips together, 'then come on, let's do it.'

'What?' I ask, suddenly nervous.

'Are we climbing this thing or not?' Jay asks, and without waiting for me to reply he starts to move, stepping sideways along the cable.

'What are you doing?' I yell.

'Come on,' he shouts back, taking another step. 'We've got to do it before it gets light or the police are going to spot us.'

Panic floods through me. 'Jay, what are you doing? Come back!' I scream, then catch a movement out of the corner of my eye. In the distance someone is jogging down the walkway towards us.

'Why?' Jay asks, not looking at me, but keeping on moving along the cable.

'Because . . .' I shout. Do I really need to give him a reason? He's going to fall and he's going to *die*. 'Please,' I beg. Shit. He's going to fall. And it will be *my* fault.

'Why?' he asks again.

'Because I'm scared for you,' I shout back, so furious that lights flash at the corner of my vision.

He stops then. Finally. Looks directly at me. 'Why?' he demands.

'Because I don't want you to fall,' I scream.

'So what if I do?' he asks me. Even from a distance I see the defiance in his eyes. The challenge. He wants me to answer him.

'I don't want you to,' I yell. I'm so mad now half of me wants to walk out along the cable and push him off.

'But if I do fall, that's got nothing to do with you,' Jay says, shrugging like he doesn't get it.

'Yes it does.'

He looks at me confused. 'No it doesn't. Why does it have anything to do with you?'

'Because you're here because of me,' I shout.

He waits until the thunder from a passing lorry dies away. 'No,' he says. 'I'm here because I chose to be. I'm climbing this ridiculously thin cable suspended one hundred foot above certain death because I *choose* to do it. If I fall, it's on me. Not on you.'

Anger licks at me but I can't let him see. I need to stay calm, reel him back in. 'I get what you're trying to do,' I say, lowering my voice, my eyes darting to the jogger who's getting nearer. There's no way he won't see us. And then he'll call the police.

'What am I trying to do?' Jay asks.

'You're trying to prove to me that I'm not responsible for what happens to other people.'

'Is it working?' he asks.

I don't answer.

Still staring at me, Jay slowly lets go of the cable above him. 'Look, no hands,' he says, showing me his palms.

'Jay!' I scream.

He sways so hard that I'm certain he's lost his balance and my stomach plummets as my heart leaps into my mouth, but he manages at the last moment to grab hold of the cable and stop himself from falling.

'My choice, Liva,' he says. 'Just like it was that man's choice to shoot up a police station. And the people that died – they didn't die because of you. Felix didn't die because of you. He died because shit happens. And none of it is your fault.'

I'm trembling so hard I can barely hold on and tears fill my eyes, blurring my vision. I blink them away but they keep coming.

'I'm scared,' I suddenly say, the words just tumbling out.

'It's OK to be scared,' Jay says, his voice gentle now.

The knotted cable starts to tremble in my hands. 'No it's not,' I say.

He's beside me again somehow. His hand covers mine. 'Liva,' he says softly, 'it's OK to feel afraid. It's OK not to know what's going to happen.'

I grip the cable tighter, feel it cutting into my palms.

'You have to let go of this idea that we're in control of life. We're not.'

I squeeze my eyes shut. 'I don't want to feel any of this. I want it all to go away. I can't think like this. I can't live like this.'

'Come on,' he says, gently pulling at my arms. 'Let's get down.'

I let him turn me carefully around and lead me over the guard-rail. He jumps down ahead of me, waving at the jogger who is just now passing by. He stares at us in slack-jawed bewilderment, slowing his pace, but Jay's smile persuades him we're fine and so he keeps on jogging, darting us several more looks over his shoulder, as though checking we're not about to free dive once his back is turned.

Jay holds his hands out to me and I drop down into them. He doesn't let me go even when I try to struggle free. I don't want him to hold me. When he holds me I feel I might unravel.

'It's OK to feel things, Liva,' he says. 'We're *meant* to feel things – we're meant to feel *everything* – hurt, pain, anger, rage, grief.'

My eyes burn. I shake my head furiously. 'I don't want to feel those things. I can't. It's too much.' And suddenly I'm sobbing, endlessly, without relief.

Jay holds me around the waist with one arm and uses his free hand to lift my chin. 'Liva,' he says, 'if you don't allow yourself to feel those things, then you'll never be able to feel the good things either – happiness, or joy, or love. You can't have one without the other. That's life. That's how it works.'

I try again to break free. I don't want to hear any of this. But Jay refuses to let me go. His grip just tightens.

'Life's unfair,' he says. 'And it really goddamn hurts at times. It hurts more than you think you can handle. But in the end, it's worth it.'

But that's the thing, the thing that cracks my heart in two. 'How do you know?' I ask sadly, because it isn't. It isn't worth it.

Jay studies me for a second and then he smiles like he's just won the debate, even though he hasn't, because he can't prove it. There's nothing he can say that will convince me that life is worth this much pain and hurt.

But then he kisses me. Softly, and so gently that my heart sighs. And everything does unravel.

When he finally stops kissing me and I open my eyes, I find him staring down at me – his expression a fine balance between joy and pain and happiness and grief – all those emotions he just talked about.

'It's worth it,' he says again, his forehead pressed to mine.

And this time, I believe him.

39

Jay is sitting on the grass with his elbows resting on his knees. He's staring out across the park, over the water, towards the skyline of Manhattan that's gradually growing crisper against the dawn sky. A day ago we were walking across the bridge into the city on the way to my dad's apartment. I was wearing pyjama shorts and an NYPD sweater. I didn't know anything about the boy now sitting beside me other than the fact he'd been arrested and that his name was Jaime. I knew enough to judge him, though. To think he was a murderer. And now I sit beside him, wearing a borrowed black dress, feeling like I've known him a hundred years. I feel that old. Worn out. Too tired to keep running. Too tired for any more secrets or surprises.

Jay turns to me then, and I notice that he looks older too. His face is drawn with tiredness, but even though his eyes are dark-ringed they blaze bright and I can read every one of his thoughts as they pass across his face: the disbelief and the disgust and the tiredness and, when he looks at me, the empathy and the hurt and the sorrow too. But most of all when I look at him I see the resilience that's part of who he is. Despite all we've been through, despite all I've told him and despite all that awaits him, there's no sign of resignation or of quitting. It's not in him to give up on anything, including me.

I stare at him in wonder, still trying to get my head around the fact that in a city the size of New York he found me. But not only that, he escaped custody for a second time to do it. Well, practically. The cops were banging on Marisa's door, so he took a leaf out of the Olivia Harvey escape manual, he told me proudly, and climbed out the window and up on to the roof.

He told me the story grinning like he'd just won the lotto, even though fleeing arrest could potentially earn him more time behind bars. In return, I told him everything Agent Kassel had told me, about his mother being safe and all about the trafficking ring my father's involved in. I described the photographs and the witness statements in detail. I didn't leave anything out. And he hasn't said a word since.

But now finally he does. He turns to me, his elbows still resting on his knees, and stares at me for a long beat. 'You have to do it,' he says.

I turn away from him and stare at the bridge. To think I almost climbed that. Maybe one day I'll come back and try it for real. Though even as I consider the idea, it loses its appeal.

Jay puts his hand on my shoulder and gently strokes a strand of hair behind my ear. At his touch I close my eyes and let out a sigh. I wish I could stay here with him. I wish we could lie down in the grass and sleep and let the world spin on without us.

'I don't think I can,' I say.

'Liva,' Jay says, 'remember when I first met you? I told you you had heart?'

I nod.

'It was the first thing I saw when I looked at you,' he says. 'Actually the second. First thing was your legs.'

I sneak a look at him. He pulls a face at me as if to say *hey, I'm a guy, cut me a break.*

'I seem to remember you thinking I was an uptight rich chick.'

'With heart,' he says, smiling and flashing his dimples. 'You were sitting in that chair in the homicide department,' he continues, 'and you were staring at the board – the one with all the murder cases on it. And the look on your face . . . It was like you knew every single one of those people personally.'

I frown at him, not understanding.

'That's why I know you'll do the right thing now,' he says, holding my gaze with those bewilderingly green eyes. 'Because you got heart.'

I turn my head back to the horizon but all I see in my mind's eye is the chalkboard. And the policeman carefully writing the Goldmans' names in block letters along the bottom. I think of the space beside it left blank for the words *case closed.*

I know Jay is right. There was never any other option. Not from the moment Agent Kassel left me in the room with that folder. Not since I saw the photograph of my father shaking hands with the man who killed the Goldmans and all the people in that police station. Not since I read those girls' witness statements.

Jay stuck by me from the start, because he believed he was doing the right thing. And sometimes that's all you can try to do, I guess, *the right thing*. Sometimes it's simple. Sometimes it's not. But either way, you should never have to think about what the right thing is. You just have to listen to your heart. The difficulty is in then acting on it.

I stand up. 'Come on,' I say to Jay. 'We're going to be late.'

The Staten Island ferry terminal sits beside Battery Park. At six-thirty it's swarmed with commuters piling off the ferry, heading to work in the city. Jay and I approach on foot from two blocks away. I have dug the binoculars out of the go-bag. Jay has the Glock he

266

took off the dead cop, which is good as Agent Kassel never gave me back the Smith & Wesson. But it's my father, I remind myself, what am I going to need a gun for?

The binoculars are to make sure he's not being followed. The fact that my dad had no idea he was under surveillance by the FBI for the last six weeks makes me wonder at his skill in shaking off a tail.

Beside the terminal is a Wells Fargo bank. Jay and I hide in the shadow of one of its massive marble pillars and I pick up the binoculars and scan the people heading into the terminal. Most people are heading out, into the city for work, so it's easy to keep track of those heading in. It's just a smattering of tourists catching the outbound ferry to enjoy the views it offers back over Manhattan and towards the Statue of Liberty. I check the time on the phone. It's twenty minutes to seven.

At five minutes to seven my stomach is twisted into several knots and I'm holding my breath. What if my father didn't get the note I left for him in the safe? What if he didn't understand it? What if he doesn't remember where we bought the Statue of Liberty statuette? I refocus the binoculars on the terminal doors and then I catch sight of someone moving fast against the flow, purposefully, striding as though he's late for an urgent meeting. A half foot taller than everyone else, my father stands out in any crowd, but among all the tourists wearing shorts and brightly-coloured T-shirts he stands out even more. He has his back to me so I can't get a look at his face, but everything about his body language shrieks dread – panic barely contained.

'That's him,' I tell Jay, pointing him out as he pushes through the doors and enters the building. 'The tall one with the dark hair, wearing the grey suit.'

'OK,' Jay says. He squeezes my hand and kisses me quickly on the cheek. And then he disappears, jogging towards the terminal. I take out my phone and hit send on the message I already programmed, telling my dad to meet me on the ferry. He might not buy it. He won't recognise the number and he'll naturally be suspicious, but hopefully his need to find me will outweigh any suspicions.

I switch out the SIM card and place a new one in the phone, crushing the first one under my heel. As soon as I turn the phone back on it vibrates in my hand. I answer on the first ring.

'He bought it. He's getting on the ferry,' Jay says. 'Hurry.'

I run up the steps to the terminal building. A blast of ice-cold air hits me as I walk through the doors. I spy Jay waiting at the top of the escalator and I start sprinting up it, hitting dial on the phone as I go. The operator picks up instantly and I ask for Agent Kassel. The operator puts me right through to her cell phone. When she answers I cut straight in.

'It's Olivia.'

'Where are you?' she demands.

'Staten Island ferry. Meet us at the Staten Island end at seven-thirty a.m. You wanted my father? Come get him,' I tell her.

She covers the mouthpiece and I hear her murmuring something to someone else in the background, giving orders.

'And Agent Kassel,' I say. 'Keep the line open. You want proof? I'll get you what you need.'

40

Jay falls into stride a few paces behind me and we join the last stragglers boarding the ferry. I slide the phone into the side pocket of the bag and toss it over my shoulder. As we step on board the engines start to thrum and, before we even make it up the first flight of stairs, the ferry is pushing off from the pier and speeding out across the water. Jay splits off at the top of the first staircase. He takes a seat in the centre of a row of empty chairs and I walk out on to the narrow outside viewing deck. It's empty on this side of the ferry. Most people are over the other side of the boat, admiring the view of the Statue of Liberty and downtown. I also chose the furthest and lowest deck, knowing that most people would head for the higher levels. Just to make sure we're not disturbed, once my dad follows me out on to the deck, Jay is going to borrow a plastic *no entry* sign from somewhere and place it in front of the door to ward off interruptions.

I wait, gripping the railing. My heart flutters in my throat. I gaze down at the churning water below, the white tips of the waves spewing up in our wake, and wonder if I'm going to be sick.

'Liva!'

I jerk around. My father stands in the doorway. His shoulders drop when he sees me, relief washing across his face. My first thought is that in the space of a week he has aged fifty years, His face is grey and pouchy, the lines across his forehead gouged knife-deep. Grey stubble speckles his jaw and cheeks and it makes me pause – I've never seen my dad unshaven.

'Liva,' he says again, my name a sob on his lips, and he's suddenly moving towards me, arms outstretched. He draws in a deep breath that wracks his whole body and then he pulls me into his arms and crushes me to his chest. I smell his familiar scent – expensive cologne, coffee, dry cleaning starch. 'Oh my God, I've been worried out of my mind,' he murmurs, still clutching me tight, his lips pressed to my hair.

I freeze, my muscles locking in total paralysis. But I don't want him to get suspicious, so I force my arms up and around his waist and give him a feeble hug back, the whole time thinking *Who is this man?*

'Dad,' I say, the word sticking like a barb in my throat.

He takes me by the top of my arms and holds me at a distance so he can look me in the face. 'Are you OK?' he asks. 'Did anyone hurt you?' The terror flashes once more over his face, as though he's picturing the worst. And I guess he knows exactly what that would look like.

I shake my head, hoping it hides my shudder. 'I'm OK,' I stammer. I study him. His blue-grey eyes, the exact same shade as mine. The familiar knot of worry between his eyes, the relief and gratitude in his gaze as the realisation that I'm unharmed sinks in. How can he not be who I thought he was? It's as if I've just discovered an actor has been playing the part of my father for the last seventeen years. He's searching my face and I realise that now the relief has passed he's becoming suspicious.

'Why'd you tell me to meet you on the ferry?' he asks. He glances over his shoulder then reaches for me as though to pull me inside. 'I need to get you somewhere safe.'

'I thought it was safer to meet here than in the terminal,' I answer, pressing back against the railing. 'I was in a hurry. It was the first place I thought of.'

'They broke into the apartment. I thought they must have found you . . .' His voice cracks; he draws a deep wracking breath.

'No. We escaped,' I tell him, my mind replaying the images of the girls from the containers. The girls who also escaped.

'We?' my dad asks, his head flying up.

'Yeah,' I say. 'I escaped with someone from the police station.'

'Where are they now?' my dad asks, glancing around, suddenly wary.

'He's not here,' I say quickly. I need to wrestle control of the conversation back before he gets too suspicious. 'Why am I being chased?' I blurt.

My dad considers me carefully, slipping on his authoritative face, the one he uses to chair meetings and give orders to staff. 'I don't know. But we're going to find out. And now I'm here no one is going to hurt you. No one's going to get near you.' There's an edge to his voice. A cold shiver runs up my spine. Because despite everything, I hear the love in his voice. The barely disguised anger that someone has tried to hurt me.

'Who's Vladimir Demitri Bezrukov?' I ask before I can allow myself to feel anything more for him than the hatred he deserves.

My dad blanches. For just a split second. His face goes slack, panic flares brightly in his eyes, but then the shutters fall and the mask is back in place. He looks at me half quizzically, bemused. But behind his sharp blue eyes I can almost see the cogs spinning as he tries to figure out what exactly I know and how exactly I know it. 'How did you find out his name?' my dad asks, his voice even.

'Who is he?' I press.

'He's a very bad man.'

I give him a look. 'I'm not six years old. Don't patronise me.'

My dad nods, licks his lips. He decides to give me more. 'He's the right-hand man of a man called Andrei Radchanka, who runs a Belarusian crime syndicate. He gets the dirty work done. Now are you going to tell me how you know his name?'

'Are you involved in trafficking?' I ask.

My dad blinks once, but otherwise his face reminds completely composed. 'Yes. I'm working on the GRATS task force.'

'No,' I say, clutching hold of the railing to stop my hands from shaking. 'Are you involved in trafficking human beings into the USA?'

My dad straightens up. He studies me as an interrogator would, eyes drilling right through me, calculating his next move, his next question, yet at the same time revealing nothing. 'Did the police put you up to this?' he asks after a stone-cold beat of silence. 'The FBI?'

I keep my face poker blank, as Felix taught me.

'Where have you been for the last twenty-four hours?' my dad asks.

'You didn't answer the question,' I say.

He smiles tightly, almost a wince. The muscle by his eye twitches. He's nervous. Wrong-footed. 'I can't believe they tried to use my own daughter against me,' he says, taking a small step back from me and shaking his head ruefully. His eyes dart to the side, lighting on the doorway behind us. He's already calculating his escape routes and that more than anything he could have said or done sticks like a dagger in my gut.

'They haven't,' I say. 'I'm here of my own accord. My choice. There are no FBI agents around.'

He scans the deck, the water, the roof of the ferry.

'Did they make you wear a wire?' my dad asks.

I hold out my arms horizontal like I'm on a cross, inviting him to pat me down. I can't believe it when he actually does. His hands move fast, methodically and I have to fight to stay still and not push him away. These are not the actions of an innocent man. The knife in my gut twists another turn. I realise I was still clinging to a fragile hope that maybe it was all a mistake, that Agent Kassel had it wrong. But as my dad's gaze drops to the go-bag, propped at my feet, I know without a shadow of a doubt that he is guilty. My dad moves for the bag, just as I remember the phone in the side pocket. I snatch it just before he can reach it and start unzipping it.

'They have the proof, Dad,' I say, hoping that my words will be enough to distract him. 'They showed it to me. Photographs, witness statements, bank accounts.'

'Liva,' my dad says, and it sounds like my name could be a million things to him – a prayer, a curse, an admonition, an apology or even a goodbye, and I have no idea which it is. Or which I want it to be.

'What's this?' I ask, pulling out the sheet of paper from the go-bag with the numbers on it.

His face turns deathly white.

'Why keep that in your go-bag?' I demand. 'Everything else in there is an essential. What's this for?' I wave it in his face. 'Bank details in case you ever had to flee the country?'

'Liva,' he says, half pleading. But pleading for me to what? To stop? To understand? To give him the bag?

'Why?' I ask him.

'It's not what you think,' he says.

273

'Then why are they chasing me? Why me? You're not that important. Unless of course,' I tip my head to one side and smile sadly, 'you are.'

'Liva,' he says, through gritted teeth. Now there's no mistaking his tone.

'The truth,' I spit, ignoring him. 'I want the truth.'

'Why?' he asks.

'Because I deserve it.' I glare at him. Hatred is as sudden as regret. You don't fall into hatred slowly like you do with love, it doesn't give you a new lens through which to see the world, it overcomes you in a riptide of anger and violence, blinding you with its force, then scarring your vision for evermore.

The hatred I feel in that second towards my father makes me want to throw myself on him and start pummelling him to the ground. It makes me want to shred him into a million pieces. It's like a death. His *and* mine. And it doesn't just destroy the present it destroys the past. And it makes me wonder whether there can ever be a future. Every memory I have of him and of my past is now tainted.

My dad flinches as he sees the expressions passing across my face but through the savage rage I'm feeling I keep sight of the fact that I still remain his one weakness. He's trying to work out how to hold on to me, how to deflect the hatred. He doesn't want to lose me. And that's the only way I am going to get him to tell me the truth.

'If you lie to me I swear to God I will never speak to you again for the rest of your life,' I spit.

My dad searches my face and I see him acknowledge the truth that I'm not bluffing and a small light goes out in his eyes, his muscles slacken.

'Liva, it's just a business deal,' he says quietly. 'The trafficking was always going to happen. I don't create the demand.'

I stare at him unblinking, too stunned to say a word. *That's* his reasoning? That's his excuse?

'I'm just a businessman who saw an opportunity,' he explains as though we're in some college enterprise class.

I shake my head at him, astonished. 'Are you really standing here trying to justify to me why you're involved in a human trafficking syndicate? You're selling people. PEOPLE!' I yell.

He doesn't answer.

'Why did you leave me here alone?' I ask him, pushing on. It's been preying on my mind this whole time. If he knew he was about to double-cross his business partner, a business partner who also happens to be a stone-cold murdering psychopath, why'd he leave me here unprotected?

'I didn't leave you unprotected. There were two people watching over the Goldmans' house.'

'What?' I ask.

'They were taken out.' He says it so offhandedly that it takes me a few seconds to realise he means they were killed. For a moment I struggle to breathe. Even more people to add to the tally. When is it going to stop?

'I had surveillance running on Bezrukov too,' my dad continues. 'Believe me, Liva, I would never have put you in harm's way. I had to go to Nigeria. There was no way of getting out of it.' He seems almost more apologetic about this than he does about everything else.

'Why, did you have a shipment of girls to pay for?'

My dad blinks at me once in surprise, flinching back, then he shakes his head, looking at me sadly. 'Please, Liva,' he says, reaching his hand slowly towards me.

I look down at it and know that this is my chance. I hold his gaze, letting him believe I'm considering forgiving him and then I nod, swallowing the lump in my throat, and slide my hand into his. He smiles instantly with relief, gripping me tightly, and even though I'm repulsed I grip his fingers tighter and watch as his smile starts to falter and is replaced with a look of surprise as I snap the plastic cuff I took from the bag around his wrist.

There's a moment of pure bewilderment as he stares down at it and then up at me, not understanding, then he takes a step backwards. Straightaway though he freezes, his hands moving slowly upwards, palms facing outward.

I nod at Jay, who stands behind my dad. Though I can't see it, I know Jay has the Glock pressed against my dad's spine. My father could easily disarm Jay. He's an ex-marine. He could probably fight his way through an entire battalion of soldiers single-handed, but I think he's too shocked by my betrayal to move. And he doesn't know who Jay is, can't even see him. For all he knows, Jay could be an FBI agent and he could be surrounded on all sides.

Before he has time to assess the situation I snatch his hand and cuff him to the railing. Then, keeping my eyes locked on his face, I reach inside his suit jacket for the gun I know he'll be carrying. I pull it free from its shoulder holster. It's cocked and locked, showing me exactly how nervous he was about this meeting. I put the safety on and slip it into my bag. Behind my dad's shoulder I can see Jay is pressing close, keeping his back to the door, trying to hide the gun from anyone who might happen to pass by.

I reach down into the bag, slide the phone free then bring it to my ear. 'Did you get that?' I ask.

Someone, not Kassel, tells me yes. I hang up. My dad's expression hardens, his mouth tightening in a line. He looks like he wants to say something but is biting back the words.

When I bend to put the phone back in the bag my dad finally reacts. He kicks the bag, sending it spinning along the deck far out of reach and at the same time he throws all his weight backwards, into Jay, knocking him into the row of seats behind. Before Jay can get back on his feet, my dad spins and roundhouse kicks the gun straight out of Jay's hand. It clips the railing and tumbles into the waves below. Jay leaps forwards and I let out a scream as my dad rams his elbow into Jay's face. He goes sprawling backwards, blood spurting from a cut above his eye.

I know there's only one option. I dive backwards for the bag, dragging it on to my lap and tugging frantically at the zip. A quick glance upwards reveals my father reaching into the inside of his jacket and in the next second I catch the glimmer of a blade as he starts sawing through the plastic cuff tying him to the railing. My hand closes around the butt of the gun in the same instant and I drag it free.

Hearing the hammer cock and a bullet dropping into the chamber, my dad looks up startled. Behind him I see Jay back on his feet, using his forearm to swipe at the blood pouring down his face. I stand slowly, aiming the gun straight at my dad's chest. I see a moment's doubt flare in his eyes, but then he looks down and keeps sawing, discounting the threat, banking on the fact I won't shoot him.

The thing Felix taught me about poker is that your best play is when your opponent underestimates you, when they think they can read your every bluff and know exactly what cards you're holding. My dad knew me a day ago. He doesn't know who I am now.

I breathe out, shift the gun four inches to the left and up and I pull the trigger. The gun has a silencer which slows the bullet, but I aimed at the fleshy part of my dad's shoulder and it goes right through, tearing a hole in suit and muscle.

My dad is blown back by the blast and the knife flies out of his hand, skidding beneath the row of seats lining the deck. I lower the gun with a shaking hand, ignoring Jay who's standing there staring at me in total shock, arms dropped to his sides and blood coursing down the side of his face. My father is gritting his teeth, crumpling against the railing. Sweat prickles his brow. He clutches his free hand to the wound as blood starts flowing, darkening the arm of his suit.

'Jay, hold this,' I say, handing him my father's gun.

Jay takes it without a word and moves to face my father, training the gun on him but careful to stand out of kicking range. With his free arm he tries to blot the blood trickling down his face.

I pull the cord out of the go-bag and start tying my dad to the railing, using the most complicated knot Felix ever taught me. My dad grunts with pain as I pull the cord tight, but I ignore him. I refuse to look at him. I can't.

When I'm done, I realise I'm panting. I take a step back and only then do I look at my father, knowing it will be the last time that I ever do. I stare him straight in the eye, unflinching, until he understands he will never see me again. He bows his head and sinks to the deck.

41

The voice over the tannoy announces we're approaching the Staten Island ferry terminal. Jay slips his hand into mine and pulls me gently backwards away from my father and out the door. I can't take my eyes off him, collapsed on the ground, one arm raised perpendicular where it's tied to the railing, but then the door clangs shut and he's gone.

Jay makes a sudden hissing sound through his teeth and I turn to him and wince. My dad managed to open up an inch-long tear above his eye. It almost meets the other scar that dissects his eyebrow.

'I'm sorry,' I murmur, taking his face in my hands to inspect the damage.

Jay shrugs and offers me a weak smile. 'You weren't the one who elbowed me in the face.' He shuffles us into the shadow of the stairs so no one can see us and I drop to my knees and rummage through the bag, hiding away the gun and pulling out the balled-up NYPD sweater. I use the sleeve doused in some water from the bottle to mop up the blood. Jay hisses through his teeth and curses as I staunch the flow as best I can.

The boat's engines cut out. A hydraulic shunt signals our arrival. The tannoy warns all passengers to disembark. Jay and I stay huddled in the shadows and I feel time slipping away, pouring through my hands like quicksand.

I take a deep breath and look into his eyes, still holding the sweater against his forehead even though it's stopped bleeding. 'Are you ready?' I ask. As soon as the FBI board the ferry we know that Jay is going to be arrested. Knowing it doesn't make it any easier to face.

Jay stares at me and nods. My stomach plummets and I feel all of a sudden like I'm going to cry. He catches my arm as it drops to my side and pulls me against his body. His hand curls around my neck and he gazes at me fiercely, possessively, his lips pursed. It's like he's trying to tell me a thousand things but can't find the words. But it doesn't matter. He doesn't need to say them. He doesn't need to say anything. I get it.

'It's gonna be OK,' he tells me. He presses his forehead against mine. 'It's gonna be OK,' he says again. And then he kisses me – one hard, firm kiss that I know I'll remember forever – before he lets me go.

'I'm going to get you help,' I say.

He nods, but I can tell he's not putting much hope in that. And maybe he's right not to. Why would anyone help me, knowing who my father is? That route is lost to me now. Hopelessness and despair batter me, making me want to sink to my knees. I've had enough. I can't go on any more.

A final call for passengers to disembark drowns out the sound of a phone ringing. Finally we hear it and both of us frown, looking around for the source. Eventually Jay realises it's his phone ringing and he pulls it out of his back pocket, staring at it like it's a foreign object.

He puts it to his ear. 'Hello?' He listens for a beat. 'Yeah, I'm with her now,' Jay says, glancing at me. I frown at him. Who's he talking to? Jay suddenly tenses, the blood draining from his face. 'What?' he says. 'When?'

Fear rakes talon claws through my insides.

Jay closes his eyes and sways slightly.

'What?' I ask him.

Jay has the phone still stuck to his ear. He looks at me as though seeing a ghost. 'They took Risa,' he says.

'Who?' I ask. But I already know. The only person I can think that Jay would have given this number to would be Yoyo or Risa.

'Teo told the Blades about you and me. They told the Russians. And they came for Risa. This morning. Told Yoyo to give me the message.'

The breath is sucked clean out of my body. 'What message?' I ask. I know already what it is, but I need to hear it.

On the other end of the phone Yoyo is still yelling, screaming something into Jay's ear. Jay drops the phone to his side and stares vacantly at me. 'They want to exchange her for you.'

I take that in without really feeling anything. My body's gone cold. Then I reach out and take the phone from Jay's limp hand. Yoyo is still screaming hysterically on the other end.

'Yoyo, it's me. It's Liva,' I say.

He starts crying hysterically, his words a stream I can barely keep up with.

'OK, calm down. Say that again. Where and when?' I ask, already kneeling and rummaging in the go-bag for the notepad and marker.

I write down what he tells me and then I hang up the phone and hand it back to Jay. I'm aware of every single movement I make. Hyper-aware. My body has slipped into autopilot. I feel numb but my mind is surprisingly clear.

'We need to tell the FBI,' Jay says, glancing over my shoulder. 'We need to get help.'

'No,' I say, zipping up the bag and throwing it on to my back.

'What do you mean?' Jay asks.

'They said we had to come alone. That they'd be checking. Any sign we were being followed and they'll kill her.'

'But—'

I shake my head and grab his hand. We need to hide. The thunder of dozens of footsteps storming up a metal staircase deafens us suddenly. Shit. I spin on the spot. We need to move, but Jay is still digging his heels in.

'Jay,' I growl at him, 'trust me.'

He opens his mouth to say something but then just nods and we run, flying around the corner just as a wave of blue-coated FBI agents washes over the lip of the stairs and storms out on to the deck. The door clanks against metal, sounding like a death knell, and we hear someone yelling that they've found him and then someone else shouting for a paramedic. Jay and I jog to the far end of the ferry and take the stairs down to the disembarkation point.

We make it off the ferry, throwing our arms around each other and acting like a loved-up couple of teens to make it past the FBI agents stationed at the exit. Jay pokes his finger into my side, making me yelp, and he hisses at me to laugh as he ducks his head against mine to hide his bloodied face.

On the street I come to a halt. What's the quickest way to 125th Street from here? I don't have a map of Manhattan in my head. I can't think. Jay suddenly moves in front of me, blocking my path.

'Liva, you can't do this,' he says.

'Yes I can,' I say. 'Jay, you're the one told me life isn't fair and I couldn't stop shit happening to other people. I buy that. But I don't buy this. I can stop this from happening. So I'm going to.'

I march off. I need to find a cab.

Jay keeps pace with me. 'Wait,' he says. 'Just wait. Let's figure something out.'

I don't stop. He grabs me by the shoulder, forcing me to slow. 'Where are we meeting them?'

'125th Street. Uptown platform.'

'And they're expecting me to be taking you there against your will?'

I shrug. 'I guess so.'

Jay grimaces; his hands are fisted, his body vibrating with energy. He glances around. There's a queue of taxis snaking past the entrance. I head to the front of the taxi queue. I have an hour to get all the way uptown. I'm never going to make it.

'What if they find out your father just got arrested?' Jay says, seeing where I'm going and trying to head me off.

I sidestep around him. 'Then I'm no use to them and neither is Marisa. So let's hope they haven't and that they don't. Not until you get Marisa back.'

Jay stands in front of the taxi door, blocking me. 'I'm not letting you go with them,' he says.

'It's not your choice to make,' I say.

He can't argue with that. I reach past him for the door handle, but he grabs my hand.

'Get off!' I yell.

'No,' he says, pulling me away. 'We have an hour to get there. You need someone who knows how to drive.'

Before I can say a word he starts jogging in the other direction, dragging me with him. I open my mouth to ask what he's thinking of doing because I really don't like the sound of whatever it is, and then I see the four blacked-out sedan cars that have been abandoned by the entrance with their doors flung open. FBI cars. And I know exactly what Jay is thinking.

I dig in my heels and come to a halt. Jay stares at me impatiently. 'Clock's ticking,' he says.

I glance over his shoulder. 'You can't steal an FBI car!' I hiss. 'And there are two agents standing twenty metres away to your right,' I add, praying they don't look this way.

'Got it handled,' Jay says, moving instantly towards them, leaving me standing there open-mouthed. He turns to face me, even as he keeps walking towards the agents, and indicates the closest car with an inclination of his head.

Oh God. I watch him turn back to the agents and run over to them. He is pointing at his bloody face and saying something. Then he points back towards the ferry terminal. The two agents exchange a look and then go running past Jay and up the stairs. Jay watches them go and then speeds over to the car which I am standing beside.

'Get in!' he yells at me, as he dives behind the wheel.

When Jay told me driving was like an escape for him, I didn't quite appreciate the truth in his words. He drives like a man trying to outrun death itself. His foot is flat to the floor, and it's all I can do to clutch hold of the sides of the car and pray.

Even when we hit a line of traffic Jay doesn't let up, he rides one side of the car up on to the sidewalk and overtakes on the inside, ignoring the fanfare of honks that blasts in our wake.

'We're going to get pulled over,' I yell at him over the noise.

'Only if they can catch us,' he answers through gritted teeth. His face is a mask of perfect concentration as he jolts us down the kerb and across an intersection.

Once on the expressway he weaves in and out of traffic, careful to keep his eyes on the mirror. He switches on the police scanner on the dash and, though it all sounds like gibberish to me, Jay manages to make sense of it, swinging us off at one exit, down a ramp and through some backstreets before rejoining the expressway in time to take the Brooklyn Bridge.

I glance up at the pedestrian walkway above us, filled with people, and at the strung cables of the bridge set against the stubborn blue sky. Then it's gone and we're on to the Manhattan side.

Jay takes us a block before we slam into traffic. Nothing's moving in any direction. Jay tries to manoeuvre us left then right, but there's no room, no way of cutting through Manhattan's gridlock. Jay slaps the wheel with the heel of his hand and swears loudly. He glances in the rear-view mirror and makes a quick calculation. Instinctively I brace myself as he jerks the wheel hard. We fly up on to the sidewalk, almost ploughing into the front window of a bagel store. Jay rams on the handbrake and throws open his door.

'Come on,' he shouts, beckoning to me.

My hands fumble for the seatbelt. I throw open my door, grab the go-bag and jump out the car, running around to join him. The owner of the bagel store has burst out the door and has started remonstrating, but Jay just tosses him the keys to the car, grabs my hand, and starts pulling me down the street.

'Where are we going?' I ask, out of breath already, a pain lodged in my chest making it hard to run.

'Subway,' he says, eyes straight ahead.

This time both of us hop the turnstile, not even a word passing between us. Jay doesn't let go of my hand once we're through, pulling me down on to the uptown platform. We jump on the next train. It's an express and it's heaving. There are no seats. Jay takes hold of the metal rail that runs down the centre of the train with one hand and pulls me to him with his other. I press my head under his chin and close my eyes, breathing him in, trying not to let my thoughts stray, trying just to focus on breathing in and breathing out.

I count down the stations in my head. At 116th I stretch on to tiptoe and, holding on to Jay's shoulders, I lean in close and whisper in his ear. 'Just take Marisa, OK? Just take her and go.'

Jay doesn't answer. He wraps his arm around my waist and pulls me back against his chest, holding me so tightly it's as if he doesn't ever want to let me go.

125th Street isn't a busy station. We get off the train. Jay takes hold of my arm. He's playing along. Acting as if he's bringing me against my will. He has the go-bag on his back.

We spot them straightaway. They're standing twenty metres ahead of us with Marisa sandwiched between them. She's wide-eyed with terror, her whole body trembling, and looks like she's barely holding it together, but when she sees us she gives an audible gasp that cuts out and becomes a whimper when Bezrukov prods her. Behind me I feel Jay tense and exhale sharply.

She doesn't look like she's been hurt though, thankfully; there are no scratches or bruises visible. I catch a glint of metal. Bezrukov is holding a gun to the small of her back. He moved it briefly so we could see it; a brazen warning. He isn't wearing the cop uniform, but I would have recognised him anywhere. Even from this distance I can make out the arctic blue of his eyes. The other guy is shorter, squatter, with thick brown hair, a nose that looks like it's been moulded out of dough and pitted skin.

We stand there, facing them, and for a moment that feels as long as eternity no one moves. A train comes rumbling through the station and the sound of it jars my bones, or maybe I'm just shaking from nerves, I can't tell.

I keep my eyes fixed on the man holding Marisa and listen as the train's doors hiss open. People flood past heading to the stairs, oblivious to us standing like statues in the midst of them.

The man holding Marisa gestures with his head towards the train.

Jay and I step sideways towards the nearest door and climb on board.

A half second before the doors bang shut the three of them step on board too, Marisa still sandwiched between them, her shoulders hunched. Half a carriage separates us from them.

It's crowded, all the seats taken, and about half a dozen people are standing in the gangway between the seats, holding on to the overhead rails and swaying hard as the train jolts and screams into a tunnel.

Down the far end of the carriage a man bangs a homemade drum. The metallic sound reverberates inside my skull. My pulse keeps time. My hands are sweating so much I have to wipe them on my dress. Jay's grip on me is so tight it hurts, but it's the only thing holding me to any kind of reality.

What are we supposed to do now? Aren't they supposed to let Marisa go? I fight the urge to turn to Jay. He's pressed against me and I can feel the steel-hard flat of his stomach and that's enough to steady me.

The one who isn't Bezrukov is holding Marisa by the top of the arm and suddenly he motions to me with a rough jerk of his head. He wants me to walk towards them. I glance at Jay. His fingers don't loosen on my arm and I have to tug myself free. I do it without looking at him. I can't look at him. I just move forwards, pushing past the people holding on to the overhead rails, until I'm standing a foot in front of Marisa. She stares at me with huge eyes, brimming with tears. I smile weakly at her, trying to convey to her that everything is going to be OK, but she doesn't smile back. She lets out another small whimper and I glance up.

Behind her Bezrukov stands watching me and, once he has my full attention, he drops his gaze deliberately and lets his eyes travel up my body in a way that chills me to the core. A smile eases across his face and I have to fight the urge to run back to Jay.

The train starts to brake as we enter another subway station and I lurch forwards, grabbing hold of the metal pole closest to me. The doors open and a dozen people get off, none of them even trading a backwards glance at us. I watch Bezrukov. What are they planning on doing? Are we going to ride this train until the end of the line?

The second man, the one with the brown hair and mushy lump of a nose, takes hold of Marisa and walks with her to the door. He shoves her on to the platform and she stumbles to a stop, shaking violently. She stands there with her back to us, not moving, her head bowed as though awaiting execution. Then the doors slam shut and I let out a sigh of relief. She's OK. She's free. As we pull out of the station I see her through the window turning slowly around, still cowering, as though she expects the guy with the gun to still be there and then, when she realises she is alone, she clutches a hand to her chest and then we hit a tunnel and in the blink of an eye she's out of sight.

42

I turn back to the man with the dead blue eyes. Bezrukov. He smiles at me, showing nicotine-stained teeth. Fear infuses every cell in my body.

The other guy rejoins us and motions to Bezrukov. I turn. Jay is still standing in the exact same spot. He hasn't moved an inch. They expected him to get off the train with Marisa. Now they're wondering what he's doing. As am I.

With a jerk of his chin Bezrukov tells me to move. I do. I turn so that I'm standing beside him, slightly in front, and he presses the muzzle of his gun into the soft flesh above my hip. I close my eyes as a tremor rides up my spine. Bezrukov's hand grabs my other hip, drawing me closer, and the muzzle of the gun imprints against bone. It's a threat. Don't draw attention to myself. Don't do anything that will get me or anyone else on this train killed. My eyes dart down the length of the train. Most people got off at the last stop; there are maybe twenty people still on board, all studiously ignoring one another. A few are leaning back against the scratched-up windows, sleeping; others are nodding their heads in time to music playing through headphones. The guy with the drum hasn't let up. He still pounds out an angry rhythm that seems to escalate right along with my heartbeat.

My attention skips back to Jay. He's taken a half-step forwards, his eyes fixed on my hip, his face stricken. I will him not to take another step. He doesn't. We stare at each other for an endless beat before the lights overhead flicker and go out, plunging us into darkness as we hurtle down what feels like another endless tunnel.

At the next stop Bezrukov exchanges a few words in Russian with his partner. I understand. They're saying something about a car that's waiting for them. For *us*. They nudge me off the train. My body resists, all my muscles turning to stone.

I turn my head to watch Jay as they drag me from the train. He doesn't move. He's not going to get off. A part of me wants to cry with relief but another part, a bigger part, wants to scream his name and yearns for him to follow me, feels betrayed that he's stayed put.

Bezrukov's hand is planted on my shoulder, the gun digs into my side. They pull me along the platform. I try to look back, to snatch one last glance at Jay, but the train's pulling away and I'm being forced towards the stairs.

Panic rears up like a wild animal inside me. I start to struggle despite the gun, casting around for help, but there's no one in sight. I'm not going with them. I'm not getting in that car. I remember my dad's warnings when I was barely bigger than a toddler, to never ever get into a car with an abductor. It's game over from that point but, before, you still have a chance. I dig my heels in and, when Bezrukov turns snarling towards me trying to make me move, I rake my nails down his cheek and then curl my fingers and shove them into his eye socket.

He howls and from out of nowhere a fist smashes into my temple, nearly knocking me to the ground. The world explodes, lights sparking bright at the edges of my vision. I'm caught and hauled upright, my ears ringing so loudly that I don't hear it at first. But then it comes again. A shout.

'Let her go.'

Bezrukov, with beads of blood bubbling on his cheek from where my nails tore his skin, hauls me around and I see him, standing at the far end of the platform.

'Jay,' I whisper, his name a sob.

He's standing next to a metal pillar, half shielded. He has the gun in his hand and it's cocked and aimed at Bezrukov's head. I feel a dizzying spike of elation that he hasn't abandoned me, followed by a bone-numbing dread.

'Put the gun down,' Bezrukov answers in a thickly-accented voice. He brings his own gun up and levels it at my head, pushing it against my ear. I let out a whimper and bite my tongue. 'Fire that gun and we kill her,' he says. 'Then you.'

Jay shakes his head, refusing to take his eyes off Bezrukov. 'You need her. You're not about to shoot her,' he answers.

Bezrukov sighs and mutters something under his breath.

'You realise who you have there, don't you?' Jay shouts.

Bezrukov shoots a look at the other guy who snickers, mutters something in Russian, then brings up his gun ready to fire at Jay. 'Yes, we realise,' he says. 'Daniel Harvey's daughter.'

'No,' Jay says. 'You got Rambo, actually,' and his eyes fly to mine.

I understand exactly what he means to do. And more importantly what he means for me to do. I nod, so slightly it's not even a nod. And then I throw myself sideways as Jay fires the gun. I hear the crack and at the same time I ram my clasped hands upwards as hard as I can into Bezrukov's crotch.

291

I stumble to my feet as Bezrukov doubles over, screaming. The other guy is firing at Jay, who has ducked behind the pillar. 'Run!' Jay shouts.

I stand there for a second, unable to move. I can't just leave him. But then I see that the only way I can draw their fire away from him, the only way I can save him, is if I do what he's saying. So I turn and I run.

I make it ten metres and then I'm hit by what feels like a freight train and go flying. My left arm and shoulder smash into a pillar and I fall to the ground, so close to the track I can hear the rail buzzing like a hornet's nest. A hand closes around my ankle and I kick out, making contact with something hard and hearing a bellow of surprise and pain. The grip on my ankle loosens and I stagger once more to my feet. Bezrukov is on his knees lunging towards me, blood gushing from his nose. I dart out of his way.

Behind him I see the other guy stalking towards Jay, firing off round after round. Jay is trying to shelter behind the narrow strip of a pillar as bullets ping and zing around him. He ducks at one point and fires his own gun, but the bullet goes wide. And then the guy is on him, his gun held at point-blank range.

The space explodes suddenly with thunderous noise. A train is hurtling towards us. I start to run towards Jay, but Bezrukov blocks my way. I try to dart past him but he darts in front of me, a smile on his face.

'Jay!' I scream.

The guy looks my way, distracted, and in that split second Jay lowers his head and rams him in the chest, and they both go flying to the ground. The other guy is heavier though. He rolls, grappling Jay in a body hug, and they struggle until Jay's just an inch from the platform edge.

A bullet suddenly roars over the thunder, shattering off the tiled walls. My heart slams to a halt as Jay's body goes suddenly limp and then the other guy collapses and rolls off him. I let out a guttural sob that is drowned by the noise of the train. I'm aware that Bezrukov has turned and is grinning at me, but I can't tear my eyes away from Jay's limp body.

He's dead. He's dead. Jay's dead. I can't compute. My knees give way and I collapse on to the platform, a dead weight myself. The thundering roar of the train fills my head, every cell in my body vibrates with it, and as Bezrukov looms in front of me, his hand reaching for me, I stare at the cold hunk of metal in his hand and I want to die too. I just want this nightmare to finally end. I've had enough. I don't look at Bezrukov as his fingers grip my arm to pull me to my feet and I don't struggle either as he drags me towards the stairs. I look back over my shoulder, keeping my eyes on Jay as the tears start to fall thick and hot and fast.

But then he moves. I blink. Jay's leg twitches again. He rolls on to his side and staggers to his feet and I draw in a breath that diffuses the pain in my chest. He's alive! The gun dangles from his hand and he stares over at the guy on the ground, who isn't moving because, now I realise, Jay must have shot him.

Bezrukov wheels around, spots Jay and lets out a curse in Russian. He lets me go and swings his gun in Jay's direction. I throw all my weight against him and the bullet goes wide. Jay dives behind a pillar as Bezrukov elbows me aside and fires again. The bullet ricochets off the subway wall with a loud crack that's drowned by the sound of the train finally roaring into the station and coming to a screeching halt.

It spits out a handful of passengers, including a woman who screams at the sight of the body lying on the platform leaking blood. More people join in and a crowd starts to form. Bezrukov lunges for me, fury on his face. I throw one last glance back down the platform before I turn and run, not up the stairs, which I can't reach, but towards the end of the platform, towards the tunnel entrance.

43

There's a metal barrier at the end of the platform. I hurdle it, smacking my knee hard, but feeling it only as a dull thud. I jump down on to the tracks and start running. Behind me I hear a blast of gunshots. One. Two. Three bullets. I count them, each one feeling like it's slamming into my own body. They're followed by screams. Is it Jay firing? Or is he the one being shot at? Did he get hit? Oh God. Oh God. I stumble on a brick, catch myself and keep running, tripping over planks of wood and metal rails. It's pitch-black other than for a few lights glimmering in the distance – the next subway station along the track.

Behind me I hear footsteps gaining fast. I stifle the sob as I pitch forward over another brick and almost fall. My breathing is loud and rasping in my ears, sticking in my chest.

There's a track to my left and another about fifty metres over. I catch glimpses of it through brick archways, the metal gleaming like phosphorescence.

The air is hot, hellish, foul. I can't get enough of it.

As I run I glance backwards. A dark silhouette is briefly lit up by the firework sparks bursting off a rail. I move faster. To my right a side tunnel opens up, just wide enough for a man to pass through. The entrance is almost unnoticeable. I dive down it.

It's dark as a grave inside and fetid damp. My feet are instantly buried in dirt and inches of rubbish. I rest my hand against the bricks. They're coated in something mosslike. Something scurries beside me in the coal-black dark.

I slide down against the wall and try to make myself small. Hopefully Bezrukov will run right past me. Footsteps echo down the tunnel, coming closer. It's hard to tell how far away they are because the sound bounces off the tunnel walls and the constant rumble of trains above and below is disorientating.

I squeeze my eyes shut and start praying silently. I haven't prayed in years but I pray now. I pray to God that Jay is OK. I make silent bargains that I will do anything, be anything, take any amount more of suffering if only Jay is OK. Surely someone has called the police already? Where are they?

The footsteps slow, then stop. I wait, holding my breath. Whatever it is that's scampering in the tunnel starts snuffling at my foot and my stomach rolls over as I feel its tiny claws and whiskers brush my skin. I swallow a scream. How long have I been here? A train goes suddenly rushing past, shaking the ground underfoot. The rat lets out a squeak and goes scuttling into the furthest, darkest recesses of the tunnel. I peer after it. Should I head down there after it?

I don't get to choose.

Bezrukov stands in the tunnel entrance. Blood coats his face like a Halloween mask. He sees me crouching down in the dirt and something flickers behind his eyes. I know instinctively that it's pleasure at seeing me cowering there.

I rise to my feet, not willing to give him any kind of pleasure whatsoever. He smiles at me, that thin-lipped, eerie smile that turns my blood to ice. I feint forwards and then dart backwards, following the rat into the darkest depths of the tunnel. But Bezrukov is quicker. One hand closes around my waist, the other

296

hand grabs for my ponytail and he drags me, kicking and screaming out of the tunnel.

My nails scrape the walls as I fight him. I kick and scream and twist and heave but I've got no hope. He's so much stronger than me. In a panic, I lower my chin and sink my teeth into the soft flesh of his hand.

He lets out a roar and smashes me in the temple with his fist. Stars ricochet off my skull, pierce my eyeballs. I stagger against him, vomit filling my mouth. Then I'm slammed against the wall and suddenly I can't breathe. His fingers are clamped around my throat. I start choking. Blood pounds in my head. My hands flap ineffectually against him. He just keeps smiling.

Then he raises the gun and presses it to my forehead.

I stare him straight in the eye. I'm not going to die showing him I'm afraid. I'm not going to give him that.

The world starts to blur at the edges, the tunnel shrinking around us. I can hear my heart panicking for lack of oxygen. Pain wracks my body. But then his hand loosens and I'm suddenly sucking in air – hot rank air, but it's air, and I fill my lungs as the tunnel stretches wide again and the thundering of the trains overcomes the roar in my head.

'No,' he says to me. 'Why waste such a pretty face? You're worth more to me breathing.'

He takes my wrist and starts pulling me away. I fight, my screams swallowed by the noise of a passing train. Sparks from the rail fly up, bursting like a Catherine wheel around Bezrukov's head. He waits for the last carriage to pass and then he starts dragging me across the track, away from the tunnel, further into darkness.

'Drop the gun.'

Bezrukov freezes. I draw in a breath.

'I said drop the gun,' Jay repeats.

He's standing behind Bezrukov, merging with the shadow, but I can see he's holding something against Bezrukov's neck.

After a few seconds Bezrukov releases me. Jay pokes him harder and he stumbles forward and his gun clatters to the ground. I pick it up. My hands are shaking like I've lost control of my muscles.

'Now start walking,' Jay barks at Bezrukov, prodding him down the tracks the way we just came. I glance over at Jay. His left arm is bleeding, hanging uselessly at his side. He's been shot. But he's still alive. I want to burst into tears but I don't. I clutch Jay's hand and keep the gun trained on Bezrukov the whole way.

44

'So let me get this straight?' Agent Kassel says. 'You shot the first guy and then you apprehended the second one, Bezrukov, with a doorstopper?'

'Yes.' Jay nods, wincing as the paramedic presses a gauze bandage to his arm. 'I ran out of bullets. And I grabbed the first thing I could find from the bag.'

He glances over at me. I'm sitting on the bottom step of the platform watching everything going on around me. Someone placed a blanket over my shoulders at one point. I'm covered in blood. Jay's blood.

The paramedic crew checked me over and gave me the all-clear for physical injuries. I am covered in bruises, including a fresh one on my temple from where Bezrukov punched me, and my knee is black from where I hit the barrier, but I hardly notice it. A paramedic hovers close by. I think they're worried that I'm about to keel over from the effects of shock. But I refuse to move until Jay can come with me. I can't take my eyes off him. They cut his T-shirt off to treat his arm. The paramedics wanted to take both of us straight to the ER, but the FBI wanted us to walk through everything that happened step by step and insisted they treat us here.

Jay looks over at me then and smiles, though the smile doesn't make it to his eyes. Maybe we've both seen too much? Or maybe it's because neither of us knows what happens next? A thousand more silent words pass between us. I want nothing more than to walk over to him and curl up against his chest and tell him everything will be OK, just like he told me back on the ferry, and I'm rising to my feet to do just that when Agent Parker sits himself down beside me with a loud sigh.

'You OK?' he asks.

I glance sideways at him.

'You did a really brave thing today. Stupid. But brave. Helped a lot of people, a lot of girls.'

I don't say anything.

'Bezrukov will get life. Lucky there's no death penalty in New York or he'd be straight to the chair.'

I pull the blanket closer around me.

Agent Parker doesn't say anything for a bit. 'They're processing your father, in case you're interested. He won't make bail.'

'And Marisa and Jay's mum?' I ask, struggling to find my voice. 'Are they OK?'

'Yes, they're OK. Doing fine. Both of them back at home. Jaime's mother has been notified and someone's spoken to your mom too. She's already on her way here.'

I contemplate that. What will happen to me now? Will I have to move back to Oman? I glance over at Jay and realise that I no longer care what happens to me, so long as I find a way of helping him.

Someone steps in front of me barring my view. I look up. It's Agent Kassel. I can't help but glare at her, even though technically she's not to blame for anything.

'Liva,' she says, 'we're going to need to take statements from both you and Jaime down at the station.'

300

I nod. 'OK, fine,' I say. 'But what about Jay? Are you going to arrest him again?'

Agent Kassel shrugs at me. 'I'm sorry, Liva, process is process. Soon as we're finished taking his statement we're handing him over to the NYPD."

I scowl at her. She already knows what I think of her process.

45

Because of something they call jurisdiction they take us to the nearest police station to give our statements, even though we already gave them in the subway station. Apparently there's still more paperwork to complete. The police station's somewhere in Harlem. The view from the roof sweeps all the way to Central Park.

I gave my third statement, excused myself to go to the bathroom, found the fire-escape door and headed up here to the roof. I didn't want to be there to see them take Jay away. I told them everything he'd done to save me, to save Marisa and to catch Bezrukov, but they just shrugged at me as though none of it mattered. Frustration eats at me. The only thing I can do is wait for my mum to get here and then make her do something to help him. A tiny voice in my head tells me she's not going to do anything. She's most likely going to be hysterical – and she's not even qualified to practise law in the US. She'll claim she can't do anything. I know it. I grit my teeth. After everything we did, after everything Jay did, how can he be the one going to jail?

I stand on the roof edge in my bare feet, feeling the asphalt burning like hot tar beneath my toes. Warm air from an air-conditioning vent rises up and blasts me. I feel I could topple forwards and it would float me back up on a current. I'm swaying and realise that I'm so tired that balancing here is an act of crazy stupidity. But I can't seem to step away from the edge.

My mind chugs desperately, trying to piece together all the events of the last thirty or so hours, probing to see where the fear has gone. I come up empty. There's no more fear. Gently it tests to see what else I'm feeling. Am I still numb? No. There's an unrelenting pain in my chest, like a bullet has tracked a path right through me, and lodged in my heart. There's hurt and grief and guilt and regret thrown into the mix too. And I can't imagine those are ever going to disappear either. Every night when I go to bed, every time I give my last name, every time I have to explain who my father is, I'll have to dredge through a thousand memories. I can't even think about my dad right now. I close my eyes and Jay's words spring into my head.

I can't live my life feeling responsible for choices others made. Easier said than done. And a whole lot easier when Jay was there to look me in the eye and tell me it.

No, I repeat to myself like a mantra. I wasn't in control of any of it. I can't control life. The only thing I can do is open myself up and accept everything it throws at me, wholeheartedly. Defiantly. I don't get to quit, not when so many other people didn't even get the choice.

Behind me, the door eases open. I knew they'd find me eventually. I turn with a sigh, expecting to see Agent Kassel. But it's not her. It's Jay.

'I knew I'd find you up here,' he says.

I stare at him in shock. He's wearing an FBI T-shirt. The bandage on his arm is soaked with blood and the cut above his eye has been cleaned and butterfly-stitched shut. 'What are you doing?' I ask, breathless.

'Looking for you,' he says walking towards me. He moves gingerly as though he's bruised all over.

'They told me they were processing you,' I say, looking over his shoulder expecting to see a cop waving some handcuffs at him. Has he come to say goodbye? My heart aches as though it's as bruised all over as Jay. It would have been easier if he'd just left. That's partly why I was on the roof. To avoid the goodbye. I can't handle it.

'They processed me already,' he says reaching my side.

'So why are you here?' I ask him. Please don't touch me, I think to myself. I can't take that, not if I know it's going to be the last time.

Jay smiles at me, pulls me away from the edge. 'You mean instead of wearing a hot orange jumpsuit and on my way to the county jail?'

'Yeah.'

His arms wrap around my waist. 'They processed me and let me go.'

I blink at him in confusion. 'Let you go?'

He gives me that half-smile. 'Yeah. Dropped all charges. On account of how I'm a hero.'

My eyebrows shoot up. Lightness fills me. 'A hero?' I say, smiling back at him.

'Yeah, didn't you know?'

I laugh, shaking my head at him.

He narrows his eyes in mock annoyance, pulls me tighter against him.

'I do know one thing though,' I tell him as his eyes fall to my lips.

'Yeah? What's that?' he asks, his mind elsewhere.

I take a deep breath, feeling like I'm free-falling off the roof.

'You were right,' I say.

Jay looks at me quizzically.

I reach up on tiptoe, bringing my lips to his. 'It *is* worth it.'

Acknowledgements

So many thanks go to the following people:

Lauren, for telling me a story involving the New York subway which whetted my appetite for setting a story there. And then for traipsing around the city with me, exploring. I've never had so much fun.

Kent and Tara for lending us their fabulous house in Brooklyn, complete with chickens and the best coffee known to man.

John and Alula, as always, for just existing and sharing the love.

Nicola J for giving early feedback.

Jaime Burnell for the security information.

Daniella Burr for the Mexican slang and translation – you rock, sister.

Craig for the brain-boosting acupuncture sessions.

Vic and Nic for your endless support and enthusiasm for every sentence I write.

My parents for giving me the travel bug.

Amanda, the best agent on the planet.

Ellie, Venetia and everyone at Simon & Schuster for all their hard work and support.

Information on Human Trafficking

Sex trafficking is one of most shocking crimes on the planet, one that currently affects around 2.4 million people at any given moment, mainly women and girls.

There are many books that tell the stories (both fictionalised and real) of people who have been victims of human trafficking. I urge you to read them, learn as much as you can, and then start speaking out, because it's only when individuals speak up that change can happen.

If you want to read more I highly recommend the books *Sold* by Patricia McCormick and *Not for Sale: The Return of the Human Slave Trade* by David Batstone.

Other ways you can get involved in the fight against trafficking and slavery:

Visit Notforsale.org, a campaign tackling slavery in all its forms.

Check out Equality Now's website and get involved in their mission to achieve legal and systemic change that addresses violence and discrimination against women and girls around the world.

Join the Half The Sky Movement and organise a showing of one of their fantastic documentaries at your school or in your local community.

Support the charity unseen.org.uk

Take action via the Coalition Against Trafficking in Women and learn how to donate to their cause via your eBay sales. http://www.catwinternational.org/Help

http://www.stopthetraffick.org/ has a brilliant website, with numerous ways to get involved and help support their goal of stopping slavery and trafficking at a local and global level.

Get involved in the UN's Blue Heart Campaign. http://www.unodc.org/blueheart/en/campaign-tools.html